W9-BTP-157

You Don't Know Me But I Know You

REBECCA BARROW

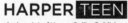
HARPER TEEN

An Imprint of HarperCollinsPublishers

HarperTeen is an imprint of HarperCollins Publishers.

You Don't Know Me but I Know You
Copyright © 2017 by Rebecca Barrow
All rights reserved. Printed in the United States of America.
No part of this book may be used or reproduced in any manner whatsoever without written permission except in the case of brief quotations embodied in critical
articles and reviews. For information address HarperCollins Children's Books, a
division of HarperCollins Publishers, 195 Broadway, New York, NY 10007.
www.epicreads.com

ISBN 978-0-06-249419-1 (trade bdg.)

Typography by Torborg Davern
17 18 19 20 21   PC/LSCH   10 9 8 7 6 5 4 3 2 1
❖
First Edition

R0450137055

You Don't Know Me But I Know You

ONE

Audrey sipped her third lukewarm beer and tossed her head back, shaking her hips to the bass-heavy music thrumming through the house. Barely two feet away, the band held their instruments like long-lost loves, enchanting a slick, sexy-infused rock from battered guitars and crackling mics.

Audrey closed her eyes to feel it all. The sweat on the back of her neck tickled as it inched down into her shirt, but she barely noticed. How could she when she was having so much *fun*?

(The three beers might have had something to do with that.)

(Okay, and the vodka.)

An achingly familiar voice made Audrey open her eyes again, and she focused on the lone boy grabbing the mic away from the girl with the orange guitar. "This is a new one," he said in a hoarse voice, jerking dark hair out of his face. "You'll get it. Izzy—"

The girl ripped into a frenetic riff on that guitar. Audrey watched the boy—her boy—lift his shirt to wipe the sweat from his forehead before starting up a killer bass line, and then the girl in shiny, black knee-high boots began to sing.

Audrey felt the beat in the pit of her stomach and smiled. Next to her, Rose whipped her long, messy hair back and forth and ignored the annoyed glances as she bumped into the surrounding people. The den of Cooper's extravagant house hummed with energy, crowded with kids eager to see the band play, to spill their drinks on the cream carpet as they thrashed around. That was exactly the way Audrey liked it: surrounded by air thick with body heat, sweat, and perfume, wrapped up in the heartbeat of it all.

They danced through another few songs until the girl with the orange guitar announced they were done. "I'm Izzy. This is Julian, Dasha, and Jasmin. We're Hera," she said to raucous cheers. "Thanks for having us, Coop."

The sudden buzzing quiet was quickly filled with electro coming from the ceiling-mounted speakers. Audrey caught Julian's eye and held up her red cup, pointing to it. *Drink?* she mouthed.

He nodded as he lifted his guitar strap over his head, then held up two fingers. *Water*, he mouthed back.

Audrey slung an arm around Rose's neck, pulling her best friend close to speak rushed words into her ear. "Kitchen! Coming?"

They elbowed out of the crush and found their winding way to the kitchen. Audrey ignored the table groaning with illicitly acquired beer and opened the refrigerator, grabbing two bottles of water. Cooper's mom wouldn't mind—not that she'd ever know, since Coop was an expert in postparty cleanup. By tomorrow afternoon the house would be pristine, fridge restocked, china released from under the sink, and—party? What party?

It was quieter in here, more talk than music. Audrey took Rose's hand and pulled her over to the granite-topped island where María was perched, her skirt riding high as she lectured Jen, the fourth member of their quartet. "So what if it's part of the canon?" she was saying, adjusting her pink-framed glasses. "If I have to read another book by an old white guy about a dead teenage girl, I will throw up."

Audrey laughed and poked María's leg. "You know we're at a party, right?" she teased. "You can leave the literature smackdown for later."

Jen nodded, her high ponytail swinging, the dyed bright red of it dramatic with her winter-morning-white skin. "Here, this will be more fun," she said. "Let me read your palm."

"Since when do you know how to read palms?" Rose said.

"Since we had an astrologist come to church," Jen said. "Now, let me see your lifeline, Ree. I want to know if you're going to die before me."

Audrey watched as Rose snagged two lime-green Jell-O shots from a passing plate. "Sometimes Jen truly astounds me," Audrey said.

Rose handed Audrey one of the shots. "You love it. Drink."

They clicked the tiny plastic cups together and threw back their heads in perfect sync, downing their shots. Audrey shimmied as the sour shock hit her. "More!"

Rose laughed. "Okay, hold on a—" She cut off suddenly, and her face went from giddy glee to thunder in a split second. "Really? Is she fucking serious?"

"What?" Audrey followed her friend's knife-sharp gaze and twisted to see a beautiful, dark-skinned girl with braids to her ass walking through the doorway. "Oh, shit. Hey—" She put her hands on Rose's shoulders and forcibly turned her away. "Ignore her."

"What, Saint Francis doesn't have their own parties?" Rose pulled in a ragged breath, her eyes still fixed on a point past Audrey. "She has to come slum it all the way over here?"

"Ignore her," Audrey repeated. "Don't let it get to you."

"I'm not!" Rose twitched out of Audrey's grip, and her focus came back, flicking around to their friends' curious faces. She stood up straight and shook her head, her face momentarily hidden behind the curtain of her hair. When it was visible again, her smile was back and the angry flash gone from her eyes. "I mean, come on," Rose said, and she laughed now. "She knows this is my place. These are my friends. God—how *desperate*."

"Who's desperate?" Jen leaned between them and saw the subject of their disdain. "Wait, is that Aisha? What is *she* doing here?"

"The more important question is, who cares?" Rose turned away, her bravado fully reengaged. "Hmm. Do you think she follows all her exes around, or am I special?" She batted her eyelashes at María, who laughed loudly. "I mean, we only went out for, like, a couple months. She needs to get a life."

Audrey watched Aisha, now moving through the party with the grace of a gazelle, trailed by her private-school friends. Rose made it sound like no big deal. But it had been a big enough deal when it was happening—enough for Rose to whisper to Audrey that she was falling for this girl. Enough to leave Rose a sobbing, sad mess when Aisha unceremoniously dumped her soon after.

Rose rubbed her gloss-wet lips together and sighed. "Whatever. Let's talk about something *actually* interesting," she said. "Like how Pete Krakoz is totally checking you out right now, Ree."

María rolled her eyes. "No thanks."

"Why not?"

"He's creepy! He still snaps people's bra straps. Like, we're not twelve years old."

Audrey remembered the water sweating on the countertop and grabbed the bottles. She hip-bumped Rose. "I'm going to find Julian," she said. "I'll be back."

After a circuit of the entire house with no sign of her boyfriend, Audrey ventured outside. The French doors clicked shut behind her, and Audrey paused on the patio, inhaling the crisp suburban New York night air. The sky above glittered with stars—well, the few that were visible with the neon glow of streetlights. There were things Audrey liked about living in Kennedy (river walks, the excellent independent music scene, early-morning sunrises) and things she didn't, like how she couldn't pick out the constellations in the sky. Like how Kennedy was somehow big enough that not everybody knew everybody else, but still small enough for secrets and rumors to travel venom-slick. The kind of town where if you weren't driving the right kind of car or bringing in your trash cans fast enough or turning out for the neighborhood association meetings—well, no one would say anything. No one would do anything. But you'd be marked in some invisible way as Wrong. Not One of Us.

She didn't want to be One of Them anyway: judgmental and uptight, wasting energy caring about this nowhere place? No thanks. The other side was *so* much better.

Audrey's hands twitched at her sides, longing for the camera that she'd left at home. She lifted her hands so they framed the cluster of pinpoint lights and squeezed an imaginary shutter—*click*.

Imaginary was better anyway, because her real version would most likely have been grainy and impossible to make out. She didn't have a problem finding things she wanted to capture, but making the image reflect what she'd seen? That was where the trouble started. Sometimes she wished she could forget about composition and aperture speeds, light versus dark, and all the other technical shit that tripped her up. *If only it was that easy*, she thought.

She was still staring up when she felt long fingers creep around her waist and squeeze hard, shocking her enough that she jumped and her heart kicked into double time. "What—"

"Wait, it's me!" Julian grinned at her, his dark eyes gleaming. "Aud, it's only me. Relax."

Audrey punched his shoulder semiplayfully. "You know I hate when you do that."

Julian put two fingers under her chin and tilted her face up. "Let me make it up to you," he said, and kissed her. Audrey pressed her hands against his chest and rose up on her toes to return the kiss, sighing as his hands skimmed over her hips. Kissing Julian was like plugging herself into an electric circuit, lighting up her veins and sending shocks to the tips of her toes.

She pulled away, sinking back down until she was fully grounded again. That was more like it.

Although . . . "Did you smoke?" she asked, leaning away from him. She saw the way his eyes widened and lifted a finger in warning. "Don't lie."

"One," Julian admitted. "Half of one, really. What?"

"You know what," Audrey said. "You quit, remember?"

"I'm not smoking," he said, and in his voice Audrey could hear the annoyance of having this argument—*discussion*—again. "It was one."

Audrey knew her nagging pissed him off, but she'd stopped caring. Before they'd started dating, Julian had always had a cigarette in his hand; Audrey would see him underneath the bleachers or hiding from the rain at the bus stop, and God, she'd thought he was so hot, with his guitar strapped to his back and hair curling into his eyes and his mouth blowing smoke rings.

But then they'd started dating, and Audrey had discovered that as sexy as it looked, in reality the whole thing was gross. She'd come home with her clothes smelling of smoke, and shivering outside while she waited for him to finish his cigarette was beyond boring. Plus, she couldn't stop picturing his lungs turning black, and it had freaked her out enough that she'd made him promise to quit. Which he had, except for times like now when he cheated.

Julian frowned, pulling her back close to him. "Don't give me the lecture," he said. "I'll be good from now on. I promise."

The buzzed part of her wanted to believe that, and the sensible part of her said that he meant it, too. So she let her body press into his and smiled. "You were good tonight," she said. "You need to start bringing stuff for people to buy again. More EPs and whatever else."

"We're trying," Julian said. "Dasha's brother's helping us with shirts."

"I can help, too," Audrey said. "Pictures, posters, whatever. Tell Izzy."

"I will," Julian said. "What are you doing out here anyway? You were miles away."

"I was looking for you," Audrey said, tipping her head back and inhaling deeply. "What's your excuse?"

Julian gestured to somewhere behind him. "I was talking to Cooper and Davis."

Audrey leaned past him, looking to the far side of the patio where Cooper and Davis, plus some others, were congregated, the glowing tips of their cigarettes the only things giving them away. "*Talking*. Oh, I see."

Julian rolled his eyes, lacing his fingers through her other hand. "All right, all right," he said. "Come on, let's go inside. You must be freezing."

Audrey glanced down at her bare legs, her bleached denim shorts and thin cotton T-shirt, and then at Julian in his jeans, shirt, sweater, and leather jacket. "No," she said truthfully. Three beers and a beautiful boy would do that to a girl.

She lifted their joined hands, wishing again for her camera. She loved the way their hands looked together: his long, piano-playing fingers pale against her brown skin and glitter-painted nails. *Click.* "My mom and Adam are out tonight," she said, looking back up at him. "In the city."

"So they won't be home till late," Julian said, raising his eyebrows.

"Yup. Which means I have the house all to myself."

"Hmm." He nodded, a knowing smile appearing on his face. "Interesting."

"Very interesting," Audrey said, and stroked her thumb against his palm. "I mean, we'd have to be quick, because Rose is supposed to stay—"

But Julian was one step ahead of her, whipping his keys out of his back pocket and tripping toward the French doors as her laughter pealed into the night. "Let's go."

TWO

The blaring alarm rudely woke Audrey, and she would have ignored it if not for the pillow that landed on her head a second later. "Mmph," Rose groaned. "Shut it off."

"All right," Audrey said, her voice late-night raspy, and she tossed the pillow away. "Why are you always such an ass in the morning?"

"Not always," Rose mumbled. "Only when hungover."

She rolled over, taking Audrey's half of the covers with her, and Audrey swung her legs to the floor. "I'm going to take a shower," she said through a yawn. She stood up and gazed around her room, stretching her arms high above her head as she took in the dark-purple-painted walls, decorated with her own artwork: collages of her photos interspersed with paper printouts, tacked-up portraits of Old Hollywood starlets, posters of her mom's movies. Hanging from the ceiling were spiraling sculptures she'd made out of Julian's old guitar strings, pretty, wild things. Having her space to decorate however she liked was her favorite thing about their house. "I told Jen we'd be there at ten." She poked the lump that was Rose underneath the covers. "Don't go back to sleep. We need to get energized! Knitting! Let's go!"

When Audrey came back from the bathroom, Rose had made the bed and was rifling through the bottom drawer of Audrey's closet, the one that held a small collection of Rose's things. Rose did not have that stereotypical big, wildly loving Italian family—her parents were of the always-absent variety, too busy being a surgeon and a lawyer to check whether Rose was in by curfew or to do anything more than leave money for dinner. And ever since her sister, Gia, had left for college and then a job in Singapore, Rose had started staying over at Audrey's more and more. She spent enough time there already that it barely made a difference—just that now a bottle of her expensive shampoo lived in the bathroom, and when the coffee machine broke in the morning, there was someone in the house who actually knew how to fix it.

Rose held up an olive-green sweater. "This or the black shirt?" Rose was a dancer, but not the willowy, elegant ballerina type. ("Trust me, the American Ballet Theatre is never going to want this much T and A," Rose had once said.) She was more powerful—athletic muscle where Audrey was curves and softness—and Rose towered over her, but it didn't stop them from switching and swapping clothes all the time. The perks of best friendship meant no repercussions for a shirt with the chest stretched out or hems permanently rolled up.

"That," Audrey said. "Can I borrow the lipstick you were wearing last night?" She stepped over Rose to get to her clothes and picked out one of her standard outfits: worn blue jeans, a plain white tank, and a slouchy gray sweater to go over the top. She stuck with the basics mostly, and let her hair and lipstick do the talking for her. The hair, in her natural kinky, coily curls, said, *Yes, I'm aware of my skin color, and I don't need you to point it out to me.* The lipstick said, *If you touch me I will hurt you.* And plus, the purplish red looked excellent against her brown skin.

Eventually they were ready to go—only fifteen minutes behind Audrey's schedule. They blew through the kitchen, where her mom and Adam were eating breakfast, and Audrey grabbed two lemon poppy-seed muffins from the basket. "See you later," Audrey said. "Julian's coming for dinner."

"Okay," her mom said, twisting her red hair into a knot on top of her head. "Where are you two going?"

"Knit-a-thon," Rose answered. "At Jen's church."

"Raging," Adam said, grinning. "Have fun."

Outside, the bright morning sun glared high in the sky. Audrey got into the passenger side and slipped on one of the many pairs of sunglasses Rose kept in her car's glove box. "My head is killing me," she said. "I can't believe we did Jell-O shots. Not a good idea."

"I know. My mouth tastes like ass," Rose said. "Remind me why we agreed to this again?"

Audrey slumped down and tucked her hands inside her sweater sleeves. "Because Jen's our friend, and we love her. Quit complaining."

"Okay." Rose laughed as they cruised through a yellow light. "But only because I love her."

They pulled up outside Jen's church: a pretty, understated white building with flowers creeping around the doors and only a small sign out front. Inside, the place bustled with activity, and they found their way through it all to the sign-in table where Jen's mom sat.

"Hi, girls," she said, white teeth shining behind her glossy-red lipstick. "Thank you *so* much for coming today."

"Hi, Mrs. Archer." Audrey wrote her name at the bottom of the sign-in sheet, and Rose's beneath it. "We're happy to help out. I don't know how much help I'm actually going to be since I can't really knit, but I'm willing to try."

"Don't you worry," Mrs. Archer said. "It's not as difficult as it looks, and even if you only get one square done, that'll be great." She handed them each a set of needles, a small ball of yarn, and a pair of scissors. "Jen will get you all set up—she's over by the piano with María. Have fun!"

"Thanks," Audrey said, and she jabbed Rose in the side as they headed off in search of their friends. "Rose, would it kill you to say hi?"

Rose twirled one knitting needle between her fingers. "She scares me."

"Everyone's mom scares you," Audrey said. "Except for mine. But she's boss, so that's understandable."

"I don't know," Rose said. "I feel like I'm always one wrong word away from getting in trouble. Like they're going to ground me or take away my allowance."

Audrey spotted María waving and raised her hand. "That's ridiculous. *Your* parents don't even ground you."

Rose snorted. "Yeah, they'd have to actually *be* at home to keep me there."

"Hey!" Jen said. She and María were set up in the corner—Jen had orange yarn wrapped around her arm and orange fuzz in her hair, and María looked thoroughly annoyed already. "You're late."

"Barely," Audrey said. "But we're here, and we're willing."

"Very willing," Rose said. "One thing: what exactly is this for, again?"

"The women's refuge and the NICU at the hospital," Jen explained. "They always need blankets and baby things. All we have to do is knit a bunch of little squares, and then they'll get put together into bigger pieces later. It's really easy."

María let out a frustrated groan and dropped her needles with a clatter. "Easy? You're such a liar."

"Don't be ridiculous," Jen said as Audrey bent to pick up María's needles. "Look, let's go through it again. You all follow what I'm doing, okay?"

Audrey and Rose pulled a couple of chairs over to complete the circle. Audrey carefully watched Jen's hands as she wound a length of gray yarn around her hand and slipped one needle through it, saying things like "cast on" and "stocking stitch" as she lifted and twisted the yarn around, a neat row of stitches emerging before Audrey's eyes. She made it look simple, and at first Audrey couldn't figure out how to keep her stitches from sliding off and unraveling, but after an hour or so she got the hang of it. Her first couple of squares came out misshapen—"Psychedelic knitwear," Rose called it—but eventually they evened out, and it was kind of hypnotic: that clicking of the needles, the rhythmic pulling and twisting of the yarn, the hum of talk all through the room. They took a break for lunch and walked across the street for pizza, where they pulled apart the events of last night's party over double mushroom and pepperoni. When María brought up the Aisha Forrester sighting, Rose only rolled her eyes. "Whatever," she said. "You know what's more important than that? I heard *someone*"—here she elbowed Jen—"was getting high in the bathroom with Lilia George."

"I took one drag," Jen said. "I hardly think that counts as getting high. Plus, I don't think I like pot. It tastes weird."

María hooked a caramel wave behind her ear. "Did you know they're doing clinical trials in Washington to see if pot can be used to treat schizophrenia?"

Audrey tipped her head to the side and stared at María. "No, Ree. Only you would know that. I read *Elle*, not *New Scientist*."

María stuck out her tongue as Jen and Rose laughed. "Sorry for finding medical innovations fascinating," she quipped, and then, "I read *Elle*, too."

"Of course," Rose said. "That's why you have the best hair on the debate team."

María smoothed her hands over her black Peter Pan–collared dress—with the pink-framed glasses, she was the perfect Mexican American Wednesday Addams–Barbie hybrid. "Duh."

They headed back to the church then and worked for another few hours, until a guy in a Dead Kennedys shirt stood up in the middle of the room and told everybody to start piecing the squares together.

Needle-and-thread sewing Audrey could do, so she was put to work with Jen stitching baby blankets while Rose and María helped clean up. It was fun, and when the whole thing began to wind down, Audrey was impressed with what they'd managed to make. They packed the blankets into boxes and loaded them into the back of a rainbow-painted van, and when it was time to leave, Jen hugged them all. "Thanks for doing this," she said, clasping her hands together in front of her chest. "It means a lot to me."

"You mean a lot to us," Audrey said. "Anytime you need us, we're there. And now we know how to knit!"

"Speak for yourself," María said, picking a thread from her jacket sleeve. "Next time let's cook something. I'm real good at weighing shit out."

Jen laughed. "Sure thing. See you on Monday."

Audrey and Rose waved as they got into Rose's car, and Rose cranked the heating. "We should actually volunteer at the women's refuge," she said. "This was good."

"Yeah." Audrey flipped down the visor and inspected her lipstick in the mirror. "Let's check it out."

Rose turned off the engine. "I can't believe she was there last night."

Audrey looked at Rose sideways, measuring what to say next. She didn't want to scare Rose off, now that she actually wanted to talk.

Sometimes Rose volunteered secrets, in the middle of the night, whispered between movie previews, or out of the blue like this. These moments were delicate—Audrey had to handle them carefully. Mostly Audrey pulled the confessions out, word by slow word. She had a lot of Rose locked away in her head. That was okay: better in Audrey than in Rose, stacking up until it all spilled over, a waterfall of anger and truth. "You mean Aisha?"

Rose stared straight ahead at the white walls of the church. "Yeah," she said, an exhalation. "Aisha."

"I'm sorry, Rose. I don't think Cooper invited her, if that helps."

"It's not fair." Rose drummed her fingers on the steering wheel, her painted nails flashing in the setting sunlight. "Isn't one of the rules of breaking up that you stay away from each other's places? How come she's allowed to come to *my* friends' parties, listen to *my* friends' band, walk around like she did absolutely nothing wrong?" She laughed, a soft but bitter sound. "I guess maybe the breakup rules only apply in the case of an actual breakup. Two people fooling around for a few months doesn't exactly qualify as a couple, does it? And you can't break up if you were never together in the first place."

Audrey flipped the mirror away and twisted as much as she could to face Rose. "I don't care about the 'breakup rules' or how 'official' you two were. She treated you like shit, and you deserved way better than that."

"Did I?"

"Yes!"

"We never even went on a real date. We would just go to the

drive-through, and if she wanted to be romantic, she'd buy me a sundae." Rose shook her head. "Do you think I'll ever find somebody who, like . . . loves me or whatever?"

"Duh, of course you will," Audrey said. "We're seventeen. You have your whole entire life to find someone who, like, loves you or whatever."

That got a laugh out of her. "Don't make fun of me," Rose said, fighting a smile. "It's not nice."

"I'm being deadly serious." Audrey reached across the gear stick and put her hand on Rose's wrist. "Listen, someday—tomorrow, or ten years from now, or maybe even thirty—you're going to meet someone who's totally head over heels in love with you. And whoever that person is—boy, girl, someone somewhere in between—they'll be lucky to have you."

"Don't make me barf," Rose said drily, but her cheeks were pink, and she'd given up on fighting that smile.

Audrey pulled Rose's lipstick out of her bag. "And who knows?" She uncapped it and touched up the faded lines on her bottom lip without looking. "Maybe they'll even take you *inside* the restaurant."

"Jerk." Rose flipped Audrey the bird and then cranked the engine again. "You think you're so funny, don't you?"

THREE

Audrey chopped the green peppers the way Adam had shown her, careful with the sharp blade of the knife (she'd had more than enough accidents carving clay in art class not to be). The cat wound himself around her ankles while she worked. "Hey, Marmalade. You hungry, boy?"

"He's always hungry," Julian said from his position at the stove next to Adam. "He's a chunk."

"A cute little chunk," Audrey said. "Adam, is this enough?"

Adam left his sauce long enough to inspect Audrey's work. "Plenty," he said. "Okay, toss 'em in with the onions."

Audrey added the peppers to the pan of onions and fragrant garlic Julian was stirring. They were Adam's assistants for the night, helping him cook the sticky glazed chicken and sautéed potatoes with spinach that Audrey loved. She put her hands on Julian's waist and stood on tiptoes to peer over his shoulder at the pans there. "What next?"

When dinner was ready, Audrey set the table and called her mom down from her office. Laura descended the stairs dressed in slouchy draped pants and a T-shirt declaring her Queen of the Desert. "Dinner smells amazing," she said, delving into the cabinets and coming out with a bottle of wine. "I'm starved! Let's eat."

They arranged themselves around the table in their by-now familiar formation: Audrey with her back to the stove, next to Adam and across from Julian, with Laura on his left.

"Julian, pass the Parmesan?" Adam asked. "Thanks."

Audrey took two pieces of garlic bread from the bowl in the middle. "Mom, how's the show prep going?"

Her mom made a clicking noise with her tongue. "Slow. And painful. The script is beautiful, *so* evocative, but trying to get the cast to stop overacting it is killing me."

"Didn't we see that other one by the same writer?" Adam said. "The one with the marigolds and the dead father?"

"No, that's a different company," her mom said. "This play is so heart wrenching, honestly—you'll see when it's ready. If we're ever ready. I swear to God, if I have to talk to them one more time about being *understated*, I'm going to cry."

Audrey shook her head. "This is why I can't watch movies with you—you analyze them to death."

"That's what happens when you make an art your life," Laura said. "You can't see it any other way."

Audrey rolled her eyes but smiled. "Whatever."

Her mom was right, she knew: she had a lifetime as an actress to back her up. Laura Vale Spencer had once upon a time been a Hollywood darling, the girl who left school to become a sociopathic killer, a runaway mother, a queen. Upstairs, copies of her films slept tucked inside storage boxes, next to Audrey's childhood books (for her future grandchildren, Laura said) and props she'd stolen over the years. Her mom acted like those days were so long ago, like people around town didn't still give her strange looks as she walked around the grocery store—and yeah, it'd been a few years since Laura had taken on any acting jobs, preferring to stay behind the scenes at the theater she ran now. But no matter how far away from that time it got, to Audrey, Laura was every inch the star she'd always been. Sometimes when Audrey's friends stayed over, they'd sneak movies out of that box and revel in the sheer weirdness that was Audrey's mom on screen, pretending to be somebody else. Audrey would find herself mouthing the lines along with her mom: *What is it, Frank? You want the knife? Fine. Come and get it.*

Sometimes Audrey wondered exactly what it was that had made her mom distance herself from that world, decide to adopt a baby solo, and move to the other side of the country. She'd had a life and a career that so many people would *kill* for. But if Audrey ever asked, Laura would smile and say simply, "I wanted a baby so bad, and I was lucky enough to be given you. Nothing else compared to that." Which Audrey was more than grateful for, because even though Laura was still a star to Audrey, first and foremost she was the best mom in the world.

They talked between mouthfuls of the delicious dinner: about Julian's band and their fund-raising for a recording session, Adam's sister and her divorce, Laura's plans for their first lake house vacation in the summer. These were her favorite times, sitting around with her family, so easy and simple. In the past she had looked at her friends' families and thought how weird it must be to have so many people in your life—like Julian with his two brothers or Jen and all her many stepsiblings and -parents. Back then Audrey had only had her mom, and Marmalade, who they'd adopted from the shelter, and she'd thought that was perfect. But now it was weird to think that not so long ago it had been just the two of them—no Adam, and certainly no Julian. Not that things hadn't felt easy and simple then, too, but . . . there was something about having these two people become part of their home that made Audrey indescribably happy. That was all.

She chewed her food thoughtfully and scrunched up her nose. "Hey, Adam?" Audrey swallowed. Something wasn't quite right. "Did you do something different with the sauce this time?"

Adam shook his head. "Same as always. You saw. Why, is it not good?"

"Tastes good to me," her mom said, and as if to demonstrate scooped another spoonful onto her plate.

"Huh." Audrey scraped the tines of her fork across her plate, resulting in a hideous screeching sound. "Must be me."

Julian reached over, fork at the ready. "If you don't want it . . ."

Audrey waved him on. "Go ahead." She poured a glass of water and then swished it around inside her mouth. This was what she got for mixing beer and cheap vodka at parties: the hell of an all-day hang-over. She grimaced. *When will I ever learn?*

After dinner Julian had to go to a late-night practice session, and Audrey kissed him good-bye at the front door. "See you tomorrow," she said, touching her thumb to his deliciously full lower lip. "Try not to start any fights with Izzy, okay?"

"I *always* try," Julian said with an innocent look on his face. "What are you implying?"

Audrey laughed and pushed him away. "Whatever. Go on—you're going to be late."

"All right. Tell your mom and Adam bye for me." He turned and ran down the steps, almost slipping but catching himself right before falling. "Love you!"

Audrey swore under her breath, watching him right himself. What a loser. "Love you, too," she called out.

FOUR

On Monday morning Audrey was in art class, planted in front of one of the shiny iMacs donated by someone's overly generous parent. Not that she was complaining about said generosity—fancy computers equaled fancy photo-editing software, and *that* equaled a very satisfied Audrey. Kennedy High had slowly but surely shed its eighties' all-sports-all-the-time skin for its current arts-heavy, creative-encouragement version. Perfect for Audrey, for Julian and his musical talents, for Rose and her dancing. Not so much for those on the AP-everything track, like María, but like she always said, the nonspeaking role in the spring play was worth it if it made her application essays look more "diverse."

Audrey plugged her camera into the computer, but the progress bar of her loading pictures crawled along painfully slow, and staring at it didn't make for thrilling entertainment. She spun around on her stool to see what her classmates were doing: painting (neon-bright still life), chatting (about Saturday night and who'd hooked up with whom), and sculpting (something involving clay and doll parts). Art freaks—they were the best.

"Audrey, could I borrow you for a minute?"

Audrey looked to her left to see her art teacher, Ms. Fitzgerald, approaching, trailed by an Asian girl with an unfamiliar face. "Sure thing." Like Audrey would have said no—Ms. Fitz was her favorite teacher, even when she was harsh on Audrey's photography, which was often.

"Audrey, this is Olivia Lee." Ms. Fitz nodded at the girl beside her, who gave Audrey the tiniest smile. "She's joining us from . . ."

The girl jumped in when Ms. Fitz trailed off. "Florida. Orlando."

"That's right, Orlando." The teacher looked at Audrey. "Since Olivia is new, I thought that you might be able to tell her how we do things in class and, you know, welcome her. Okay?"

Now the girl looked at her feet, her cheeks flushing pink, and Audrey's heart swelled. She knew what it was like to be the new girl, could remember standing by the jungle gym in too-white sneakers and tight, tiny braids at the beginning of fourth grade. There'd been a girl playing alone on the far side of the playground, skipping with muddy knees. Audrey had liked her T-shirt: blue with pink birds flying across it. When the bell rang and they filed back into the classroom, that girl found a note from Audrey on her desk and, to Audrey's relief, responded with a gap-toothed grin. And that was how she and Rose had become Audrey-and-Rose.

"No problem," Audrey said, and Ms. Fitz clapped her hands together so enthusiastically that half the class looked up, which the new girl must have absolutely *loved*.

"Excellent!" she said. "Okay, Olivia, I'll leave you in the capable hands of Ms. Spencer here, and if you need me for anything, don't be afraid to come and ask."

Ms. Fitz turned and made her way back to the front of the classroom, the girl—Olivia—looking after her forlornly. Audrey pushed out the stool next to her, and the scraping noise it made caught Olivia's attention. "Here, sit." She smiled. "I'm nice. Promise."

"Thanks." Olivia dropped her messenger bag on the floor and hopped up. "Audrey, right?"

"Yep," Audrey said. "I love your hair."

Olivia touched a hand (bitten violet nails, thin silver band on her middle finger) to her head. Her licorice-black hair was cut short so it fell around her ears, with strands of aqua blue peeking out, and neat bangs snipped high across her forehead. "Thanks," she said again, offering another shy smile that made deep dimples appear in her cheeks. "I like yours, too."

Audrey smiled, trying to figure out the best way to coax this girl out of her shell without pushing too hard.

But then Olivia spoke again, in a voice that sounded musical once it got going. "My dad didn't like it so much," she said. "Which is why I moved here with my mom after the divorce was final."

"Oh," Audrey said. "That's, um—"

Olivia laughed, a bubbly sound. "I'm kidding, of course," she said.

"Not about my dad not liking my hair, because he did threaten to send me to my grandmother in Taiwan if I kept up the weird hair and piercings, but the divorce thing isn't true. Although my parents *are* divorced, but I moved with my mom because . . . well, she's my mom. And also because my dad didn't appreciate me changing my last name to match hers. And besides, if I'm not with him, he can't send me to my grandmother, which would be a disaster because she doesn't know I'm gay yet and I think she might have a heart attack when she finds out."

"I see," Audrey said. Initial judgment revised: Olivia Lee was clearly *not* shy.

"Did you take those?"

"What?" Audrey followed Olivia's gaze and turned back to the computer, where her photographs now filled the screen. "Oh. Yeah, I did."

Olivia nodded, pushing her cat-eye glasses up her nose. "They're really interesting."

Interesting. Translation: *they're not great, but I'm a nice person, so I'm not going to say anything.* "Oh, I don't know," Audrey said. "I'm only learning, and my composition is completely—" She cleared her throat. *Don't bore her to death.* "What do you do?"

"Draw, mostly," Olivia answered, but she was still looking at Audrey's photos. "I like this one," she said, tapping her finger on the computer screen. "Who is she?"

The picture that Olivia was pointing at was of Rose: Audrey had taken it when they were getting ready for the party the other night. Rose was peering into the mirror in Audrey's room, her mouth hanging open as she painted shadow over her lids, a green that Audrey had managed to catch the shimmer of. The framing was all wrong, though, and the whole thing was overblown. But it was such a rare moment to see—Rose with her guard completely down—that it was special, maybe, and Audrey almost felt wrong letting this new person see it. Like she was giving her something she hadn't earned yet.

Audrey clicked out of the program. "That's Rose. You'll get to know her."

"I will?"

Audrey smiled. Well, she'd get to know exactly however much Rose chose to give. "Oh, yeah. She's my best friend."

"Oh, right. She's pretty." Olivia turned to Audrey, nodding seriously. "They're great pictures. Honestly."

"Thanks," Audrey said, and then, changing the subject, "So, let me tell you about Kennedy High." Nothing made her more embarrassed than talking about her work—she dreaded their monthly crit sessions in class. Like it wasn't bad enough pulling apart her pictures by herself—listening to other people do it usually felt like having her insides spilling onto the floor for everyone to pick at. And worse than that was the showing they did at the end of every semester, where Audrey got to see exactly how far behind some of her classmates she really was.

"Rule number one," Audrey said. "Don't believe the graffiti in the second-floor bathrooms. It's not true at all, I swear."

FIVE

Audrey guided Olivia through the lunch line and into the maze of tables, giving the new girl a rundown as they went. "Lunch is thirty-five minutes, and we have the same period as the seniors," she explained. "But they get to go off campus, so we are the only ones stuck in this *beautiful* place." Audrey kicked the metal leg of a bright-orange chair. "As you can see, the theme in here is Give-You-Nightmares Bright."

She waved at the girls they sometimes chilled with at parties. "That's Lilia and her group," Audrey said to Olivia. "They're cool. And those guys by the windows? They're our friends, when they're not being complete assholes. The blond one throwing pretzels, that's Cooper." She turned to Olivia and raised her eyebrows. "You'll get to know *all* about Cooper. And see the one trying to catch the pretzels in his mouth?"

Olivia nodded, looking a little bemused. "Yeah?"

"That one would be my boyfriend." Audrey shook her head. "Trust me, he's not as annoying as he seems right now. Although I'm beginning to wonder."

She headed toward their usual table. Rose, Jen, and María were messing around and laughing; a shiny red apple flew from María's hand, narrowly missing Rose, and Audrey felt herself smile. "Come on," she said, sensing Olivia's hesitation. "I'll introduce you to my friends."

She wove her way between the tables. "Hey!" Dropping into the seat next to Rose, Audrey nodded at Olivia, trying to let her know without words that it was okay for her to sit. When she did, Audrey turned back to the girls. "This is Olivia. She's new. We're in art together. She just moved here from . . ." Shit. Was it Philadelphia? Fort Worth?

"Florida," Olivia filled in.

Right.

Jen and María leaned in, the cross and crescent moon pendants around Jen's neck making music, while Rose gave a halfhearted wave. Audrey picked up her fork and twisted it into her noodles. "This is Jen," she said, pointing so Olivia could follow. "That's María, and sunshine here is Rose." She jabbed a finger into her best friend's arm in the hope that it might get her to at least feign interest. "Don't be scared of them. They only look mean."

"Except for Rose," María said with a laugh. "Don't get on her bad side."

"Shut up," Rose's automatic snap back came, and Audrey glanced at Olivia, half expecting her to be ready to flee.

But actually, she was laughing. "I'll remember that," she said. "Rose." Her head tilted to the side. "From the pictures, right?"

Audrey stared down at her food, across the table at María, anywhere except at Rose. It wasn't that Rose didn't like having her picture taken—more that over the years, Rose had featured in most of Audrey's photographs and had lately started saying, "If you don't put the camera down, I will smash that shit up myself." Meant with love, Audrey was sure.

Rose's sigh echoed in Audrey's ear. "I'm going to guess yes," she said, her voice surprisingly soft. "Thank you, Audrey."

"I'm sorry," Olivia said quickly. "I didn't mean to—you shouldn't be mad. They were beautiful."

Audrey waited to see how Rose reacted, absorbing Olivia's compliment. A pink flush appeared on Rose's cheeks, and when she said, "Thanks," it was short and high.

That was the thing with Rose: most people thought she was a bitch. (Or at the very least *bitchy*.) And maybe she was (who wasn't?) but often it was shyness that made her snappy, short-tempered. But you had to really get to know Rose to know that about her, and Rose kept her circle small. So most people watched from afar, simultaneously disliking her and wanting to be close to her. It was a strange thing for Audrey to watch, being on her side of things—the one person Rose ever opened up to, told secrets not even Jen and María were allowed to know. But it also felt kind of nice—like Rose didn't belong to anybody but her.

She knocked her foot into Rose's leg under the table. "Hey," Audrey said, a lilt to her voice. "She doesn't bite."

María launched into an interrogation of Olivia that took up the rest of the lunch period: Why had she moved from Florida to New York state? Did the ring in her nose hurt? What about the bar through the top of her ear? And what was her schedule like?

Audrey picked at her food as Olivia talked about her mom's new job at an art gallery in the city, how New York was her real home and the year in Orlando was a failed experiment. The holes in her ears hadn't hurt but the nose ring had, enough to make her cry, she said. And she didn't know her schedule yet, but she had a lit class next period, America in the Twentieth Century or something.

"That's my class," Rose said. "With Dr. Bennett?"

Olivia fished inside her messenger bag and produced an illustrated notebook, the cover filled with pencil-shaded magical creatures. "That's what it says," Olivia said, running a finger across the inside cover. She looked up at Rose and smiled. "At least I'll have one nonhostile."

Audrey held back her snort. Rose, nonhostile? That was a nice idea.

Jen grabbed Olivia's notebook and studied the rest of her schedule. "You're in my biology class," she said. "And Spanish."

"I'm in Spanish, too," Audrey said with a smile. "This is working out good for you."

Olivia nodded, her gaze focused somewhere past Audrey. "Yeah," she said. "It seems like it is."

The bell rang then, sending the cafeteria into a scramble as everyone hurried to their next class. Rose followed behind Audrey as they took their trays over to the trash. "Hey," she said. "You hardly ate. You okay?"

Audrey frowned at the leftover food on her tray and pressed a hand to her stomach to quell the queasiness stirring within. "I think I'm coming down with something," she said. "I've been feeling sick since last week."

María pushed past them, laughing. "It's called a hangover," she said. "You little lush."

Rose laughed, too, and Audrey wanted to join in, but the most she could manage was a halfhearted smile. Because she had been feeling sick all weekend, maybe even before that. And she was dead tired all of a sudden. And her boobs were spilling out of all her bras.

Lining up all those facts like that made Audrey feel stupid, like someone had given her a checklist of clichés and she'd run through them all, ticking every box.

But they were clichés for a reason.

Audrey left her tray and threw her bag over her shoulder, following her friends out into the hall. *It's probably nothing,* she told herself. *No need to panic.*

Right. Tell that to the alarm bells screaming, shrill and insistent, in the back of her mind.

SIX

Audrey stared blankly at her math homework, chewing the end of her pencil. If only they could figure out brain switching and María's mind could do this work for her.

"Audrey?" There was a knock on her bedroom door, and then it swung open a few inches, enough for Adam to step one foot inside. "I'm ordering dinner; what do you want?"

She sat up on her bed, knocking her notebook onto the floor. "What are we having?"

"Thai." Adam came fully into her room, waving a menu. "From the place on Charleston," he added. "Your favorite."

Audrey's stomach rolled, and she clenched her teeth. Normally she would've snatched the menu right out of his hand, pretending like she was going to order something other than her usual tom yum soup with chicken-and-vegetable spring rolls, but the thought of any of it made her feel like she was about to throw up. "You know, I'm not hungry right now," she told Adam. "I'm not feeling so great." That part came out before she could stop it, and she wanted to kick herself. Now Adam would tell her mom, and her mom would come upstairs, and she'd have to lie even more because no way in hell was she about to admit what she was thinking it might be.

"Really?" Adam pressed the back of his hand against her forehead. "You don't feel warm. I don't think."

Audrey squeezed out a laugh. "Who are you, Florence Nightingale? Your idea of sick is when you ate too many hot dogs at a baseball game. I've seen you drink a beer because you thought it would help with your allergic reaction to a *banana*."

"Hey, I can be nurturing," Adam protested. "Don't you remember that time I brought your mom soup when she had the flu?"

"That was, like, three years ago," Audrey said. "And you only did it because you'd just started dating, and you needed her to think you were sweet. And"—she put up her hand—"before you start denying it, you told that story at Mom's theater party last Christmas, so don't even."

Adam ran a hand through his dirty-blond hair, giving her a sheepish grin. "I need to learn to keep my mouth shut, don't I?"

Audrey nodded solemnly. "Yes."

"All right, point taken." Adam turned to leave, then paused in the doorway. "You want me to bring something up? Toast, ginger ale . . ."

Audrey shook her head. "I'll come down in a minute. Thanks, though."

Adam closed the door on his way out, and Audrey flopped back over onto her stomach. As much as she teased him, Adam was sweet—the first of her mom's boyfriends to ever last past a couple of dates, the first to be invited into their house for dinner. Certainly the only one who'd ever gotten to know Audrey well enough to learn her favorite takeout and that she liked her orange juice with pulp. The fact that he also happened to be twelve years younger than her mom paled in comparison to all that, not that it'd ever bothered Audrey. She was already well accustomed to a less-than-normal life: Adopted? Check. Movie star parent? Check. Mother with fair skin and red hair about a thousand degrees removed from her own brown skin and mass of curls? Check and check. So in the grand scheme of things, the age gap was kind of boring.

She dug her hands into her covers, listening to Adam's footsteps going down the stairs and into the kitchen. She'd better do what she needed to quickly.

Audrey jumped up from her bed and kicked her way through the clothes blanketing the carpet to get to her desk. Her planner was already flipped open to the day's date, and she licked her finger before flicking back—a month? Two?

The kitchen was too far away from her attic room for her to hear any voices, but the bottom step of the second staircase had a loud creak that let Audrey know whenever someone was on their way up. She only had to listen for it.

She yanked out the second drawer in her desk, where she kept her birth control pills. This pack was almost half empty, so—she counted on her fingers, looking up at the ceiling. Eleven days ago was a Friday, and yeah, they'd stolen an hour in Julian's bedroom with the door locked, but that wasn't it. That couldn't have been it, because that would be way too early for her to know. Right?

They were always careful: Audrey took her pill every day like clockwork, had been since the trip to the doctor with her mom last January. If they ever thought they needed more than that—like the time Audrey got a shot before her vacation—then they used condoms. Always, *always*.

So stupid, she thought. *How could we be so stupid?*

She couldn't imagine what would happen if It was happening. What her mom would say—God, what Rose would say. She'd be so— Actually, Audrey didn't know what she'd be. Would she be more disappointed in Audrey's foolishness, or annoyed? Shit.

She closed her eyes. She couldn't pretend this wasn't happening.

"Audrey, honey." Her mom's voice floated up, and then there was the telltale creak. "Are you okay?"

Shit.

Audrey grabbed her phone and typed a text to Julian: Need to talk. Call me when you get this.

His response came back almost immediately: At practice, what's up?

She inhaled sharply. How to phrase it so it wouldn't sound like drama? Come over later, she settled on typing.

She managed to press Send and place her phone facedown on the desk a second before the door opened and her mom entered, her hair twisted up and held in place with a pencil. All these years and it was still the same shade of rich red that Audrey saw in the red carpet photos online. "Hey," she said gently, "Adam said you're not feeling good. Do you feel sick? Headache?"

Audrey looked at her mom, worry wrinkling the skin around her eyes, and felt her stomach twist again. "I'm fine," she said. "It's nothing, honestly. I'm coming down now."

Laura smiled, tipping her head to the side. "Okay. I'll fix you something—apple slices and crackers."

"Oh," Audrey said. "Like—"

Her phone vibrated twice in quick succession, and without thinking she snatched it up to look. They were both from Julian, the first:

Everything okay? I'll swing by when we're done. (If Izzy
ever lets me leave.)

And the second:

I love you.

"Like what?" Laura said.

Audrey clasped her phone tightly as she stood, smiling at her mom with a brightness that she definitely wasn't feeling. "Apples and crackers," she said, starting toward the door. "Like when I was little."

At the sound of the doorbell Audrey jumped off the couch, earning a look from Adam. He glanced at his watch pointedly. "Do I have to ask who that is?"

"Nope." She opened the front door to Julian, standing there with his hands jammed into his pockets and the wind whipping his dark hair into his eyes.

"Hey, I came as—"

Audrey didn't let him finish, grabbing his arm and yanking him inside the house. "Upstairs."

"Audrey?" Her mom's voice floated out of the kitchen, and then she stepped out, a beer in her hand. Her eyebrows rose when she looked past Audrey, and she raised the bottle to her lips. "Hi, Julian."

"Hey," he said. "Sorry, I know it's late."

She dipped her chin in a nod, her gaze floating to her daughter. "He's right, Audrey," her mom said. "It's nine."

"I know."

"Don't we have rules about school nights?"

"I *know*," Audrey said again. "But—ten minutes. Fifteen, max. Please?"

For a moment Laura looked like she was going to say no, the lines creasing her forehead a clear indicator, but then she sighed and pointed at them. "Ten minutes," she said. "And Julian, if I catch you here after that, I'm cutting you off from Adam's record collection."

Julian gave a mock salute. "Yes, ma'am," he said, and Laura swatted at him.

"Ten minutes," she said again, a warning. "Go on."

Audrey raced up the stairs and into her room, Julian close behind her. On her bed Marmalade kneaded his paws into the comforter, purring loudly. "Hey, buddy." Julian lay across the bed and scratched the cat's head before looking at Audrey. "What's up?"

Audrey fluttered her hands in front of her face. Now, she trusted Julian, loved him, let him know all her secrets and hidden sides. And she knew him. She thought she knew how he would react when she said it, but—what if she was wrong? What if she didn't know him as well as she thought she did?

"Audrey." Julian sounded impatient. "What is it? You made it sound all urgent and now—"

"You're going to think this is ridiculous," she interrupted. "You're going to think *I'm* ridiculous, but—I think I might be, maybe, a little . . . pregnant?"

She didn't mean for her voice to go up at the end the way it did, turning her statement into a question—as if Julian had the answer.

He sat up now, Marmalade following his hand and meowing indignantly when Julian didn't begin scratching him again. "What? But—" His voice cracked a little, and he cleared his throat. "Pregnant?"

Audrey exhaled, lowering slowly into her desk chair. "Yeah. I think so."

"Shit," he said. "But we—"

"I know."

"And that's not—?"

"I guess not," Audrey said. She moved to sit next to Julian on the edge of her bed. "Look, I need you to tell me right now that everything's going to be okay and I don't need to freak out; otherwise I'm going to do exactly that. Okay?"

His smile was a touch too wide to be even a tiny bit believable. "Everything's going to be okay," he said. "You don't need to freak out."

Audrey closed her eyes and felt her heart rate slow, the blood pulsing through her body less like rapids now. "What are we going to do?"

"Did you take a test?"

"No." She hadn't gotten that far, had gotten stuck at allowing herself to believe this could be happening.

"Okay," Julian said, and Audrey could hear it in his voice, his brain clicking into problem-solving mode, the same way he sounded when he was figuring out why that chord progression didn't sound right or how to make his amp stop buzzing. "We'll go after school tomorrow, get a test, take the test. . . ." He paused. "And it'll probably be negative, and we'll have worried about it for nothing."

Audrey wished she could believe that, but it seemed way too simple. Easy. "And if it's positive?" she asked. "Then what? Because I feel pretty Positive." Yeah, the sore boobs and the nausea and the exhaustion, that all seemed to point one way.

"Then . . ." Julian seemed stumped for a second, and he raked his hands through his windswept hair. "We'll work it out," he said after a moment. "Yeah?"

He slung his arm over Audrey's shoulder and pulled her into him, pressing a kiss to her temple where her soft baby hairs grew. "Don't worry," he said, sounding more confident now. "It'll be okay."

Audrey closed her eyes against the feeling of his words on her skin and nodded. Even though she could hear the nerves in his voice, could see his foot tapping a staccato rhythm on the floor, she wanted to believe what he was saying. If she followed the steps he laid out, if she didn't freak out, if her body didn't betray them, then he'd be right. Everything would be okay.

Marmalade crept onto Audrey's lap, his claws snagging at her tights. "Off," she said, gently shoving him away. She looked at Julian. "You'd better go, too. Unless you want the wrath of Laura Vale

Spencer to rain down on you."

Julian laughed. "I'm good." He got up, bringing Audrey to her feet with him, and kissed her once on the mouth before pulling away, looking thoughtful. "Although compared to what she might rain down on me if it turns out I knocked up her daughter..."

"Shh," Audrey hissed, and widened her eyes. "Really? Is this the time for jokes?"

He raised his eyebrows and gave her the smile she could never resist, even though she hated how weak it made her feel. "Lighten up, Aud. I mean, it's laugh or cry, right?" It was weird how their positions were switched: usually Audrey was the calm, things-will-figure-themselves-out one, and Julian was the one fixating on the issue, driving himself to the point of anxiety with that methodical mind. That alone tripped a little panic wire in her. But then, she always told Julian things would be fine, and he believed her. Couldn't she do the same?

She walked him downstairs and kissed him again on the front step, sliding her hand around the back of his neck while his fingers tickled at her waist, until the porch light flicked on and off three times very deliberately.

Audrey stepped back, wrapping her arms around herself. "See you tomorrow," she said. "I love you."

"Love you, too," Julian said. "And remember what I said, yeah? Everything's going to be okay."

"Right." Audrey looked down at her feet, the smile she tried too tight. "I'll remember."

SEVEN

The ticking of the clock beat along in perfect time with Audrey's drumming fingers. They were taking a quiz, on covalent bonds or something, but she'd given up fifteen minutes into it. What was the point in trying when she couldn't focus at all?

She bit the inside of her cheek and looked up at the clock: two minutes left.

People were starting to rustle around, surreptitiously slipping pencils into backpacks and sitting up straight, ready to make a quick exit. Audrey watched Mr. Vargas at his desk, making sure he didn't see her folding up her quiz and putting it into her bag. No need to hand it in when she already knew she'd be getting a zero, right?

The bell rang—finally, thankfully—and the room exploded into movement. "Okay, people!" Mr. Vargas yelled over the squeaking chairs and sudden chatter. "Leave your quizzes on your desks, and, guys—don't forget about the chapter for Thursday, all right? I don't want to have to go over it yet again. . . ."

Audrey was already one step out of the room when he started speaking. Okay. She'd done it, day over. Now all she had to do was buy a pregnancy test, take it, and learn whether she'd landed herself in a monumental fuckup of a situation or not.

Not, she thought. *Please, please not.*

"Audrey!"

Her first thought on hearing Rose's voice: *Please, not right now. I cannot deal with you right now.*

"Audrey! Hello?"

Audrey hurried along across the parking lot, her book-laden bag smacking against her hip. *Almost there, almost there, almost there.*

"Audrey Spencer, I know you hear me! I swear to God, if you don't turn around right now, I'm going to come over to your house in the middle of the night and—"

"Jesus," Audrey hissed under her breath. But she came to a stop, pulling her jacket close around her, and then turned, feigning surprise. "Hey! What's up?"

Rose ambled toward her, a thick chunk of her hair slipping over her shoulder and a pair of tap shoes swinging from her fingers.

"Hey." Rose gave her a suspicious look. "Didn't you hear me calling you?"

Audrey shrugged. "I guess not."

"Whatever." Rose didn't look at all convinced. "Where were you at lunch? You totally disappeared today."

"Oh, um . . ."

She'd been with Julian, holed up in his car with her legs up on the dash and the cassette player—that's how old Julian's car was, it had a tape deck in it—singing the one Cure song she liked over and over. They'd been working out which pharmacy to go to: not the Walgreens downtown—too close to the theater that Audrey's mom was director of. And the one closest to school was out, too, since the manager and Julian's mom belonged to the same book club. They might as well put up a billboard announcing it.

She looked up at Rose. Usually they told each other everything, good and bad, like how Rose missed her sister a painful amount, or how Audrey had walked in on Adam in the shower. Audrey was the first person Rose had told she was bisexual; Rose was the only person who knew Audrey's first kiss had been with a *way* older art student.

This, though. Something about this felt different.

"I had to make up a test," she lied. "I thought I told you."

"Speaking of homework," Rose said. "My Government paper?"

"Shit." Audrey found it in her bag and handed it over. She'd borrowed it for inspiration, but she hadn't even started writing her own paper yet. "Sorry, I completely forgot."

Rose held her shoes under her arm as she tucked the plastic, wallet-protected paper into her bag. "It's fine. But don't do it again, or you'll lose all intelligence-borrowing privileges."

Audrey attempted a smile. "Sorry."

"Forget it," Rose said. "I have something better to talk to you about anyway. So, if you had been at lunch today, you would have witnessed Olivia . . ."

Audrey glanced down at her beat-up watch, the leather band so worn that it hung loosely around her wrist. They had to get to the pharmacy, get back to Audrey's house, and be done with everything before Julian had to get to his shift at his restaurant job.

"What?" Rose snapped. "Am I keeping you?"

Audrey looked up into Rose's pissed-off face. "Um . . ."

"Are you kidding?" Rose lifted her hands to the sky. "You've been MIA all day, and now you can't spare five minutes to listen to me? God, you're worse than my sister."

"It's not like that," Audrey said. "I really have to go. Because I have . . . an eye doctor appointment." *Wow*. Talk about unconvincing. Her mom's acting talent clearly hadn't rubbed off on her. "But I'll call you later and you can tell me all about it. Okay?"

Rose huffed and flipped the hood of her jacket up against the rain that had begun. "Fine."

"Sorry." Audrey sidestepped a tall kid bouncing a basketball, flicking cold rainwater over her shoes. "Talk later. Promise."

She glanced down at her watch again—she was supposed to meet Julian at his car, and he was going to be soaked if she made him wait any longer.

"Go on," Rose said. "I don't want to make you late."

Audrey tossed her rain-dampened hair out of her eyes and smiled wanly. No way had Rose bought her eye appointment lie, but she didn't have the energy to worry about that right this minute. She had more pressing matters to attend to.

Pregnancy test–taking matters. *Happy happy*, Audrey thought as she left Rose behind. *Joy joy*.

EIGHT

Audrey stared at the selection of brightly colored boxes stacked on the shelves in front of her. "Wow."

Julian whistled, a sharp, tight sound. "Wow is right. I didn't know there were so many different kinds."

This pharmacy was smack-bang between both of their houses, so hopefully safe from nosy neighbors and gossip-mongering PTA members. The pink-haired girl behind the counter had smiled at them when they'd walked in, but other than that she hadn't paid any attention to them.

"I didn't know they were so *expensive,*" Audrey said, picking up one that promised "unmistakably clear results instantly!" "Twenty-three dollars? It's a stick that you pee on!"

Julian took the box from her, squinting to read the tiny writing on the back. "This has three in it. Do we need three?"

"Probably not, but . . ." Audrey made a face. At least if she took all three of them, she'd have a better chance of feeling certain about whatever it told her. She'd definitely have to take more than one, because what if she got a false positive? Or a false negative, for that matter? On second thought, three was an excellent idea. "Let's get this one." Audrey held out her empty hand. "I only have my debit card."

"Okay," Julian said. "So . . . ?"

"So—" Audrey pointed up at the counter and the sign stuck to the register: CARD READER OUT OF ORDER. CASH ONLY. Because of *course* they would pick the one pharmacy apparently stuck in the Dark Ages.

"Oh, right." Julian patted his pocket and his face dropped. "Shit."

"What?"

"I don't have my wallet," he said. "Don't you have cash?"

Audrey dragged her nails across the tiny bumps of Braille on the back of the pregnancy test box. "No," she said. "I thought you got paid last Friday."

"I forgot my *wallet*, Audrey; when I got paid isn't the point."

"Okay, well, I don't have any cash on me! It's not like I could ask my mom, is it? 'Hey, can I borrow twenty bucks? I think I might be knocked up.'"

Julian leaned in, his gaze jumping around. "Keep your voice down."

A contrary part of Audrey wanted to yell even louder now, and she narrowed her eyes. "Don't tell me what to do."

"You're the one who doesn't want anybody to know! Isn't that why we had to come all the way out here? And now you're screaming it to the whole place."

"I'm not—" Audrey caught herself—why was she fighting him over this? So stupid—and stopped, pulling in a deep breath. "Okay. Look, I'll go find an ATM. Problem solved."

She fumbled in her bag until she found her battered wallet and slid the card out. But as soon as she had it in her fingers, Julian snatched it right from her grip. "I'll go."

"J."

"I said I'll go, all right? I know your PIN." He sidestepped out of reach of Audrey's hand. "I'll be back in a minute."

Audrey watched him leave, watched him walk past the store windows with his hands shoved into his jacket pockets and his jaw set in this hard line. She placed her fingertips on the shelf edge and strained on her tiptoes until she couldn't see Julian anymore, only a blurry shape like him disappearing between two buildings.

"Do you need any help?"

Audrey fell back onto flat feet and gripped the box of tests tight in her hand as she looked at the pink-haired sales assistant standing there. How long had she been there? And wasn't it against store policy or something to creep up on the customers? "No," Audrey said.

The girl raised her perfectly drawn-in eyebrows. "No?"

"No. Thank you," Audrey remembered this time. "I'm just . . . waiting."

The girl—Lindy, her name tag read—did this flourish of her fingers and laughed, a pack-a-day rasp. "Oh, I've been there. Word of advice: don't wait too long. One day you'll open your eyes and he'll be long gone and you'll be here. Waiting."

The judgment in that one word fell heavily on Audrey, and she almost shook herself to shake the weight and the bitterness of it off. "Oh, no," she said, making her voice deliberately light. "It's not like that."

"It never is." Lindy shrugged, pulling a hand through her pink ponytail. "But what do I know?"

She turned and made her way down the aisle back toward the counter, and the fluorescents made her hair shine almost neon.

Yeah, Audrey wanted to call after her. *What the fuck do you know?*

But it would only be for the sake of being pissed off, for the anger of being called out. She knew exactly why this stranger had taken it on herself to hand out those pearls of wisdom, because Audrey would have done the same thing if their positions were reversed. Well, maybe Audrey wouldn't have said it out loud, but she for sure would have thought it: *Look at her, waiting on some boy. Please get some self-respect.*

It was what she thought when she saw girls hanging around at parties while their boyfriends dealt little tabs and Baggies, when they were crying in the school bathrooms because they had cheated on them, when she saw people her mom's age talking about the house they were going to buy and the wedding they were going to have "as soon as he leaves his wife" or whatever other excuse they had been given. And she knew it was harsh, so not sisterhood, to judge these girls, but so often it was sadness more than scorn that coursed through her. Because they didn't need those boys, those waiting girls: they were smart and strong and had the entire world at their feet, if only they could see it. If only those boys weren't blocking their sight.

Audrey had never thought she was one of them. When Julian had band practice, she didn't hang around—he could come and find her when he was done. At parties she took shots with her friends while he played beer pong with his, perfectly happy. But now, here she was.

With a pregnancy test in her hand, and a boy walking away from her, and maybe this was it.

She backed out of the aisle toward the cheap makeup. *No. I'm not like that. Julian isn't going to be like that.* He was here with her, wasn't he? And that already made him different from all those depressing teen parent statistics—right?

Audrey occupied herself by looking at the metallic eye shadows she already had in three colors until Julian returned. He handed back her card with a tight smile that only half of his mouth moved into. "Sorry."

Audrey replaced the cap on the pencil in her hand. "Me too."

"We good?"

He held out his hand and Audrey looked at it for a second. Were they good?

They were about to find out, right?

She threaded her fingers through his, ignoring the way his palms were sweat damp, and nodded. "Of course."

At the counter Lindy rang them up, her nails clacking on the register. "That'll be twenty-two ninety-nine."

Julian handed over the cash while Audrey avoided the girl's eyes, staring at her nails instead. They were painted the exact same pink as her hair and were covered in tiny silver polka dots. Pretty.

"Here you go," she said, handing over a plastic bag that hung limply with their one purchase inside it. "Have a nice day."

Audrey took the bag, looping it around her wrist. *Does it seem like I'm having a nice goddamn day?* "Thanks."

They stopped off at a 7-Eleven on the way to Audrey's house, where she almost bought a Big Gulp of Diet Coke before she got distracted with wondering whether you could drink soda when you were pregnant, which led to wondering what else she wouldn't be able to drink—coffee? What about tea? Beer, obviously.

And *that* led her to wonder whether her thinking of all this meant something, because if she didn't care about the possibility that there was a tiny bundle of cells that would become a baby inside of her, would she even be considering what was good or bad for it?

Eventually she gave up and bought the biggest bottle of orange juice that she could find. Vitamin C couldn't hurt.

Could it?

Audrey stood in her bathroom, staring at herself in the mirror. If her life were a movie, now would be the point when she lifted her shirt, pressed her hand flat against her abdomen, and turned side on, as if she'd be able to feel anything other than the regular soft and yielding flesh of her belly. *Why do they always do that?* she wondered idly. *Like it's not happening if they can't see it with their own eyes? And of course they never have an ounce of surplus fat on their bodies, and they usually look superhot, and they're always, always half naked, too. What is with that? Who takes a pregnancy test in their fanciest lingerie or—*

"Audrey?"

Julian's voice pulled her back from her dreamland, and she began clawing at the box containing the tests as she answered him. "What?"

"Can I come in?"

She paused. "Um . . ." She'd always drawn the line there—*some* kind of mystery would be nice.

However, Julian had seen her naked more times than she could count, had touched her places no one else ever had, and quite possibly had knocked her up. The time for shyness was long past.

Audrey unlocked the door, and Julian stepped inside, one hand tangled in his hair. "Sorry," he said. "But I was freaking out by myself out there."

"That's okay." Audrey managed a tiny laugh as she finally ripped open the package and sent the contents clattering into the sink. "I was freaking out in here."

Julian sat on the edge of the bathtub, peering up at her with his forehead creased and cheeks flushed patchy white and red. "It's probably nothing, right? We use protection. It could be your body being weird, right?"

Audrey nodded. "Probably." She didn't want to tell him about all the stories she'd read on the internet where women had said the exact same thing as him only to find out they were wrong.

Audrey tapped her nails on the sink, muted clicks on the porcelain. "Can't put it off any longer, can we?"

Julian stood and put his hands on her waist. "It's okay," he said quietly. "No matter what it says, it'll be okay."

Audrey felt the way his fingers gripped her tightly, betraying the calm in his voice, but forced a smiled anyway. "You're right. We'll be fine."

NINE

Audrey's heart was drumming so hard and so fast that when she put her hand on her chest, pressed her palm flat there, it felt as if it were about to burst out. She had that hollow feeling in the pit of her stomach, too, an emptiness. *How much longer could it take?*

Julian laced his fingers through Audrey's other hand, his palm clammy-cold. They stared at the three plastic sticks—*They really are almost nothing,* Audrey thought; *how can my future rest on such slight little things?* Her future. Art school, maybe; Rhode Island School of Design, that was the place she dreamed about, the dream she kept quiet because it was crazy hard to get into and embarrassing, almost, to admit that she even wanted to try. But that didn't matter now; whatever she'd been imagining—RISD or Syracuse or Illinois, photography or illustration or a *very* useful liberal arts degree—might be gone.

It felt like way longer than the two minutes the directions said, but eventually it happened. First the one in the middle, then the left, and then the right. All three the same.

Three big, fat positives.

Julian took a deep breath and squeezed her hand. "It's okay. We'll be okay."

Audrey squeezed back, his clammy fingers damp in her grip.

I wish he'd stop saying that.

They weren't much of a surprise, those positives. Not truthfully. Since she'd thought it, thought she might be pregnant, she'd *known* it was happening. Audrey could feel the trouble brewing in the pit of her belly, all the way down in the blood streaming in her veins.

"You should go." She registered the confused look on Julian's face and amended her words. "To work. You're going to be late."

Julian checked his watch and groaned. "Shit."

"It's all right," Audrey said, slipping her hand out of his—but only so she could loop her arms around his neck instead and kiss him. "We'll talk about it later."

Julian kissed her back with a fervor that, for a second, made Audrey forget all about the *P* word.

"It's all right," he said. "I know this is scary, but it's going to be okay. We'll figure it out. We'll be fine."

Who is he trying to convince, Audrey wondered, *me, or himself?*

But as soon as Julian left to go wait tables, as soon as she'd disposed of any and all incriminating evidence, when she was lying facedown on her bed, the reality came rushing back.

Pregnant.

I am pregnant.

But it's okay, she reasoned. *Because things are going to be okay. Julian said so. Julian's never wrong. He never lies.*

She pressed her face into the pillows so her world-weary, soul-deep moaning couldn't be heard. *Fuck. Fucking fuck shit fuck.*

Okay. She had to calm down. She had to relax. And most of all, she had to forget about that tiny thrill, of nerves and disbelief and something almost like excitement, that she'd felt in the split second between seeing the results and Julian squeezing her hand.

Easy.

TEN

Sitting in a cracked vinyl booth opposite María and next to Rose, Audrey tried not to look too much like she wanted to disappear. Which wasn't easy, because if she could have figured out some way to make the ground open up and let her in, she would have.

Then again, she was hungry, and Bettie's was the best place to get burgers after school (which was why half their class was crammed into the place). And since she now seemed to be nauseous more often than hungry, she had to take advantage of this moment.

"I think I have the perfect costume for Friday," María said over the seventies hair metal playing over the speakers. "One word: *Flashdance.*"

Audrey ripped the paper off her straw. "Is that one word or two?"

"*Flashdance*?" Rose asked. "So, leg warmers and underwear?"

María shook her head. "Overalls and a welding mask. I will be comfortable, citing an iconic pop culture moment, and refusing to pander to the male gaze all at the same time."

"It's Halloween," Rose said, picking up her milk shake. "What better time to strengthen our feminist ideals?"

María grinned, mischievous eyes behind her pink-framed glasses. "Exactly." She turned to Audrey. "Have you decided yet?"

Audrey made a face. Last year she and Rose had gone *Clueless*, rocking knee-high socks and supershort pleated skirts as Dionne and Cher, and two years ago the theme had been Prohibition-era gangsters—Laura had let them raid the costumes at the theater for wide elastic suspenders and painted on sharp mustaches for them. Usually Audrey loved it all, but this time around she was kind of lacking inspiration.

Juno? Maybe a little too on-the-nose.

The server kid, a sophomore fellow art freak, arrived at their booth then and set down their food. "Careful," he warned. "Onion rings are fresh out of the fryer."

As he left, Jen appeared with Olivia in tow. "Hey," Jen said, and she waved toward Olivia. "Sit wherever. Do you want anything? I'm going to order."

"Um . . ." Olivia looked at the board, her eyebrows furrowing. "I don't know. What's good here?"

"Everything," Audrey said, and she brandished an onion ring as if to illustrate her point. "But if you want the *best* thing, get the bacon cheeseburger. It'll change your life."

Olivia laughed. "Okay, I guess I'll have one bacon cheeseburger."

Jen nodded. "Excellent choice."

She headed up to the counter, and Olivia hovered there, looking uncertain. "Come on," María said, and she patted the bench. "We're discussing Halloween."

"We're T-minus three days," Rose said, "and still have no costume. I mean, I wanted us to be Heathers, but Audrey thinks it'll go over everyone's heads."

Jen came bounding back and pulled up a chair. "What's a Heather?" she asked.

"See?" Audrey said. "My point exactly."

Olivia smiled. "A Heather is cool," she said. "But Veronica would be cooler."

"Finally," Rose said, allowing her lips to curve into a half smile. "Someone who *gets* me."

Audrey picked up her burger and eyed the gloopy mustard spilling out of the bun. God, was she starving, but everything tasted so weird to her now. Now that she was pregnant. Every time she'd remembered that today—every four seconds or so—she'd inexplicably heard the snotty voice of her ninth-grade health teacher reverberating in her head: *The only one hundred percent effective birth control is abstinence! AB-STI-NENCE.*

Which, yes, was true, but God was it ridiculous. Even ninth-grade Audrey had known that. People—teachers, parents, old-white-guy politicians—liked to say that if you were going to have sex, you needed to be prepared to deal with the consequences.

Well, no shit, Audrey thought. *Of course you did.* But what they actually meant was that if you got knocked up, you'd better not complain about missing out on your teenage years, because it was only your (bad, very bad) decisions that got you in that (bad, very bad) situation. She knew what those people would say about her now. She was trying not to care.

Audrey forced that to the back of her mind and made herself take a big bite of her burger. Had to maintain as normal an appearance as possible; otherwise her friends would start to notice. Rose had already started to notice, before Audrey even had, and if she didn't get her act together, it would become obvious. She wasn't ready for that—she and Julian hadn't even talked about what they were going to do about this piece of news. No, if she could just pretend like everything was normal, then maybe everything would *be* normal.

Jen stole an onion ring. "So, Olivia, are you bored of this place yet?" Then, in her typical Jen way, she continued without pausing to let Olivia answer. "Are you coming to the Halloween party? It's going to be excellent; I can already tell."

Olivia shrugged. "I'm not sure," she said. "I mean, I've heard about it, but . . . it's only my second week here. And I don't want to crash."

"Cooper won't care," María said. "Is he here? Oh, there he is. Coop! Hey!"

A backward-baseball-hatted head popped up from a table near the windows, and Cooper looked in their general direction, pointing at himself questioningly.

"Yes, you!" María let out an exaggerated sigh. "What other Cooper could I mean?" She turned back, sinking into her seat again and nodding at Olivia, who seemed bemused by everything. "Trust me," María said. "It's fine."

Audrey watched as Cooper made his way over to them, catching wide-eyed stares from a group of freshman girls too shiny-new to know better. Sure, he had that Pretty White Boy thing going on, but that faded once you got to know the inside of his dirty mind. He was fun, though, Audrey couldn't deny that.

He climbed into the booth behind them and leaned over between Rose and Audrey. "What's up, Cortez?"

"Halloween is what's up," María said. "Your party. You don't mind if Olivia comes, do you?"

"That depends," Cooper said. "Who's Olivia?"

Olivia cleared her throat, leaning forward. "Me."

"Oh, *right*." Cooper stared, a slow smile spreading over his face. "The new girl. I've been wondering when I'd get to meet you."

"Her name is Olivia, not New Girl," Audrey said shortly. "And can you answer the question?"

"All right! Jeez, Audrey, who got your panties in a bunch?" he said. "No, I don't mind. Olivia—last name?"

"Lee."

"Olivia Lee!" He extended his hand in an enthusiastically theatrical manner, almost smacking Audrey in the face. "It would be my greatest honor to have you in attendance at my Halloween party. Costumes mandatory—the smaller the better," he added.

Audrey rolled her eyes as María said, "Don't be a skeeze, Coop."

But Olivia was laughing along with Jen. "Thanks," she told him, and looked over at Rose. "Are you going?"

"Wouldn't miss it for the world," Rose said.

Olivia looked like she was giving it serious thought, her teeth digging into her bottom lip and her eyebrows sloping together, before she finally nodded. "Okay," she said. "I guess I'll be there."

Cooper bounced to his feet, grinning mischievously as he backed away from their table. "Excellent. Can't wait."

Audrey watched him leave while she twisted her napkin into ribbons. She did not want to be at that party.

But if she wasn't there, she'd have to give Rose a reason, and what was she going to say?

Jen clapped gleefully, interrupting Audrey's thoughts. "I think someone has an admirer."

"I agree," María said, nudging Olivia. "Cooper was totally checking you out."

Jen laughed. "Of course, Coop checks everyone out, but . . ."

Olivia laughed, a small flush appearing in her cheeks. "He's not really my type."

"Too pretty?" María asked.

"Too loudmouthed?" Jen said.

Olivia shook her head again, the small silver hoops that dangled from her left ear swaying. "Too *boy*."

"Gotcha," Jen said. "Well, there are going to be plenty of cute girls at the party, too. Okay, mainly straight girls, but, hey—you never know, right?"

Audrey pushed away her food and forced herself to participate some more. "Right," she said. "People keep secrets."

"I hear rumors of Saint Francis in attendance," María said. "Wasn't Aisha at Coop's last time, too?"

"I have to pee," Rose said abruptly. "Audrey, move."

Audrey got up so Rose could slide out and made a face at the others as she sat again. "Oops."

"Was it something I said?" Olivia asked, and it sounded like she was half joking, half serious.

"No, no! Don't worry," Jen said. "It's Rose."

"It's Aisha Forrester," Audrey said, watching Rose cut between the tables. She had this mix of dancer grace and violent determination that made people's eyes find her without trying. Audrey would go after her in a minute, listen to her pretend not to be bothered by the mention of Aisha's name until she admitted it and came back. That was the way it usually went—Rose retreated, ran away, and Audrey found her and held her hand until she was okay again. "They went out, it didn't go well, the end. Just—" Audrey gave Olivia a pointed look. "Don't hook up with Aisha, and you'll be fine."

"Duly noted," Olivia said. "So . . . Rose is gay, too?"

"Bi," María said. "But I'm sure she'll tell you the password."

"Password?" Olivia frowned.

"To the underground network," María said seriously. "You know. Of girls who like girls."

A smile dawned on Olivia's face. "Ha," she said. "Well, I think I'm going to need it, so she'd better spill."

The server came back with Jen's and Olivia's food this time, and

Olivia picked up her burger and stared at it, hard. "Okay," she said to it. "I have high expectations for you. Impress me, burger."

Audrey watched as Olivia took a bite, her eyes at first thoughtful and then widening as she chewed. Audrey grinned. "Good, right? I told you."

Olivia finished chewing and shook her head at Audrey. "Remind me never to doubt you."

"That's a good policy," Audrey laughed. "Stick to it and you'll do well."

ELEVEN

Audrey shoved her textbooks into her locker while trying (unsuccessfully) to avoid the skeleton hanging on her neighbor's locker. There was no doubting it: her Halloween spirit had been completely wiped out. Even Ms. Fitz dressed as eighties Madonna—fingerless lace gloves, ropes of fake pearls around her neck, a shiny tiered skirt that bounced as she danced around the art room, *and* a drawn-on mole—hadn't brought a smile to her face. All she wanted to do was go home, lock herself in her bedroom, and scarf all the candy her mom had bought for trick-or-treaters. And maybe try not to fixate on the fact that she was pregnant.

She pushed an old sketchbook to the side, squeezing her math book next to it, and then slammed her locker shut. As if she could think of anything else *but* that; as if she'd let anything besides that enter her mind for the past week.

A touch on her waist made her jump, and suddenly Julian was beside her. "Jesus, Julian," she hissed. "Do you always have to do that?"

"Sorry," he said, sounding anything but. "What time do you want me to pick you up tonight?"

Audrey hitched her bag onto her shoulders. "I don't—I'm not going."

"What?"

"I'm not going," Audrey repeated. "I don't feel good. I just want to stay home."

"But you said you wanted to act as normal as possible," Julian said. "The other day, you said—"

"I know what I said, but I don't want to go," Audrey snapped.

Julian was silent for a second. Then he said, "Fine. But have you told Rose? Because she's going to be pissed."

"I'll tell her." Audrey started walking down the hall. "I just have to figure out *what* to tell her."

Julian fell into step beside her. "You could always actually—"

"Don't." Audrey halted in the middle of the hall, then ducked into the alcove under the stairs. "Don't say I should tell her *that*. I can't. Not yet."

The way Julian looked at her right then initiated a spiraling guilt inside her. Like she needed any more nausea—the morning sickness had kicked in hard last Friday, as if her body had been waiting for her to take those three tests before giving her that lovely gift. Plus, whoever named it morning sickness clearly never suffered themselves, because Audrey's throw-up sessions came right in the middle of art class. (And right when she got home, and once more before bed, for good measure.) She was only lucky that Ms. Fitz gave them free rein in class and that so far nobody had noticed her jaunts to the bathroom.

"Rose isn't stupid," Julian said. "She's going to know something's up."

"Probably." *Definitely.*

It was weird. Usually Rose was the first to know any and all of Audrey's secrets, and at first she'd thought this would be no different. But this secret wasn't only hers; it belonged to Julian, too. And now Audrey had begun to be afraid of Rose's reaction—would she think Audrey was so pathetic for getting into this situation? Maybe she'd think Audrey was crazy for entertaining, even for a second, the idea of keeping the baby. Or maybe she'd go the complete opposite way and look down on Audrey if she even mentioned getting rid of it.

All these things that she hadn't realized she'd feel had begun piling on top of everything else. And in a strange way it was nice to have a secret of her own for once, taking up space normally occupied by Rose's issues. Something that belonged to her. She'd keep it a secret a little while longer, maybe. Because deep down she knew what Rose would say: *You're pregnant? Jesus Christ, I guess I'm going to have to give you The Talk again. All right. What are you going to do? Let's make a list.*

"I'll tell her." Audrey slouched against the wall, her shoulders heavy. "But not right now. Not when we only just found out." She paused. Okay, maybe "only just" was an understatement, because somehow an entire week had blurred by since those lines had shown up. "And when *we* haven't even talked about it."

Now Julian looked guilty. No, beyond him saying "How are you?" five times a day and Audrey either shrugging or saying "Fine," they most definitely hadn't discussed it. Who had known they were such masters of avoidance? "I thought you might need to wait a little," he said. "Before we . . . decided anything."

Yeah, sure, Audrey thought. *Because I might need to wait.* Like he wasn't freaking out, too, and running over all the options in his head until he felt more confused than when he'd begun. Audrey knew him, knew how his mind worked—this was the boy who regularly took so long to decide which movie to see that all the showings had started by the time he'd picked one. At least he hadn't turned into one of those boyfriends saying "But you're going to get rid of it, right?"—or worse, those ones who denied any and all responsibility and completely bailed. Hopefully he'd be able to put his logical mind to good use and think rationally about which path they were going to take. Because Audrey had no fucking idea what to do, and the really scary thing was that her instinctive response had been the opposite of how she'd ever imagined she would feel.

And so far, it wasn't going away.

She sighed, reaching across the space between them to sweep Julian's hair out of his eyes. They were the same dark brown as her own, like looking into a mirror. "Sorry," she said softly. "I don't mean to be a bitch."

"Like you could ever." Julian lifted one corner of his mouth. "So, you're not coming tonight."

It wasn't a question, but Audrey nodded anyway. "It would feel too weird," she said. "Besides, I'm not in the Halloween mood anymore."

"What do you want to do instead?"

"What?"

Julian raised his eyebrows. "If we're not going to the party. Should we . . . actually talk?"

"Oh, I don't— You should go. Have fun with Cooper and the others," Audrey said. "I don't want to ruin your night."

"What?" Julian looked unconvinced. "I don't know. I won't feel right going without you. Feels like an asshole move to me, partying when my"—he lowered his voice—"pregnant girlfriend is at home by herself."

It did sound like the kind of thing that douche bags did, but Julian wasn't that kind of guy, and Audrey actually *wanted* to be at home by herself. Adam and her mom had plans with some of Adam's work friends, so maybe she'd be able to Google-research to her heart's content without worrying that one of them was about to come bursting into her room and bust her.

"Not at all." She put both hands on his chest, giving him what she hoped was a reassuring smile. "I need some time to . . . process. Besides, I need *you* to keep an eye on Rose for me. Make sure she doesn't melt down if a certain ex of hers turns up."

Julian wrapped his hands around her wrists, bringing her hands to his mouth and placing a soft kiss on her knuckles. "Rose doesn't need me to watch out for her. She can more than handle herself."

Audrey raised her eyebrows. "That's what I'm worried about."

"Hey!" A shout came their way as Davis jogged by them, grinning.

"No PDA in the hall, assholes!"

Audrey managed to flip him off, muttering under her breath, "Dick." She turned her attention back to Julian, who was trying not to laugh. "You'll go tonight, right?"

"Yeah, I'll go." He laughed for real then. "I think I must have the only girlfriend in the world who *wants* her boyfriend to go to a party without her."

Audrey shook her head. "I think your girlfriend sounds pretty awesome."

"Oh, she is."

She smiled big, the tension in her muscles easing—sometimes she forgot how much she loved him. Which made the remembering so much better. And even when she was feeling shitty, Julian could make her think that goodness was hiding somewhere in her.

She stepped out of the alcove, into the emptying hall. "Give me a ride home? I don't have my car, and I don't have the energy to walk."

She didn't have the energy to do much, but she thought that making out in front of her house when Julian dropped her off was something she could manage.

Then again, maybe they shouldn't—*Isn't that how we got into this mess in the first place?*

Audrey let out a bizarre laugh at that, covering her mouth when Julian looked at her like she was being weird and asked, "What's so funny?"

"Nothing. It's stupid," she said, slipping her hand into his. "I'll tell you in the car."

TWELVE

Around ten thirty that night Audrey was regretting her decision to stay in. Turned out that abortion plus Google did not a good night make. So much political shit and extreme pro-life propaganda came flying at her that she'd had to close her laptop and put it away. Then she'd sat there zombiefied, alternating between thinking of ways the guest room across the hall could be turned into a nursery and how amazing the classes she'd dreamed of taking at RISD would be.

Eventually she couldn't stop her antsy hands, and she dialed Julian, sighing impatiently as she waited for him to answer.

"Hey!" When he finally answered, Audrey could hardly hear him, her ear suddenly filled with staticky noise. She could hear enough in his loud voice to know he was well on his way to drunk, though. "Audrey? Hello?"

"Julian?" Audrey threw herself down on her bed, the air rushing out of the covers with a whoosh. "Can you hear—"

"Hold on, I can't hear you," Julian's yell came. "One second."

Audrey watched the ceiling as she waited, her irritation ticking up. Oh, wasn't it nice for him to be out, having fun, getting drunk? Huh. That would probably be their future with a baby: Audrey in on her own on a Friday night, bored and despondent, while Julian partied it up with his friends, no worries at all. She'd watched enough repeats of *16 and Pregnant* to know that.

"Okay." Julian sounded breathless. "That's better. Hi, babe."

"Don't 'hi, babe' me," Audrey said sharply. "What are you doing?"

"What do you mean?" Julian said. "I'm at Cooper's."

Audrey was quiet for a moment before flaring up. "I can't believe you actually *went*," she snapped. "Are you out of your mind?"

"What? You told me to go!"

"I didn't mean it!" Audrey pinched herself hard on the thigh, the nervous tic that she tried so hard to keep under control. "Okay, I did, but I didn't think you would do it."

"Sorry," Julian said, sounding immediately sober and irritated. "I didn't realize I was supposed to understand that by saying you wanted me to go, you really meant that you *didn't* want me to go."

"That's not fair."

"Fair? You're the one yelling at me because I had the audacity to do what you told me to. If you didn't want me to go, why didn't you say so? I can't read your mind, Audrey. God."

"Don't talk to me like that," Audrey said. "I shouldn't have to spell out every little thing to you. Did you really think this was a good idea?"

"You told me to go!" he yelled again. "I thought this was what you wanted!"

"Well, clearly it wasn't!"

"*Clearly?*" he said. "Clear to who? I have no idea what you're—"

"I swear to God, Julian. *Why* are you being such an *asshole*?"

"Well, why shouldn't I be?" Julian said. "That's obviously the role you've cast me in already."

"No," Audrey said. "Julian—"

"Julian what? *What?*" His frustrated groan deafened her. "I shouldn't be talking to you now. I'll call you tomorrow."

"No! Don't you dare hang up." Audrey listened to his silence. "Julian?"

"I'm making it worse," he said. "I don't want to be mad at you, but I'm not exactly sober right now and it's too hard. I don't know what you want."

"I want . . . I thought I would feel better here than there but I don't." She exhaled slowly. "I want to see you."

"So come see me," he said. "There. Easy." She could hear his breathing down the line, fast and heavy. "Audrey."

They stayed there, hanging in limbo, for a minute. Then Audrey swallowed her pride, contriteness spilling into her voice. "I'm sorry," she said, curling her toes into the sheets. "*I'm* an asshole. I'm sorry, J."

He was silent again, and Audrey thought she'd pushed too far, too hard. But then he spoke, his voice calmer. "It's fine," Julian said. "I mean . . . I feel like an asshole anyway. Being here while you're there. Kind of a dick move."

Audrey shook her head even though he couldn't see her. "Truce?" she said. "Let's start over."

"Deal," Julian said, and she could hear the relief in his voice. "So. Do you want me to come over?"

"No! No." The last thing she wanted was for him to come to her house—if she spent a minute longer in there, she would choke. She'd never been one to get claustrophobic, but right now it felt like the walls of her bedroom were pressing in on her, the awesome ladies whose pictures were up there staring down at her. Ava Gardner, Lucille Ball, Josephine Baker, all judging her with their paper-soft eyes. "I have to get out of here," Audrey said. "Meet me at that playground by Coop's."

"All right," he said. "I'll be waiting."

After they hung up she curled into a ball, wrapping her arms around her knees and glancing up at her portrait ladies. "Don't look at me like that," she said. "Not a single one of us in this room is perfect."

She slammed her car door as she stepped into the chilly night, winding her scarf a little tighter around her neck. From the street the park was hidden, tucked away in the midst of family-filled houses whose occupants complained about the roaches and empty forties left there by kids with nowhere else to party. Audrey knew it would be empty tonight—it was Halloween, and that meant everyone was partying elsewhere, dressed up and drinking in costume or being scared out of their minds by movie monsters.

She heard the rattle of the swing set before she saw Julian sitting there, drifting forward and back lazily. He didn't look much in costume, wearing a baseball jacket over a white button-down and dark jeans, the thick-framed glasses on his face the only unusual thing. "Hey," she said as she neared. "Catch."

Julian shot out his left hand to easily snatch the Hershey's Kiss she'd thrown him out of the air. "You been trick-or-treating?"

"As if." Audrey lowered herself into the swing next to Julian, wrapping her hands around the cold chains. "I told my mom that I'd answer the door to all the little punks, but really I locked it, turned off all the lights, and took the candy for myself." When Julian laughed, she allowed herself a small smile. "Hey, I need it. I am eating for two, after all."

Julian laughed again, but this time there was a hollow ring to it. "Yeah," he said. "I guess you are."

They swung in silence for a while, a sudden burst of noise from nearby the only interruption: a shriek, two, followed by a cacophony of laughter. *Pranks gone right*, Audrey thought.

"You look nice."

She started. "What?" She looked down at her jeans, the ones she wore for painting that were covered in bleached patches and smears of cerulean, worn thin at the knees. "I look like a mess."

Julian reached across the gap between them, stretching for her hand. "No," he said, so urgently that Audrey turned to look at him. "You're beautiful. You're always beautiful."

"And you're drunk."

"I only had a couple beers," he said. "And one shot. I know exactly what I'm saying."

Before she could say anything, he took a deep breath. "Let's talk."

"You first," Audrey said. She knew it was a cowardly move, but a big part of her worried that if she started talking, she'd word-vomit every little thing that had gone through her head in the past ten days, and sensible, supportive Julian would see she'd lost her mind and run for the hills.

His fingers tightened around hers. "Here's what I'm thinking: we have three options, and we have to consider how we would feel if we pursued each different one. So, how we would feel if we either became parents, pursued adoption, or ended the pregnancy."

Audrey just looked at him in awe. "Jesus, J." The way he said it was so blunt, so matter-of-fact that Audrey let out a surprised giggle. "Sorry. You sound like some pamphlet."

"Well . . ."

"You didn't!" Rational, logical Julian—see, she *did* know him almost better than he knew himself.

"I was in the nurse's office ," he said, defensive. "Headache."

"Nerd."

"Be serious," Julian said, and Audrey put her feet out to stop her swinging, feeling a little like a scolded schoolchild. "Okay," he contin-ued. "So, adoption—I mean, you're the expert here, right?"

"Sure," Audrey said, nodding. "That's me." Although she'd never thought too hard about the fact that she was adopted; it had always been just that, a fact. A thing she knew about herself, as simple as knowing that her eyes were brown and her hair was curly and pine-apples made her sick. A woman—girl, really—had placed her for adoption and had chosen Laura. When she thought of it, she thought of it as an act of pure love.

There was a box of things in her mom's office that sat alongside her acting things from when Audrey was little and they'd lived in California. The box contained all kinds of sentimental stuff: some of Audrey's baby teeth, glowing report cards, the skipping rope she'd learned to do tricks with. A letter from the girl who'd given birth to her.

It was a miracle that it hadn't faded even a bit over the years, over the many times Audrey had read the letter: First with her mom lying next to her in bed, reading it out when Audrey was too little to string the words into sentences. Then when she got older, on her birthday and Christmas and sometimes Mother's Day. She could recite it in her sleep, picturing the neat, printed words on the lilac paper: *My dear sweet baby girl*, it began. *You don't know me but I know you. I'll love you forever—that's the first thing I have to say—but we can't stay together. I'll miss you when you're not with me anymore.*

It went on, about how Audrey needed to be with someone who could give her all the things she needed, and how she was going to do great things with her life, and maybe one day they'd meet again. It was equal parts sad and happy, and Audrey would be forever grateful to this girl who'd gifted her with the life she had now.

But for herself? For Julian? She wasn't sure. "Honestly," Audrey started, "I don't know. I think adoption is amazing, of course. I wouldn't be here without it, would I? Wouldn't have my mom, or Adam, or you, or my friends. But thinking about doing it myself . . ."

She paused, considering it for the first time, and the idea of it seemed alien right now. "That's scary. And *strange*. Can you imagine?" She'd be pregnant—more pregnant than she currently was. Pregnant for nine whole months while this . . . thing, this baby, grew inside her. *What might that be like?* she wondered. *Could I do it?*

"My birth mother did it." Audrey looked away from Julian again, watching the slight clouding of her breath in the cold air. "But that was her and we're us. Know what I mean?"

"Yeah," Julian said. "I get it."

"What if it wasn't even right for her?" Audrey asked, the thought occurring to her out of nowhere. That was scary, too—what if it *hadn't* been right for her? Maybe Audrey had ruined her life. Or maybe she'd made it better, in her absolute absence. "How could I know if it would be right for me, for us? I don't know. What do you think?

"I think . . . I have no idea," Julian confessed. "I don't know. Have you ever wanted to meet her? You birth mother?"

"No," Audrey said truthfully. She never had—she'd never felt like she had any reason to. Nothing felt like it was missing from her; there was no glaring reason for their reconciliation. And Audrey had her mom—the mom who, when Audrey was little, scoured bookstores for picture books featuring kids who looked like her. Who educated herself on Audrey's black heritage, learned how to do her hair. Who still tried to hold her hand when they crossed the road. Who was everything she needed. "Is that weird? It would be weirder to meet her, I think. I mean, what if she wouldn't even want to see me again?"

"That is weird," Julian said. "To even have to think about that."

"Yeah. That's why I don't." Audrey paused, looking back at the night sky. "I think the most about what she looks like. I know she was white, and my mom says she was pretty, but that's all I know. I wonder how much of me is her and how much my biological father, and then how much of me is just me. Is that weird? It's just I so obviously don't look like my mom that I wonder, sometimes," she said. "That's all." Her copper-burnished-brown skin, the wide fullness of her mouth—those things were obvious. Pieces of that biological father who was even more of a mystery than her birth mother. But the tiny gap between her front teeth, the shape of her ears? Who they belonged to, Audrey wasn't sure.

"That's not weird at all," Julian said. "I'd think about it."

Audrey kicked her feet. "Maybe she doesn't ever think about me at all. Huh. It's like . . . I don't know if she went on and did everything she wanted with her life, or if she never did any of them, the things she gave me up for so she could have a chance at them," she said. "I guess she could be perfectly happy, too. She could be one of those people who did something good and hard and is perfectly pleased with her decisions. Who knows?"

"You don't think you could be one of those people?" Julian asked. "You're good. And you can be selfless. You could do all that, if you wanted to."

Audrey flicked her gaze to him. "What do you want?"

He was silent for a minute and then shrugged. "It's your body—"

"Don't give me that," Audrey said. "Yeah, it's my body, but it's your decision, too. I'm not doing this on my own. Am I?"

"No," Julian said immediately. He ran a hand over his face and blew out a gusty sigh. "I guess—the idea of adoption feels a little weird to me. That somewhere out there someday would be a kid who might look like me, or love music and not know why, or be allergic to shellfish because of me? That's kind of bizarre."

"It doesn't always feel like that," Audrey said. "For the kid. Not for me anyway. I don't wonder all the time if the reason I like something is because my birth mother did. I hardly think about her at all, usually."

"I know that," he said. "It's like I *know* these things, but what I'm feeling is . . . I think it seems weird to me *right now*, is all. A few months down the line? If we did go that way, and we had picked people we like and knew them a little and it wasn't so . . . abstract? I think I could feel differently about it."

"Could you feel *good* about it?"

"Yeah."

"Okay," Audrey said. "And after?"

Julian took longer to answer that time. "Maybe," he said eventually. "Yeah."

"That fills me with reassurance," Audrey said drily, and Julian gave her a small laugh.

"That's the thing," he said. "We won't know."

"Exactly," Audrey said. "So what if you can't, *don't* feel good about it afterward? What if I don't? What if I can't do what she did, and I don't figure it out until after it's too late?"

Julian opened his mouth, but then his face screwed up and he shook his head. "I don't know, Audrey. I wish I had an answer for you but I don't."

Audrey pressed her hands into the chains. "It's weird. I never worried about any of this before, not knowing my birth mother or every little thing about myself," she said. "But when I think about a baby, though . . . a baby would be all me. You and me, I mean. I'd know everything about it. It'd be, like, the one thing that's all mine."

"I guess so."

"That seems so wild," Audrey said. "Having a *baby?*"

"I know." Julian said. "But we . . . y'know, there are other options."

"Right," Audrey said softly. "So. We can think about that. And we can think about the other things, too."

"Sure."

She pulled in a breath of clean, cold air and scuffed her feet in the rust-colored leaves layered on the ground. "We're only seventeen," she said. "Can you believe it?"

"We'll be seventeen whether we give it up or have it or not," Julian said now. "You know?"

"Yeah, I know," Audrey said. Yeah, seventeen was always the age she was going to remember, she already knew that. The age she got pregnant, and the age she either had a baby or didn't. *That's not something Future Me is ever going to forget.*

Julian cleared his throat. "We don't have to decide right this second."

His voice sounded strange, tight, and when Audrey glanced at him, she saw that he was watching her. Not her face—lower.

She looked down to see one hand turning circles on her stomach. *Oh, Christ. What the* fuck *am I doing?*

"No, of course not." She said this loudly, taking her hand away from her body and back to the chains of the swing. Shit, *shit.* Stupid, betraying body and hormones making her do strange things. "It has to be right. What we decide."

"I know," Julian said. "It will be."

He had this look in his eyes, sad and quiet. Sad thinking about not having it, or about having it? Audrey scuffed her feet on the worn patch of dirt beneath her. Saying "it" felt weird, but saying "baby" felt even weirder. Besides, it wasn't a baby, not yet. Only a few cells taking up residence inside her.

A loud ringing cut into the silence between them, and Audrey fumbled her phone out of her pocket to see María's name on the screen. She silenced it—whatever Ree wanted could wait.

"It's cold," Julian said. "We should go somewhere. Are you hungry? I'm hungry."

Audrey nodded, recognizing the slight change in his voice, like the way he sounded when he failed a test or missed too many baskets or couldn't master the bridge of his favorite song. It wasn't an "I'm done" voice, more an "I can't talk about it right now" thing. Which Audrey was more than okay with—all this talk was making her already-pounding head hurt even more.

"I could eat," she said lightly. "I guess."

She got off the swing and came to stand in front of Julian. A cutting wind was picking up, blowing her curls into her face, and she put up a hand so she could hold her hair back and look at him properly. Those geek glasses framing his pretty eyes. "Okay," she said. "I give up. Who are you supposed to be?"

Julian threw his hands up. "Are you kidding me?"

"What?"

"I'm Peter Parker!"

As soon as he said it, everything clicked into place for Audrey. "Oh, *duh*," she said. "Of course. Good Peter Parker, too, from the Gwen Stacy years."

"Of course," Julian said. "The *best* years."

Audrey moved her hand to his shoulder, her other hand to his knee, bending to kiss him, hard. A piece of her hair got caught between their mouths, and the chain pressed into her shoulder as he pulled her in, but it didn't matter. She was so unbelievably grateful that this boy who liked comic books and hard-core punk, who played bass guitar and the cello, who was right there with her in the pregnancy problem, was the one she'd fallen in love with.

When they parted, breathing heavily, Julian looked up at her with the slightest smile. "What was that for?"

Audrey smiled back, tipping her head forward so she could feel his breath against her cold cheeks. "For being you. Because I love you." Because she did.

THIRTEEN

The corner of the newspaper had been taken over by Audrey's sketching: a balloon swelling to bursting, a tall, loose-limbed tree, a pair of ballerina feet in perfect pointe shoes. She was tired from last night, from the playground and then eating chocolate-cream pie and fries at the café on Smith Street (well, watching Julian eat; she drank plain ice water so she wouldn't throw up everywhere).

"Hey. Kiddo." Adam's hand waved over the paper. "Are you with us today?"

Audrey dropped the pen and sat up straight, smiling at Adam across the kitchen table. "Yup. Totally."

Her mom frowned over her coffee. "You're not still feeling sick, are you? Maybe you need to go to the doctor."

Shaking her head, Audrey said, "Nope. Not feeling sick at all." Which wasn't a lie, because she'd already had her routine upchuck, right in time to come down for Saturday-morning breakfast. Saturday breakfast was sacred in their house—well, ever since Adam had come around. Before that Audrey had usually eaten cereal on the couch, while Laura had always skipped breakfast in favor of coffee.

But then Adam had started staying over, started cooking bacon and eggs, pancakes, sausage, breakfast burritos. Audrey remembered waking up to the syrup-sweet smell floating through the house, and how she'd wandered downstairs in a zombie state to find this new boyfriend, all messy blond hair and pale skin summer tan, wearing her mom's striped apron and flipping pancakes. That was when she'd decided he was a keeper.

She picked up her fork and pushed the remains of her omelet around her plate. "Do you guys have plans today?"

"Nope." Her mom twisted her long red hair on top of her head, sticking Audrey's doodling pen through it. "I thought we might go to the park, take a nice long walk. Maybe go see a movie—they're showing *À Bout de Souffle* at the Fremont."

"My favorite," Adam said drily.

Audrey laughed. "C'mon, you can pretend like you're smart and actually know what they're talking about." She flicked a chunk of green pepper at him. *"Oui?"*

Adam batted the pepper missile away and narrowed his eyes at her. "Someone could very easily stop liking you, kiddo."

"Both of you, shush," Laura said. "What about you, Audrey? Seeing the girls today?"

"I'm going shopping with Rose." That was what they needed,

Audrey had decided, to make Rose get over Audrey bailing on last night's party and for Audrey to remember that there were other things to focus on. They'd lust over pretty shoes and try on clothes they couldn't afford (well, that Audrey couldn't afford; Rose's allowance was right at the "let me buy your love" amount), and it would feel like always. Telling her could wait. She'd decide when.

Audrey took her plate over to the sink and then opened the refrigerator, taking out a bottle of water. "Okay, I gotta run. See you guys later. Don't have too much fun on your—" She shut the fridge only to see her mom perched on Adam's lap, the two of them smiling sappily as they stared into each other's eyes. "Oh, get a room, would you?"

"If you'd hurry up and leave, we'd have a whole house," Adam said without looking at her.

"Ew! Stop!" But she was laughing, as was her mom, and Audrey grabbed her coat from where she'd left it hanging over the back of her chair last night.

Today she would pretend like everything was normal. She had a boyfriend, a best friend, a best mom, and a not-quite-stepdad who made her laugh. *Pregnant? I have no idea what you're talking about.*

Audrey tossed her half-empty paper cup in the trash can, her body warmed from the bit of extrasugary hot chocolate she'd managed to drink. She and Rose had tried on dresses in the thrift store, taffeta numbers with huge, puffy sleeves and sixties shifts, Rose dancing for Audrey's camera. The only thing Audrey had actually bought, besides her hot chocolate, was a pretty shirt, long sleeved with a jeweled collar and pearly buttons to match its ivory color. It cost a little more than she would normally spend on a top, but it was superpretty, and Rose had said it made her eyes look darker than usual. Maybe she and Julian could go on a date soon—a real date, not their usual grunge band, smuggled beer, and pizza dates. Somewhere nice.

Rose linked her arm through Audrey's, bumping her hip into the paper-ribbon-tied bag that held the beautiful blouse. "I want to buy something cute, too," she said. "I'm glad you came out today."

"Me, too," Audrey said. "I'm sorry if I've been acting weird. It's . . . extreme PMS or something." The excuse tripped off Audrey's tongue, and she relaxed a little more.

"It's fine," Rose said, although Audrey could tell she didn't completely mean it. "Just don't *keep* acting weird. Oh!" She veered to the left, so suddenly that Audrey almost tripped over her own feet. "Let's go in here. They always have cute bras."

Audrey followed, trying not to think of how tender her breasts felt, how she had to glide her hands over them in the shower. She wasn't even wearing a bra today, but an old bikini top she'd dug out that didn't have any stupid wire to poke into her. But she should probably buy a sports bra or something so she didn't have to live in beachwear in winter. Or maybe she could find something nice for after.

After what?

Rose let go of her arm once they were in the store and heading for the escalators. She looked around, a blissful expression on her face, and Audrey softened. *No thinking about the Situation right now,* she reminded herself. *Fun times only.*

"I haven't even asked how last night was," she said, stepping onto the escalator after Rose. "What did you go as in the end? Anything go down that I need to know about?"

Rose half turned her body so she was looking down at Audrey, and a flicker of something passed over her face, enough to pique Audrey's interest. Scandal?

But then Rose smiled and shook her head. "Not really. María made out with that mathlete she hates from Saint Jude's all night. I think half the basketball team got into a fight with each other. And I went with the *Clueless* thing again. Couldn't think of anything else."

They spilled off the moving stairs into the lingerie department, all pastel-pink underthings hanging around, tables overflowing with brightly colored stockings. Rose picked up a neon-green thong and flicked it at Audrey. "Just your color."

Audrey caught the scrap of lace and tossed it back on the table. "Thanks, but I'm more of a neon-orange kind of girl, don't you think?"

She trailed along as Rose busied herself picking up armfuls of bras: padded and not, strapless and not, practical and decidedly not. The only thing Audrey grabbed was a two-pack of soft, nonwired, wide-strap cotton bras, which, as a plus, came in a pale-blue and dark-purple color. At least she could wrap her tits up in something nice while they were killing her.

As Rose flipped through the racks, Audrey spotted an unmistakable black-and-aqua head bobbing through the store. "Hey—isn't that Olivia?"

Before Rose could respond, Audrey stuck up her hand in the air, waving. "Olivia!"

Olivia turned, her face breaking into a grin when she saw Audrey. Next to her was a woman who Audrey immediately recognized as Olivia's mom—she was shorter, curvier, with her hair a few shades lighter than Olivia's (no blue, either) and pulled into a high ponytail; but their faces were identical.

Now it was Audrey's turn to drag Rose along, darting around other shoppers to get to Olivia. "Hey!"

"Hi," Olivia said back, a happy note in her voice. "What are you guys doing here?"

"Avoiding homework," Audrey said. "With retail therapy."

Olivia laughed. "Right. Oh—hey, this is my mom. Mom, this is—"

"Audrey and Rose," the woman said, giving them a shiny smile. "It must be." Yep—there were the dimples. She didn't actually look that much older than Olivia, and she definitely wasn't dressed like most of the moms around town who favored neat cardigans and dark jeans. Audrey remembered when she and her mom had first moved to town, how Laura had stuck out like that, too. (It hadn't taken long for them to be put on Kennedy's officially unofficial Not One of Us list.) (Coincidence that most of that list was made up of nonwhite and nonhetero and non-upper-middle-class people? Another thing Audrey violently disliked about her town.) Laura back then always wore knee-high boots with skintight leather pants and band shirts, proclaiming her Sleater-Kinney/Misfits/Joy Division love to the other parents at the playground. Nowadays she dressed much the same, except the leather pants were black jeans and there were fewer holes in her shirts, but the vibrant-red hair remained the only point of color.

Olivia's mom was less punk holdover and more hip-hop cool, with gold hoops in her ears, spike-heeled pumps, and a Knicks jacket over her plain white tee. "I know this is clichéd, but I honestly have heard so much about both of you, and I'm so glad we're running into each other." She put a hand on Olivia's arm, squeezing tight. "I want to thank you for making my girl's first couple of weeks here so good. You know, she was so nervous to come here—"

"Ma!" Olivia squirmed in her mom's grip, looking embarrassed. "Stop. Please."

Audrey smiled. "Well, I've been the new girl before. I remember what it was like. And if I hadn't had Rose here"—she elbowed Rose in the ribs, eliciting a surprised gasp from her—"I don't know what I would have done."

She expected Rose to say something then, jump in with some funny anecdote from their early days together, but she didn't. When Audrey glanced at her, she saw that Rose's gaze was flitting all around: down at the floor, up at the ceiling, at the rail of clothes next to them. Anywhere other than at Olivia and her mom.

Audrey understood that it was part of Rose to throw up this wall, but sometimes it came off as . . . plain rude. Times like this she wished telepathy existed, so Rose would hear exactly what she was thinking: *Get it together, Rose. Confidence.*

Luckily Olivia's mom didn't seem to notice Rose's lack of manners. "You girls should come over sometime," she said, her smile widening even more. "For dinner, maybe—I make the best beef rolls, don't I, Liv?"

Olivia nodded. "It's true. They're better than my grandma's even. But don't tell her that."

Olivia's mom laughed, an infectious giggle with echoes of Olivia in it. "So, anytime you want, come on over."

"Thanks, Ms. Lee," Audrey said. "That's so nice of you. We'd love to come. Wouldn't we, Rose?"

Rose finally focused on Olivia's mom, giving a tight smile. "Yeah, we'd love to come."

"Great! And please, call me Rachael," Olivia's mom said. She leaned in, conspiratorial. "Anything else makes me feel so old. I'm not ready to turn into my mother yet." She straightened up and released Olivia's arm. "Well, I'm going to go check out the shoes. Come find me when you're done, Liv."

Audrey raised her eyebrows at Olivia as her mom walked away. "Okay, your mom is so cool. Like, for real."

Olivia shrugged. "She's okay, I guess."

Okay? First name and dinner invite already? In contrast, on the rare occasions Audrey saw Rose's mom, she always insisted on being called Mrs. Vacarello and came off as supremely icy. (Clearly where Rose got it from.)

"So," Audrey said. "Did you have a good time last night? Sorry I wasn't there."

"Oh, yeah." Olivia tucked a piece of silky aqua hair behind her ear as she nodded. "Mostly I was happy that I didn't have to spend Friday night holed up in my room alone." She looked away from Audrey to Rose. "So you got home okay?"

Rose played with one of the lacy bras in her hand and nodded, her entire demeanor relaxing. "Yeah. Did you—did you have a good time?"

"Yeah," Olivia said with a smile directed only at Rose. "It was fun." Now she looked at Audrey. "Sorry you weren't feeling well. I hope you weren't outrageously sick."

Audrey swallowed and managed a wan smile. "Thanks," she said, shuffling through the lies in her head to pick the right story. "Must have been something I ate."

However see-through that excuse was, Olivia didn't seem to notice, smiling again, and then Rose spoke. "Well, we should probably—"

Olivia jumped in at the same moment, words blurring together. "I like the—"

Audrey's head spun with the back-and-forth voices. "What?"

"The pink," Olivia said with a little lilt to her voice, and Audrey watched as she reached out to pluck at one of the delicate contraptions that Rose was holding. "You should get that one. It's pretty."

A flush bloomed across Rose's cheeks, and Audrey pushed a smile down. Olivia dropped her hand and hitched her messenger bag higher on her shoulder. "Anyway, I should probably go find my mom before she buys up half the store. I'll see you guys Monday."

"Bye," Audrey said, raising one hand in a wave as Olivia began walking away.

As soon as Olivia was out of sight, Audrey pinched Rose's arm.

"Was it me, or was she flirting with you?"

"It's you." Rose turned toward the escalators, stalking along in her heels so fast that Audrey almost had to run to keep up.

"Come on, Rose—the bra thing? The look she was giving you?" Maybe something happened at the party, Audrey thought—something involving Olivia? That would be fun. She pressed on, needling Rose. "And the other day, she only said she would go to Cooper's party once you said you were going. I may not speak the Sapphic language as well as you, but I know flirting when I—"

"Audrey!" Rose whipped around, glaring with such intensity that Audrey took a step back. "Would you leave it? *Jesus.*"

Whoa. Audrey took another step back. And then there were the times when her needling did nothing but push Rose closer to eruption.

"What's your problem?" Audrey said. "I was only—"

Rose dumped her armful of bras onto one of the thong-covered tables. "You know what, I don't want these. Come on, let's go."

Audrey held up her tame sports bras. "I still need to pay."

"Fine," Rose said. "I'll meet you at the car." With that she turned and stepped onto the escalator, shoulders hunched.

Seriously? How had their fun, no-thinking-about-problems day turned from so good to so *not* good in such a short time?

Audrey stood there for an uncertain second, fiddling with the tag hanging from her bras. "Rose," she called. "Do you want the car keys?"

But the question bounced off Rose's back, and Audrey bit her lip. This was supposed to be making-up time, not yelling-at-each-other-in-a-department-store time. *What's her damage?*

FOURTEEN

There was a soft knock on Audrey's door, and then her mom's voice: "Sweetie? Can I come in?"

Audrey looked up from her laptop and did a quick scan of her room to check for any incriminating matter: no magazines flipped to pertinent articles or any of her multiple pro/con lists.

All clear.

"Come in."

Her mom entered on quiet feet. "Hey," Laura said. "How was shopping?"

With Jekyll-and-Hyde Rose? *Super-duper!* "Okay" was what she said. "Fine."

"Good. What are you up to now? Are you busy?"

Audrey shut her laptop, feigning innocence. "Editing some photos." Actually, she did need to do that, or at the very least *take* some pictures for class. They had a crit session coming up, and she needed something to turn in that wasn't a picture of Julian asleep halfway through a movie at his house, or Rose's angry expression as Audrey aimed the lens at her for the hundredth time, trying to perfect her framing and focus and the million other things that might finally make the picture she took match the image in her head.

"Good, good . . ." Her mom sat on the edge of the bed, and Audrey looked up. She was wearing one of Adam's sweatshirts that had BROWN printed across the chest. Adam had offered to take Audrey up to Rhode Island one day so she could look at RISD and he could show her the best places to hang out if she ended up going there. They'd probably never go now—what would be the point, when Audrey's chances of getting in were sliding ever closer to zero?

"I wanted to catch you before Julian got here," her mom said. "He's eating with us tonight, right?"

"If that's okay." It was such a bonus having her parents like her boyfriend, and his parents like her. They rarely went to his house, but Audrey loved going over on Jewish holidays, getting to eat his mom's cooking, hearing his music-teacher dad sing, and seeing his brothers, Nate and Ezra, forced to act like grown-ups.

They should hold on to that while they had it, Audrey realized. All that niceness was probably going to disappear once the mess came out.

She focused on her mom again, the way she was gazing around Audrey's room, the shiny peach of her cheeks. "Mom, did you want something? Or did you come to sit on my bed and not speak?"

"Hmm?" Laura looked at Audrey, a strange smile on her face. "Oh, yeah. There is something I need to talk to you about."

Audrey took in the serious tone of her mom's words and put it with the weird smile.

Did she know?

No, no way. If her mom knew, she wouldn't have said, *I need to talk to you.* She'd have said, *Is there anything you need to tell me? You know you can talk to me about anything and I won't get mad. I just wanted you to know that.*

"Okay." Her mom took a deep breath then. "I have something to give you."

She reached into her back pocket and pulled out an envelope. It was blank—no name marking the thick cream paper and no postage anywhere on it.

"For me?" Audrey pushed her laptop aside. "What is it?"

"It's a letter." Her mom paused for a long moment. "From your birth mother."

Audrey snapped back like those four words had physically caught her, snaked their way inside her body, and twisted themselves around her spine. *"What?"*

Her mom laid the envelope on the bed. "I thought—"

"She can do that?" Audrey stared at the envelope as if it were a live grenade, or a venomous creature ready to sink its teeth into her. "I thought the agreement was that things like this wouldn't happen. This isn't supposed to happen, right?" A sudden curiosity struck her. "Does she know where we live?"

"Audrey, calm down," her mom said. "No, she doesn't know where we live. And yes, we agreed on no communication. That was her choice. But she got in contact with the adoption agency, wanting to get in touch, and they let me know what happened. And I said that if she wanted to send a letter or an email or something, that was fine with me."

"You did?" Audrey spoke steadily now, her heart slowing back to a normal, steady pulse. "Oh."

She'd never expected this. They'd had an agreement, her mom had always told her, that meant no visitation. No letters; no pictures of Audrey at three with two puffy pigtails on the sides of her head, or at seven with her front teeth missing. That was what her birth mother had wanted.

So what does she want now? Audrey wondered. *Has she changed her mind?*

A wave of sickness rolled in her stomach, and Audrey clamped her lips tight shut. *Or is she psychic? She must be, to send me a letter right when I find out I'm knocked up. Jesus, talk about perfect timing.*

Her mom peered at her, concern flooding her eyes. "Sweetie?"

"I'm . . ." Audrey shook her head. She really didn't know much about the woman whose body she'd come from. She'd been young, Audrey knew that much. Sixteen, with a name to match her age: Mandy. She—Mandy—had, according to Laura, been very pretty in a hippie-ish sort of way, with long blond hair and wearing dresses that flowed to the floor over Audrey inside her belly. Over the years Audrey had added her own, fictional details to the picture: a flannel shirt worn over those dresses maybe, and perhaps a scattering of freckles on her cheeks. *Like me*, Audrey thought. *Like my mom—my here mom, my Laura mom.*

"But she said she didn't want contact," Audrey said. "That's what you told me. You were happy for her to be in my life, but she was the one who didn't want it." A clean break. The ability for this girl to move on with her life, go back to school and graduate and think of her baby growing up with a mom who loved her. *She wished she could keep you*, her mom would say. *But she wanted a life for you that was different from her own, and this was the best way she could think of to do that. And I'm so grateful that she chose me to have you.*

"I guess she's changed her mind now." Her mom toyed with a loose thread on Audrey's bedcover, looping it around her finger. "It's understandable. It has been seventeen years."

"Okay, but . . ." Audrey almost couldn't understand how this letter had gotten to her, managed to slip its way from California to New York, through the agency gatekeepers, to end up in the hands of her mom and now, on her bed. "No contact was what *she* asked for."

Her mom nodded, patient. "Yes. But, like I said, the agency got in touch with me, and then I thought—you're seventeen. Almost an adult. Old enough to make your own decisions, don't you think?" She carried on without pausing for Audrey to answer. "I think so anyway. I had to tell you. I couldn't know she'd reached out and keep it from you. That's as good as lying. Imagine twenty years from now, if I'd done that and you'd found out—God, you'd be so mad. I'd be so mad at myself. You're not a little kid, and I don't get to decide what's right for you all the time anymore. Something like this . . . I think you should be able to decide."

Audrey heard her mom say that she'd told the agency the same thing, and they'd told the girl Mandy, and the letter had passed from hand to hand until finally it was here.

The girl Mandy. She wasn't a girl anymore, was she? She'd been sixteen then, so she'd be . . . thirty-three now. *Thirty-three. A real grown-up,* Audrey thought; *maybe married, maybe not. Maybe with kids now, or maybe not.* If she was married, did her husband—or wife, perhaps—know that once upon a time she'd had a baby? If she wasn't married, did she date a lot, go drinking and dancing? Did she like to cook, or run, or read?

"Audrey, are you listening?"

"Hmm?" Audrey looked up to meet her mom's eyes, their ocean blue the opposite of Audrey's deep, almost black, brown. "Yeah, I'm listening. I hear you."

"Good. Okay. So . . ." Her mom stood, leaving wrinkles in the sheets. "I'll leave that with you, then. If you want to talk, you know I'm always listening. But this is your decision," she said again. "Your choice."

"Okay." Audrey drummed her fingers on her closed laptop, her short nails clicking against the plastic. "Thanks. I don't mean for saying that," she clarified. "For trusting me. Thank you."

"Of course." Her mom leaned in to kiss Audrey's cheek, and Audrey thought she saw a flicker of something pass over her face: anxiety? Regret? But then her mom's dark perfume filled her nose, and

Laura was pulling away, her face back to its usual caring-Mom look. "Come down in a bit, okay?"

Audrey nodded. "I'll be down soon. Need to finish this editing."

The excuse must have been satisfactory, because her mom nodded and left, the door closing with a soft click. Audrey inhaled deeply, letting the breath out again in a slow sigh. She fingered one corner of the envelope. *Do I open it now, or do I wait?*

She picked up the envelope: thick, creamy paper. Expensive. And also warm—no, hot, burning hot on her skin. Audrey launched herself from the bed and gripped the envelope with the very tips of her fingers, making as little contact as possible while she looked for someplace to put it. *Not forever*, she told herself. *Because I am going to read it. But . . . not right now. Soon.*

The bottom of her closet was the best place. She opened the door and pushed aside the clothes covering the bottom of the space, reaching past her well-loved camera collection: a Polaroid, her first ever point-and-shoot, an old film camera that used to belong to her mom. Behind them was a stack of repurposed shoe boxes, filled with birthday and valentine's cards, folded notes, ticket stubs from concerts, and empty Metro cards from birthday trips to the city.

Audrey pried open one of the boxes and slipped the envelope to the bottom; it could live there for now, out of sight and way out of mind.

Audrey's stomach clenched again, but she couldn't tell if it was from being pregnant or from the reality of her birth mother's words in an envelope intended for her. Probably both.

Yeah, she needed that letter to stay in the bottom of her closet and out of her head, because she had more important things to deal with, and right now, if she added another problem to the list? She'd probably have a nervous breakdown.

Audrey stared at her shaking hands, breathing slowly until they steadied and she could relax. "No breakdowns," she told herself. "Not today."

FIFTEEN

Audrey hung over the toilet in the graffitied stall, waiting for the spasm in her gut that would bring up her breakfast. This whole morning sickness thing was majorly pissing her off.

You wouldn't have to do this if you had an abortion, a little voice inside her said. *Wouldn't that be nice?*

Yes, it would be nice to have a break from the sore knees and raw throat. (She'd looked up cures for it, and so far nothing had worked—not saltines, not seltzer, not ginger ale. Next to try: sunflower seeds.) Yes, she'd love to be able to eat again. Yes, an abortion would be the easier option—in some ways. She wouldn't have a baby. Julian wouldn't have a baby. They could go on with their lives and not be those two assholes who got knocked up at seventeen, which would be how most of their classmates would remember them in years to come.

But would it be easy? It would be painful, probably, and scary, and maybe she'd be told all kinds of things about her baby that she didn't want to know. Like if it had eyelashes, fingernails yet; how much pain it could feel; whether it was a boy or a girl. Bullshit, most of it, but that wouldn't make it any easier. Audrey knew—she'd watched the news; she'd read the articles. That was what they made girls go through now, in so many places, no matter the circumstances.

Would it be easy, when she had that letter from her birth mother buried in her closet? When there was a woman out there thinking of her, seventeen years after the fact? It made Audrey wonder whether, if she did get rid of it, in another seventeen years' time she'd be thinking of her own baby, too.

And it wouldn't be easy because there was that stupid part of her that kept doing stupid stuff like referring to the thing as "her baby." *Not a baby*, the little voice said. *Cells. Goop. Floaty little nothing hanging out in your uterus and making you sick. Doesn't sound like a baby, does it? Babies are cute and chubby and smell good. This? Not so much.*

She heaved suddenly, emptying her stomach. A flush sounded from another stall, and as the acrid smell of her own vomit hit her, Audrey froze in place. She hadn't realized there was anyone else in here. Shit.

She grabbed a handful of toilet paper and wiped around her mouth, wiped the sweat from her forehead. *Keep it together.*

She flushed and exited the stall, walking over to the sinks like there was absolutely nothing wrong. It wasn't until she got there and focused her eyes on the mirror that she realized who the other occupant was.

Olivia nodded at her. "Hey."

Audrey stuck her hands under the water and began scrubbing. "Hey." Okay, she didn't need to worry. She considered Olivia a friend now, yeah, but Olivia didn't know her, not really. Not enough that she'd find it weird, alarming, that Audrey was on her knees barfing in the middle of the day.

They stood next to each other in silence for a minute, rinsing disinfectant-scented bubbles down the drains. Audrey had an awful taste in her mouth, metallic and sharp. She should have brought gum with her. She'd have to bum some from someone back in—

"So," Olivia said. "How far along are you?"

Audrey's hands stilled, reddening under the scalding water. "What?"

"How far along are you?" Olivia repeated softly, gently. "You know. . . ." She gestured at her stomach.

"I don't—" Audrey met Olivia's eyes in the mirror. *Fuck*. How did she know? "Wow. Is it *that* obvious?"

"No." Olivia shook her hands off and turned to Audrey. "I've seen it a ton of times with my aunts and my cousins; I know the signs, that's all. Sorry, I didn't mean to freak you out."

Audrey took a deep breath and drew her hands, now burning hot, out of the water. "Don't tell Rose." She looked at Olivia intently, pleading. "Don't tell anyone."

"I won't," Olivia said immediately. "I promise."

In the mirror Audrey could see how awful she looked: purply black circles peeked out from under her eyes, visible even with the layers of concealer she'd smeared on that morning. She hadn't had the energy to do anything with her hair except pile it on top of her head and snap three hair elastics around it (enough to keep her curls constrained). The gloss on her lips had all but disappeared after her upchuck session, and the shimmer on her cheeks looked out of place with her all-black sweater-jeans-boots combo. At least she'd tried.

"So . . . ," Olivia said. "Really, how far along are you?"

"I have no idea," Audrey said. What a great mom she would make—so in tune with the details. "I kind of haven't gotten around to that yet. I wasn't exactly prepared for this, y'know?"

"I get it," Olivia said. "Sorry for being a nosy bitch."

That made Audrey laugh, unbelievably, and she wiped her hands dry on her jeans. "That's all right. Hey, do you have any gum?"

"In my bag," Olivia said. "Come on."

When they got back into the classroom, Ms. Fitz was nowhere to be seen, and someone had turned the radio to some whiny indie station. Audrey slipped into her seat and leaned on her elbows, surveying the mess of pictures in front of her. Every year in the last week before Christmas they turned the classroom into a pseudogallery, smuggling in doughnuts and pizza while they looked at each other's work, and Audrey was already worrying about what she was going to present. For the past two years, alongside the reminders about depth of field and distortion, Audrey had gotten the same feedback from Ms. Fitz. "A theme will make everything stronger. Find a common thread and you'll see the narrative your pictures form," she'd said. "Think of each image as a sentence. Right now you have a bunch of sentences from several different stories. You need to give us that beginning-to-end version."

Olivia tossed Audrey a stick of gum as she took the seat opposite, which had quickly become her official space in the classroom. Audrey liked having Olivia at her table—she just straight-up liked Olivia. She was funny and talked art to Audrey, and had this easy, chill vibe about her that had allowed her to slip into their group as easy as pie, almost like she was meant to be there. And in the studio she worked quietly and intently, focusing on what she was drawing and not filling the hour with gossip. It made Audrey work harder—usually.

Now she kept sifting through her photographs and sighing so hard and so often that Olivia looked up from her charcoal-covered page. "Tortured, artist?"

"Very." Audrey squinted at a picture of her mom and Adam, taken when they were in the middle of an intense discussion about Adam's older sister, the one who wasn't quite cool with their relationship. Adam had this look on his face like he was about to shut down completely, while her mom laid a hand on his shoulder with frustration in her eyes. Not this one—too personal.

Then again, wasn't that the whole point?

She set it to one side, the beginning of her "yes" pile. "I'm trying to find a theme. It's harder than you'd think."

Olivia got up and came around to Audrey's side. "Do you mind?"

"Nuh-uh," Audrey said. "Maybe you'll be able to make something out of it."

Olivia began flicking through Audrey's glossy photographs, and Audrey watched her face carefully to see any reactions. But Olivia kept the same neutral expression on her face at every picture she saw.

"How come there aren't any of you?" she asked after a while.

Audrey shrugged one shoulder. "I'm always behind the camera, I guess. Besides, I don't need pictures of myself. I know what I look like."

Olivia brandished a picture of Julian lying on Audrey's bed. "You don't take pictures to remember what people look like. Don't try that on me."

"Honestly, I don't like having pictures taken of myself," Audrey said. "It's weird."

She plucked the picture Olivia was holding out of her fingers. She remembered that afternoon with Julian perfectly: the day after his sixteenth birthday, when she'd given him the limited-edition vinyl J Dilla album that had cost her almost four months' allowance. Worth it, to see the delight on Julian's face.

"Self-portraits aren't interesting anyway," she said as she slid the photo into her "yes" pile. "When I take a picture of someone else, I get to capture them off guard. In a moment when I think they look some particular way, without them posing for me or anything. That's when all the interesting parts come out of hiding." She paused, her cheeks heating—did that sound way too pretentious? She carried on, hoping there wasn't a flashing Poser Art Nerd sign above her. "Taking a picture of myself, how could I not pose? So, it's boring."

"Hmm." Olivia moved back around to her side of the table, flipping to a clean page in her sketchbook. "If you say so."

Audrey rolled her eyes but smiled. Clearly Olivia thought she was talking out of her ass, but that was fine, because Audrey knew better. She wasn't art. She was just herself.

SIXTEEN

The noise of the Kitsch house hit Audrey even before the door opened, but then it did, and Ezra—the youngest Kitsch sibling—was standing there with half an Oreo in his hand. "What up?" he asked, already walking away and leaving the door open for Audrey to follow. "He's not here, you know."

Audrey kicked off her shoes and added them to the pile by the side table. "I know," she said, combing her fingers through her hair. "I'll wait."

"Cool. There's food in the kitchen if you want."

"I'm good." She slipped into the living room after Ezra. Nate—the eldest—sat on the couch in his fancy intern outfit, the tie loosened. "Hey, Audrey," he said. "Julian's not here."

"I know," Audrey said.

Ezra punched his brother's arm. "Yeah, she knows, asswipe."

Nate used his foot to knock over the stack of Oreos next to a Coke. "Eat a dick, bro."

Ezra scrunched up his face. "You're such an asshole, Nate."

"I know." Nate grinned. He held out an Xbox controller to Audrey. "Want to play? We're defeating the locust horde."

"Always." Audrey took the controller and sat in her usual spot, cross-legged on the floor next to the old corduroy ottoman. "But Ezra, if you blow me up with that stupid bow again, I'll kill you in real life."

Ezra saluted. "Yes, ma'am."

The Kitsch boys were undeniable, and Audrey liked hanging out with them even when Julian wasn't around. They were like Xerox copies that faded a little more each time: Nate with his pure-black hair and olive skin, then to Julian's darkest-brown mess of curls, and Ezra with the hints of ash in his shoulder-length hair and freckles dotting his face. They all had the exact same mannerisms, too, and the petulance of little kids if you caught them at the wrong moment.

They played until Nate got annoyed at Ezra, and then Audrey made them watch an episode of her favorite show, about two girls trying not to fuck up everything in their lives. (She could relate.) The front door slammed, and Julian appeared in the doorway, his hat and jacket drenched from the rain. "Hey," he said, sounding surprised. He pulled off his headphones and looked at Audrey. "Did we have plans?"

Audrey shook her head as she got to her feet. "I was just bored."

His face relaxed, and he swung his guitar off his shoulder. "Cool. E, is Mom home?"

"Nah, parent-teacher thing," Ezra said.

"Dad?"

"Tutoring," Nate said. "He's bringing home pizza. Oh, and he wants you to get the boxes out of the garage."

"He specifically wants *me* to do it? Right." Julian rolled his eyes.

"It's called delegating," Nate said. "When you're a grown-up like me, maybe you'll learn something about it."

"Good one," Julian said. "Real clever."

"Nerd."

"Douche."

"Okay," Audrey said. "Good talk, everyone."

They went upstairs, ignoring the jeers that followed them, and into the bedroom that Julian shared with Ezra. As the eldest, Nate got the privilege of having his own room, and that meant Julian had to put up with Ezra's sloppy housekeeping: his side of the floor was covered in dirty clothes and shoes without pairs, empty chip bags and battered textbooks. Julian's side was spotless, his bed neatly made and one of Audrey's guitar-string mobiles hanging from the ceiling.

Audrey lay down under it, staring up at the spirals of metal. "I missed you," she said.

Julian tucked himself next to Audrey. "We just saw each other," he said, and his breath blew warm onto her face. "At school?"

"That was, like, five hours ago," Audrey said. "That's a lifetime."

"Okay, drama queen," Julian said. "Whatever you say."

His hand brushed the curls out of her eyes. "It's getting long," she said. "I need to do something with it."

"Don't cut it," Julian said immediately. "I love your hair. Especially this way."

"There's too much of it." Audrey pulled at one particularly kinky strand, narrowing her eyes. "Maybe I'll get it braided."

"I've never seen you with braids," he said. "I bet you'd look hot."

Audrey smiled. "Oh my God," she said. "Sometimes I think you only like me because I'm black and not because I'm me."

Julian widened his eyes. "Wait, you're *black*?"

"Stop!" Audrey laughed, watching the way Julian's eyes crinkled at the corners. In moments like these it was so easy to pretend that everything was fine; they were hanging out, and in a little while they might watch a movie, make out, maybe go and get something to eat. Like normal.

But things weren't normal. Tomorrow wouldn't be just another day. It would be another day she was pregnant.

Audrey touched her hand to Julian's face, smoothing her thumb over the corner of his mouth. She had to tell him. "Olivia knows."

Julian stilled. "Olivia knows what?"

"What do you think?" Audrey shifted, the mattress creaking underneath her. "I didn't tell her. I was throwing up in the middle of art and she was there. She guessed. But now she knows, so . . . I thought I should tell you."

Julian rolled onto his back, folded his arms behind his head. "Okay. So . . . I guess now would be a good time to tell you that Coop knows, too." He paused for barely any time, like he was second-guessing himself but deciding to go on. "And I *did* tell him."

"What?" Audrey snatched her hand away and sat up, her face heating. Cooper? Out of all the people he could have possibly told, he picked *Cooper*? The boy was basically the Gossip Girl of Kennedy High. Julian must have *lost* his mind. "You're kidding me, right?"

"Calm down—"

"Did you just tell me to *calm down*?" Audrey bit out the words. "*Cooper*, Julian? Out of everybody you could have picked! I haven't even told *Rose*."

Julian winced at her raised voice. "I know." He groaned, closing his eyes. "Jesus, why am I such an asshole?"

Audrey bristled. "I don't know, Julian. You tell me."

"Wait a minute," he said. "How come it's worse if I tell my friends than if you tell yours? That's not fair."

"Oh, you want to talk about fair? I'm the one who's pregnant. I'm the one throwing up all the time and lying to my parents, and I'm the one who's going to have to go through—" She stopped, struggling for the words. "I don't know. Whatever it is we decide to do!"

Julian pushed himself as far away from her as was possible in his small bed. "Fine, it's worse for you. I wasn't aware that this was a competition, but okay, you're winning. Or losing, whatever," he said, his voice rising to match hers. "But this is my life, too. Or am I not allowed to be involved anymore? You just want me to shut up and wait until you've figured it out and you can tell me what to do?"

Audrey's mouth dropped open. "I never said that. Why would you think that?"

"That's what you're acting like! We haven't talked about anything, and it's starting to feel like this is all just something you can use to throw at me when you're pissed."

"Yes, right, that's exactly what it is. I got pregnant on purpose so I could use it to punish you," Audrey yelled. "Of *course*!"

"Stop yelling," Julian said, low. "They'll hear."

Audrey's instinct was to yell even louder—he didn't *ever* tell her what to do. But then she remembered where they were—Ezra and Nate so close, his parents coming home any minute—and she forced herself to stop, counting her ragged breaths until they evened out. "Julian," she said now, quietly. "I'm sorry that I'm such a terrible person."

"Don't be like that," Julian said, his face flickering between annoyance and shame. "Come on."

"I don't know what you want me to say." Audrey rubbed at her eyes. "I don't know what to do."

"You could ask me what I want to do."

She looked at him. "What?"

"I want to *talk*," he said. "Not fight. Talk, like rational human beings. Remember how we used to do that?"

Audrey was silent for a moment, then said, "Okay."

"I'm sorry I told Cooper," he said. "But I had to talk to someone. And he might be Coop, but he's not going to tell anyone."

"I know," Audrey said. "It's just—Cooper knows. Olivia knows. Rose knows *something* is up. How long before it's not a secret anymore?"

Shit. Two weeks. It had been *two whole weeks* now, and in that time what had they done? Nothing, except drive themselves crazy thinking in circles. So—what now?

She—they—couldn't put off dealing with it any longer.

Julian held out his hand to her. "Are you mad at me?"

Audrey pulled on her bottom lip before answering. "Yes," she said. "Are you mad at me?"

"Yeah."

She took his hand anyway, holding it in both of her own. "Finally, we're on the same page." They both laughed, the sound reassuring to Audrey. She shook her head. "Since we're talking, you want to hear something wild?"

"Sure," Julian said. "What else could there be?"

Audrey dug her feet into his flannel sheets. "I got a letter the other day. From my birth mother."

"Wait, *what*?" Julian's eyes widened. "That can happen?"

Audrey shrugged. "Evidently."

"Shit," he said. "Have you read it?"

"No."

"Are you going to?"

"I don't know." Audrey counted the beats of Julian's pulse under her fingers. "I can't think about it right now."

He twined their fingers together, and Audrey looked at their hands, linked. She hadn't decided yet. It was too much, on top of all this pregnancy stuff, and school, and whatever was going on with her and Rose right now. "I feel stuck," she said finally. "Like I can't do anything yet, because it doesn't feel real to me yet. I can't decide what to do."

"I don't think it'll feel real until we tell our parents."

"I know," she said. "But when? I keep trying to find the right time—"

"Forget right time," Julian said. "There'll never be a 'right time.' It's making me all twitchy, lying to my parents. I am not a good liar."

"Oh, I know," Audrey said. "Which is why I don't even entertain the idea of worrying about you cheating on me."

Julian pulled his hand from hers and raked it through his hair, looking at her so seriously. "We should just . . . do it."

Audrey rolled her eyes. "Okay."

"No," he said, insistent. "Soon. Like . . . this weekend."

"What?" Audrey sat up, too, tucking her feet beneath herself. "No. I can't."

"We have to do it at some point," he said, catching her face between his hands. "No more putting it off."

"Seriously?" The idea sent Audrey's heart into sprint mode and started a tingling in her fingertips. The idea of telling her mom, saying the words *I'm pregnant* out loud and seeing the sure disappointment on her face—it made Audrey more nauseated than the morning sickness.

But it had to be done, before her body told the truth for her.

"My parents are going to kill me," Julian said with a laugh that Audrey didn't quite believe.

"*My* parents are going to kill you," she said, and she meant it as a joke but . . . who knew what Adam was capable of?

Kidding.

"Okay," she said after a minute, locking her eyes onto his. "Let's do it."

SEVENTEEN

I feel sick."

"Drink some ginger ale."

Audrey exhaled, putting her hand down on the stair she sat on. "Not"—she lowered her voice—"pregnant sick. Nervous sick. I don't think ginger ale helps with that."

Julian's laugh sounded anxious on the other end of the phone. "I don't think anything helps with that. Although I bet there's a pill in some lab somewhere that could do something—or if there isn't, they should make one. Maybe I could make one, and sell it before the SATs and to seniors the week of college acceptance letters. I'd make a killing."

"Hmm," Audrey murmured, tuning out his babble. College. It kept popping into her head recently, especially since Ms. Fitz had begun talking about portfolios and scholarships. Next year they'd be the ones popping Ritalin and chugging Red Bulls while they waited for the acceptances, or rejections, to come. "Hey," she said, interrupting Julian's no doubt genius plan. "We should take a trip. Over spring break, maybe, or in the summer. We could go to California and look at the schools you want to go to."

"Audrey."

"Or if California's too far," she continued, "we could keep it East Coast. Philadelphia, Boston, Rhode Island . . . Wouldn't that be fun? We'll road trip, do all the fun things." Audrey sat up straight, tapping her hand on the smooth wood of the stairs. The fantasy of California was beaches, bikinis for her and a shirtless Julian, putting sunscreen on each other, pretending like they knew how to surf. They'd stay in a cool hotel and eat disgusting amounts of room service at two a.m. "But California would be best—I could show you the things I remember from when I was a kid. I could show you our old house!"

"Audrey," Julian said again, and this time the warning was clear. "I don't think . . . Maybe we shouldn't be making any big plans. Not right now, not until everything's . . . under control."

The sick feeling returned. It was November now, and school finished in May. In summer she would—could—might be, what, eight months gone? Nine? *This is one of those times when it would be helpful to know exactly how pregnant you are*, she thought. *Impending motherhood—you're doing it right!*

"I know. You're right." Audrey looked down at her stomach, trying to imagine it all swollen and big. But even when she squeezed her eyes shut and focused all her energy, she couldn't do it. Instead she saw Julian, summer tanned and grinning. He'd look good in California.

She stood, the stairs creaking under her feet. Eleven steps down from her attic room and another thirteen down to the ground level, where her mom and Adam were making Sunday dinner. It had been easy to push all thought of this moment aside when she was with her friends this weekend, laughing with Olivia, listening to María practicing her debate speeches; but now the time was here, and there was no more avoiding it. "You ready for this?"

"Could I ever be?" Julian said, but he sounded a little more cheerful. "If you don't hear from me after, please contact the police, because it's a one hundred percent certainty that my mother will have killed me."

Audrey laughed, although at what, she wasn't sure. But the laughter felt better than the pressure in her head, so she let it roll. "Of course."

"Hopefully she'll leave the homicide for another night, and I'll be able to check in at nine," he said. "Like we planned."

"Hopefully." Audrey took her first step, her stockinged feet sliding on the wood. "I feel like I should say something, but what? Good luck? That doesn't seem right."

"I'll take it," Julian said. "And ditto. Love you."

"Love you, too," Audrey said softly. "Talk later."

She hung up and continued downstairs, holding her arms tight around her body. *Walk in there and tell them straight*, she thought. *Like a Band-Aid. Rip it off.*

Audrey heard the two of them laughing even before she got to the kitchen. When she did, she stopped in the doorway and pulled in a breath through her nose. Adam stood over a pot of boiling water, occasionally peering down at it, while her mom was next to him stirring something that smelled amazing.

She watched as Adam bobbed his head to the jazz playing out of Laura's iPod, bumping her with his hip in a way that caused Laura's arm to jerk, sending bright orangey-red liquid splattering across the cabinets. Her mom gasped, then dipped her thumb into the liquid and smeared it on Adam's cheek, sending him into childish giggles.

Audrey loved Adam, the closest thing to a father she'd ever had. Not that Adam was anything like her friends' fathers—he didn't care if she cursed, sometimes gave her a beer when they were watching the game, and thought punishment meant taking away those beers. But he was good at all the things that mattered: teaching her how to drive, listening when she and Julian had gotten into a fight. Knowing her favorite foods. Before he'd come on the scene, Audrey had worried—what would her mom do when Audrey went to college? There'd be no one to listen to her complain about her staff at the theater, the persistent calls from her manager, or the scripts filling her in-box. How would her mom come home to a silent house day after day and not get lonely?

But then Adam had come along, like magic, and Audrey stopped worrying. They were good together, she thought, watching her mom dab the tomato sauce from Adam's face, watching him pull her in for a very nonparental—but sweet—kiss. Happy.

She wished, painfully so, that what she was about to tell them wouldn't completely dent that happiness.

Audrey cleared her throat, taking a step into the kitchen. "I hate to interrupt, but . . ."

"Oh!" Laura jumped, putting her hand over her heart. "God, you're quiet. Anybody ever tell you you'd make an excellent covert agent?"

"As a matter of fact . . ." Audrey trailed off, unsure where she was going with it. "Um. No?"

Her mom turned back to the pan on the stove. "Do you want to set the table? Dinner should be about five minutes."

Audrey wrung her hands. *Rip. It. Off.* They'd agreed, it was easier that way. Like they'd agreed it would be easier if they each told their parents separately tonight, to not have the awkwardness of sitting through the same conversation twice. Or Julian's dad flipping out and calling up his terrifying grandmother to yell at them, as Julian had considered a very real possibility. Really, Audrey was relieved not to have to be there when Julian's mom found out, as pathetic as that was. Her mom's disappointment was going to be all she could handle. She didn't need another mother's sadness weighing on her conscience.

"Actually . . ." She looked away from Adam, afraid that if she met his eyes she'd lose her nerve. "I need to talk to you. Both of you."

Her mom glanced over her shoulder. "About what?"

Audrey crossed her ankles. She had to pee suddenly, and her neck itched from the tag in her shirt, and her mom had a streak of flour mixed in with the red of her hair. That smudge of flour sent a strange sadness through Audrey like she'd never felt before.

"Audrey?" Her mom sounded impatient. "Is—"

Do it.

"I'm pregnant."

Her mom turned around, painfully slow, and then there was the clang of Adam dropping the knife in his hand, a sharp echo on the countertop. Laura inhaled sharply. "You're what?"

Audrey swallowed; now that the most important part was out, she couldn't stop the rest of it from tumbling out. "It was an accident. I take my birth control, I do, and I know you know that, because you trust me. Right? That's what you say anyway, and I believe you, and I don't know why it didn't work, I guess we're in that lucky zero point one percent of people, but it happened, and so I don't want you to be mad at me for not taking precautions or being sensible because I am, we are, we were, and I don't want you to think I'm stupid—and I'm sorry I didn't tell you before tonight, not that I've known for forever or anything, only a couple weeks or so, and I kind of wanted to get my head straight before I said anything but it turns out I can't get my head straight and so—"

"Audrey." Adam crossed the kitchen in two long strides and placed his hands on her shoulders, leaning down. "Take a breath."

She did as he said, her heart slowing as she breathed out. Adam nodded, squeezing her shoulders. "And again."

Audrey inhaled, exhaled, inhaled, all the while keeping her eyes level with Adam's. So much for staying calm and clear.

She was so focused on breathing that she'd almost forgotten about the bombshell she'd dropped. Until, that was, her mom spoke again. "You're pregnant?"

Laura's voice was high, breathy, in a way that Audrey couldn't tell was good or bad. She wriggled out of Adam's grip and stepped around him, taking in the two bright spots that had appeared on her mom's cheeks and the softness of her eyes. "Mom?"

"Oh, baby." Her mom held out her arms, and Audrey rushed into them, pressing her cheek into her mom's neck. "Oh, Audrey. Always surprising me, aren't you?"

Audrey tried to stifle her laugh, but that meant it exploded from her instead, a sudden bubbly noise that caused her mom to jump. "Sorry, sorry, I know it's not funny, I know."

But then her mom's chuckle reverberated through her. "I guess it is a little funny," she said. "In an absurd way."

Audrey disentangled herself, looking from her mom to Adam and back again. "Are you mad?"

Her mom seemed to consider it for a moment before shaking her head. "No. I'm not mad."

"But you're . . . disappointed." Audrey stated it; it was easy to hear in her mom's voice.

"Well. Maybe a little," Laura said. "But not in you. Okay? Disappointed that you're . . . going through this."

Audrey pulled on her bottom lip. She didn't get the distinction, but at least her mom hadn't imploded. Not yet anyway.

She took a step toward Adam, opening her mouth to say . . . she didn't know what. *Are you disappointed? Are you mad? Are you wishing you could bail on our family because a pregnant sort-of-stepdaughter wasn't what you signed up for?*

Adam got there first, his voice sharp. "Where's Julian in all this? Why isn't he here? If he thinks he's going to—"

"He's not," Audrey said quickly. "I swear. At least, he swears. He's at home right now." She paused to tug the ends of her sweater sleeves over her cold hands. "He's telling his parents, too. We thought it would be easier this way. So everyone knows at the same time."

They fell into silence again, quiet enough to notice the pots on the stove going crazy. Laura swore as more red liquid decorated the tiles, and Adam rushed over to help turn everything down. Audrey stayed rooted to the spot, waiting for whatever was coming next and wondering how it was going for Julian. Maybe doing it separately hadn't been the best idea.

Or maybe that's the idea you should have had months ago, the voice in her head said. *Think of all the pregnancy you wouldn't be enduring if you had "Done It" separately—get it?* Audrey hid her smirk behind her sweater-covered hands. What the fuck was wrong with her?

"So." Her mom's shirt was now decorated with their dinner, a nice complement to the flour in her hair. "How many weeks are you?"

"I don't know," Audrey said. "Which is stupid, too. Sorry."

Adam's cheek twitched. "You don't have to keep apologizing, kiddo. What's done is done, and besides, what are you apologizing for, exactly? You haven't done anything to us."

Audrey nodded. "I know. Sorry." She winced.

"Well, first things first—we need to get you an appointment with Dr. Miller," her mom said, all business now. "And we'll need to get together with Julian and his parents, too, so we can talk. Have you . . ." She hesitated, her eyebrows knitting together. "Have you made any decisions yet?"

As fucking if.

But all Audrey said was "Not—no."

"Right," her mom said, nodding slowly, as if to herself. The shake in her voice was almost unnoticeable, except that Audrey knew her mom's voice better than anything in the world and so heard it clearly. "Well. I suppose it would be an understatement for me to say this won't be easy. But whatever you want to do, it's your decision," she continued, and Audrey heard the echo of what her mom had said when she'd handed over the letter from her birth mother. "We'll help you, but we're not going to make it for you or force you to do anything. And no matter what you decide, we'll support you. Won't we?"

Audrey flicked her eyes to Adam, relieved to see him nodding. "Of course we will," he said, and the smile he offered made Audrey's eyes sting. "Come on, kiddo. So this isn't ideal. But it's not the end of the world. We're all alive."

"Thanks." Audrey swallowed, folding her arms and breathing, just breathing, until she felt more in control. "I'll, um, I'll go set the table now. Okay?"

She waited only long enough for them both to say okay back and then hurried into the dining room. Lowering into her usual chair, she lifted her hands to her face and inhaled the scent of her mom's perfume lingering on her, dark and sweet.

They're not mad. It's not the end of the world. Audrey managed the world's smallest smile. Maybe things weren't quite as bad as she'd thought they were.

All through dinner, when she was washing the dishes, when she was curled up on the couch for an episode of *Twin Peaks* with her mom (not that they paid attention, Laura tracing small, soothing circles on Audrey's back instead), Audrey still felt a little unsettled. She kept checking her phone, waiting for a response from Julian. Admittedly, she'd jumped the gun a little and tried to call him at eight forty-five, but now it was thirty minutes later and she had yet to hear from him.

"Want to watch another?" Her mom glanced over with the remote in her hand, ready to press Play. "Aud?"

"Hmm?" Audrey tore her gaze away from her phone. "Oh, yeah. Sure."

Her phone vibrated in her hand then, and Audrey almost dropped it in her rush to check the message. "Shit," she muttered under her breath.

"Audrey." A warning from her mom.

"Sorry." Audrey ignored the TV and finally opened the (now multiple) texts from Julian:

Sorry I'm late—have been sitting in a lecture for an hour.
Mom upset, Dad going the disappointed route. BUT still
didn't go as bad as I thought. Think it'll be okay once they
process.
I still have a place to live, at least :)
Can't call, they're still hanging around, but glad your mom
and Adam didn't flip out either.
See you tomorrow. Love.

Audrey read through the words on the screen three times, each time her heart slowing a bit. Okay—things were okay with Julian, too. And now everyone knew everything, and it was all out in the open.

Well. Except for Rose and the others.

Audrey shook off that thought, and her fingers flew across her phone as she typed a response to Julian:

We're still alive! :)

There was no one she could imagine going through this with other than Julian. He was it.

One day you'll write a song about this and it'll be worth it.

Kidding! Kind of. See you tomorrow.

And knowing they were so together right now gave Audrey this almost invincible feeling. Like, if they could get through this, what couldn't they get through? Everything else paled in comparison. Everything else was just a distraction. That was how she felt.

We can figure this out. Right?

They would figure it out, because they were Audrey and Julian, thinking the same way, doing things right. They were.

Love you.

EIGHTEEN

*I*n the morning Audrey woke up to see the time on her phone was forty minutes past when she should have gotten up. She bolted out of bed, rubbing roughly at her eyes. "Shit," she breathed, stripping her pajamas and falling smack into the sharp edge of her desk in her rush. "Ow! *Shit.*"

A quick shower later and Audrey was back in her room, throwing on the first clean(ish) clothes she could find. She grabbed her camera and textbooks, the math problems she hadn't even started yesterday slipping onto the floor. Detention it was.

Downstairs in the kitchen there was a brown lunch bag waiting on the counter, next to a note with her name written on it. Audrey unrolled the top and peered inside: a blueberry muffin, apple slices, chunks of pale-yellow cheese, and her favorite chocolate. On top of everything lay a bright-orange flower, its stem snipped short.

Audrey looked at the scrawl of her name and smiled at her mom's trademark sloppy handwriting. She would have had to get up extra early to do this, to go out and buy the specific chocolate Audrey ate only rarely because it was so extortionately expensive, to get the pretty flower and cut it just so.

She tucked the lunch into her bag and headed out to her car, still smiling. Last night was the best night's sleep she'd gotten since seeing the plus sign appear. It felt like now she could move on—stop being so stuck on all the *maybe*s and *what if*s, the *someday*s and the *somehow*s. Not that she suddenly knew exactly what to do—*I wish*, she thought. But her head did feel clearer. She and Julian could discuss things without the . . . threat, worry, fear of their parents' reactions. And she'd finally tell Rose now. Soon.

By the time Audrey pulled into the parking lot—finding a space way at the back, next to the recycling bins—the first bell was ringing. She flipped up the hood of her jacket and dashed out into the rain, setting off at a jog that reminded her exactly how little exercise she got. Outside the front entrance Olivia's blue hair shone next to Jen's red ponytail, the others standing in a loose circle with them. She forced out an extra burst of energy and pounded up the rain-slicked steps, clutching her books to her chest. "Hey!" she panted. "I thought I would've missed you guys. I overslept."

Olivia grinned at her. "You're just in time."

Audrey fell in step with Rose as the group headed for the doors. "Hey," she said. "I didn't see you at all this weekend."

Rose folded her umbrella and shook it, spraying Audrey with a thousand icy-cold droplets. "So?"

"So nothing," Audrey said. "I was just saying. Anyway, are you busy after school? Can we do something?"

They could go get burgers and laugh at Coop, or catch a movie, maybe, one that would require zero brain power. All she wanted right now was to take a break from worrying. Keep the secret to herself a little while longer, and have some actual real-life *fun*.

But Rose shook her head, her tawny hair swirling over her shoulders. "Can't," she said shortly. "I have class. Another time."

"Sure," Audrey said, keeping her voice upbeat. *Even though that was a lie*, she thought. *Rose doesn't dance on Mondays. Ever.* "Okay," she said. "Pick a day, any day, this week."

"I'm so busy," Rose said. "With class and homework, and my dad's on my ass about SAT shit . . ."

Another lie. When did Rose's dad ever pay enough attention to talk about school shit? Audrey hadn't missed that Rose had yet to really look at her, either, a ball of trepidation forming in her stomach. But she threw a last attempt out there anyway, hating how desperate and clingy she felt. "Friday?" she said. "You can't do homework on a Friday. It's too depressing."

"Friday? Um . . ." Rose slowed her walk then. "Yeah," she said. "Friday's fine."

Inwardly Audrey sighed, relief coursing through her veins. "Okay." She smiled. "Great."

They entered the building, and Rose linked her arm through Audrey's, a rare, soft gesture. "Okay," she echoed. "Hey, maybe we could go get our nails done. I have a serious cuticle situation going on."

Audrey laughed over the sound of their shoes slapping wetly through the hall, and up ahead María turned with a curious look on her face. Audrey stuck out her tongue, goofy, and María crossed her eyes back.

It almost felt like nothing was wrong. Nothing at all.

NINETEEN

"What do you want?"

Audrey scanned the board, her nausea settled enough to let her feel actual hunger. While she could, she kind of wanted to eat everything, to make up for the time she wouldn't be able to later. But to Julian she said, "Cheeseburger and curly fries. And a Dr Pepper."

Julian kissed her cheek. "Cool. Get a table."

Audrey squeezed into the tiny booth by the kitchen, one she normally avoided because it was so small, but for only her and Julian, it was fine. She twisted the ring on her pinkie finger around, the fake jewels studded along it glittering under the fluorescent lighting. Julian came back with drinks and a handful of napkins. "Hi." He slid into the booth, and his knees bumped hers under the table. Audrey felt an electric tingle at the touch and marveled. How could she feel that at a time like this? It was incredible, and for a moment she forgot where they were. All she wanted to do was feel Julian's mouth on hers, run her fingers to the dip of his throat and make him let out that mix of a sigh and a groan in her ear.

But the bell above the door chimed, bringing her back, and she blinked at Julian staring from across the table. "What? Why are you looking at me like that?"

"You completely spaced," he said. "Did you even hear what I said?"

Audrey shook her head and Julian laughed. "It doesn't matter," he said. "But this does—do you think I'll be allowed at Saturday dinner anymore, or am I persona non grata at chez Spencer?"

"Are you out of your mind?" Audrey asked. "I think you'll be persona non grata if you *don't* come. Adam's all ready to kick your ass the second you stop being good to me."

"He's pissed, huh?"

"Nah." Audrey wrestled her camera out of her bag. "As long as you stay on my good side, you're on his good side. Easy."

"Easy," Julian repeated, smiling. "At least it's out now. I mean, I could do without the shit Nate and E are giving me, but I'll take that over keeping it a secret."

"Send them to me," Audrey said. "I'll show them what happens when you mess with my boyfriend." That made him laugh, and Audrey lifted her hair off her neck, letting it fall back slowly, spiraling twists of almost-black. "I do feel better, though. I really do. I never thought of that saying about things weighing on you as true, but it is. It's like I've had a ton of bricks balancing on me and now they've disappeared." She slid her hand across the table, curling her fingers around Julian's. "It's good."

A willowy-tall girl brought their food, and Audrey plucked a fry from the basket. "My mom made a doctor's appointment for next week," she said. "She's going to email your mom the details."

"Okay." Julian stirred his root beer straw around, his foot bumping against Audrey's under the table. "What do you think it'll be like?"

"The doctor's appointment? I have no clue."

"Do you think they'll give you a sonogram?"

"Maybe," Audrey said. "Probably. I guess they'll have to, right, to figure out all the dates?" Like she A. knew how it all worked and B. knew when the fateful occasion had been. "But it's not like we'll see anything. I'm pretty sure you have to be, like, twelve weeks for that to happen, and I'm sure I'm not that far gone." She let out a breathy laugh. "What am I talking about? There is absolutely *nothing* about this situation that I'm sure of."

Across the way two women sat at a table, one bouncing a serious-faced baby on her lap while she ate. Audrey watched the baby reach for its mother's hair and how the woman expertly unfurled the baby's fingers from her braid without any break in her conversation, giving it a straw to play with. Would she be like that one day?

Julian was watching, too, Audrey realized, and he wore this wistful expression on his face. "What?" Audrey reached across to tap the back of his hand. "Julian, what is it?"

He glanced at her, that look erased. "Nothing."

Audrey tipped her head to the side. "Have you thought about it? What it might be like to keep it?"

She didn't mean it to come out quite so bluntly, but there it was. "A little," Julian admitted. "Have you?"

"Yeah," Audrey said honestly. "A little. Mostly about what it would look like." Would their baby have her curls and Julian's strong jaw, the dark eyes they both possessed? Would it be a little boy with chubby legs and a laugh like sunshine, or a freckle-faced girl with a pensive stare? It was mesmerizing to wonder.

"I could teach it music," Julian said, a lift in his voice. "Like my dad taught me. How to play piano, read music, everything."

Audrey raised her camera and snapped a photo of Julian. "I could teach it this," she said, adjusting the focus. "Maybe it would have the natural talent I don't. Or painting. I should paint more."

Julian picked up his burger but stopped short of actually taking a bite. "Seriously, though," he said. "Do you think about it? What it would be like?"

She flicked the dials. It would be like becoming a family, a thing she only dreamed about in her most fantastical moments. But it would also mean no art school dreams becoming a reality, no California music school for Julian.

Or maybe it wouldn't. Maybe they could both go to California, go to school and work at the same time. There were schools with cool art programs out there, or maybe she'd major in something "useful" and make art on the side. Yeah—they'd have an apartment, or maybe a tiny little house if they could swing it with the jobs they got. They'd go down to the beach every day to stand with their toes touching the water. She could see it: they'd be tan and happy, each holding one hand of their brown-eyed baby, teaching him or her not to fear the waves, to love the feel of sand under their feet.

"I think . . . maybe it would be good," she said slowly. "What do you think?"

"I've always liked the name Daniel," Julian said. "For a boy."

"Oh, yeah?" Audrey almost couldn't believe they were talking about this, and talking about it this way—so casual, so simple. *But why does everything have to be difficult?* she thought. *Why do I make it all so hard?*

She took another picture of him watching her. She never quite managed to capture the Julian she saw, the way he really looked at her or the expression on his face when he got way into music mode. But it was almost better that way. It meant that no one else could see what she saw, either.

Audrey licked her lips, salty from fries, and snapped another three shots in quick succession before lowering the camera. "I like Daniel."

They could do it. Why not? Other people did it and they were happy. Why couldn't things be the same for them?

She looked up at Julian and nodded, trying to convey everything she was feeling in that one look. And maybe it worked, because Julian's face broke out into the biggest smile as he pushed his hair out of his eyes yet again. "I love you, Audrey Spencer," he said. "Like nothing else."

Audrey laughed, and the sound filled her with lightness. "Ditto," she said. "Like nothing else."

TWENTY

I should tell her now.

The thought came to Audrey as she was slicking on lip gloss in the coffee shop bathroom. She paused, the wand hovering an inch away from her mouth. Should she?

Rose was outside, ordering their drinks. She didn't seem too sharp today; at school she'd laughed at a joke Audrey made, and she'd smiled a real smile when she'd walked into the coffee shop and had let Audrey hug her hello. Good signs.

And how long had Audrey been promising herself she was going to tell Rose? Holding it back because she wasn't ready, Rose was being too Rose to talk about anything, because she liked keeping something to herself. That wasn't good, that last reason. And it didn't *feel* good anymore, either.

Rose seemed like she was in a good mood today. The kind of mood that meant she'd really listen to Audrey.

She watched herself in the mirror, taking deep breaths. She could tell the truth today. Okay.

Audrey left the bathroom and found Rose on the couches at the back, by the windows. "Hey."

Rose pushed half of a muffin toward Audrey as she sat down. "I thought we could split this."

An offering? Audrey looked at the fluffy baked good wonderingly. "Thanks," she said. Was this the universe trying to signal something to her?

"Did you hear what happened to Cooper yesterday?" Rose tore open a sugar and added it to her coffee.

"No," Audrey said. "What?"

"Evidently he's been seeing this girl from Saint Francis," Rose said. "Except she had a boyfriend who Coop swears he didn't know about. Anyway, this guy was outside the movie theater last night, waiting for Coop to come out. There was almost a full-on rumble, I swear to God."

"Shut up." Audrey laughed. "What? How did I not hear about this? What an asshole!"

"Coop?"

"No, the other guy. Coop does some stupid shit sometimes, but it's not his fault that this girl decided to lie to him and cheat on her boyfriend. And why does it always turn into some bro contest? It's so pathetic."

"Boys are pathetic," Rose said. "Most of the time anyway."

"But Coop's okay, right?" Audrey asked. "He didn't get his ass kicked, did he?"

"No. Davis and a bunch of other guys were there, and this kid left after he'd yelled at Coop some." Rose rolled her eyes. "So much drama."

There was a comfortable—on Rose's part—pause. This was the moment.

Audrey weighed the words on her tongue. *Speaking of drama*—no. Way too much. Keep it simple and direct. *I have something to tell you.*

She took a deep breath. "I—"

"God, I'm so out of it," Rose interrupted, rubbing at her eyes with this wavering smile. "Sorry."

"Out of it? Why?"

The words came automatically, and Audrey cursed in her head, pinching that spot on her thigh. That wasn't what she'd meant to say. What she'd meant was *Don't you hear me right now?* What she'd meant was *Are you really this self-centered?* What she'd meant was *Can you let me talk, for* once?

"It's nothing," Rose said, a sighing lilt to her voice. "Forget it."

And just like that they were back to normal. The normal where everything was about Rose, and Audrey came in second, every single fucking time.

But this wasn't supposed to happen today. *For once*, Audrey thought, anger building at surprising speed, *can't we talk about* me?

So instead of pushing, Audrey said, "Okay."

This look of surprise flashed across Rose's face, and she stared at

Audrey. "What?" *What, we're not going to focus on me? What, you're not falling over yourself to make me feel better?* Audrey imagined that running through Rose's mind and allowed herself to feel pleased. She let the silence linger there, tense now.

Audrey glanced at the table next to them, occupied by what her mom called the Mommy Mafia: thirty-something women in dark wash jeans and bright cashmere, tossing back venti lattes while their babies slept in expensive strollers. Definitely part of the Right People of Kennedy list. They made motherhood look like another successful accomplishment they could check off their lists, along with their degrees and beautiful homes and effortless careers. Audrey knew that she'd never be that type of mother.

She looked back at Rose, meeting her questioning eyes. "You said 'forget it,'" Audrey said, keeping her voice perfectly even. "Okay. Let's forget it."

A knock on the window right next to her ear made Audrey jump, and her head snapped around to see María standing on the other side of the glass, waving.

"Shit," Audrey said, hand pressed to her chest. "She scared me. What's she doing here?"

Rose waved back. "How should I know?"

Audrey could feel her truth crawling around her stomach, to be burned and dissolved in the acid swirling in her stomach. Maybe it was better down there, where nobody would ever find it.

It can't be a secret forever, a voice in the back of her mind whispered. *It has to end, one way or another.*

María came bounding over and threw herself onto the squishy leather couch next to Audrey. "Hey!" she said, pushing her fogged-up glasses onto her head. "I just finished tutoring, and then I saw you two in here. Cool if I join?" She reached for Audrey's half of the muffin, taking their absence of answers as an affirmative.

"God, it's cold out," María said, licking blueberry crumbs from her thumb. "I actually watched this documentary the other day about weather systems and how the oceans are going to be impacted by all this shit."

"Sounds fascinating," Rose said drily.

"Screw you, it was!" María's laughter quickly turned to a wince. "I have the world's worst cramps right now."

Oh, what Audrey would give to have cramps. "I have Midol," she said in a flat voice. "Want some?"

María shook her head. "No, I took some already. Thanks, though."

Audrey picked up her hot chocolate and took a sip, watching Rose. Rose caught her stare and raised her eyebrows. "What?" she said, exasperated. "You're being weird. What is your problem?"

What's my problem? Too late for that. *You don't get to ask me now.* "Nothing," Audrey said, and her voice was sharper than she meant it to be, but it felt good. "I have no problems at all, ever, right?" She turned to María, frozen with a chunk of muffin in her fingers and this look on her face like she was ignoring whatever fight she'd walked in on. Audrey pushed her shoulders back and pressed her mouth into a sunshine smile.

Because this was the way it always was. See, it was fine when it was Rose with the problem, when Audrey was there to make Rose talk about Aisha Forrester or her parents or her sister, spill it all so she wouldn't completely shatter. But when it was the other way around, Rose couldn't (wouldn't?) read Audrey the same way. And usually Audrey went along with it—the Vacarello family was not a family that discussed its feelings, ever, and so Rose did not know how to do it. She didn't know how to measure out her words and feelings, to let them out little by little instead of repressing until her only option was explosion. Audrey knew this, knew it was not entirely Rose's fault—but she was sick of it. And having shitty parents wasn't an excuse. That didn't make Rose completely innocent.

She doesn't listen, Audrey thought. *When I'm actually trying to tell her something, she doesn't want to hear me. Why would I want to talk?*

"So." She injected false sunshine into her voice as she turned to María. "Whatever happened with you and the mathlete?"

She could see Rose watching with narrowed eyes as María launched into the whole complicated story, as Audrey nodded along and made the right exclamations at the right moments.

Audrey didn't like lying. But lately she'd learned to lie with every part of herself, and sometimes, in moments like this when it was so easy to slip into Normal Audrey, when the lie was so much easier than the truth, it was comforting. Rose wasn't the only one who could keep her feelings inside, all pushed and folded and hidden deep down out of sight. Audrey was allowed that, too. It was only fair.

TWENTY-ONE

ere," Audrey half yelled over the noise of the Saturday-night bar crowd. She handed Olivia's phone back, the emergency 911 text they all used now programmed in. "So if you're ever in trouble or you need someone, you just send that and we'll come. No questions asked." They didn't use it often, but enough—like when María had been stranded in the city after a disastrous date with no money to get home, or when Rose had been stuck in the house with her sister's drugged-out ex pounding on the door.

Olivia leaned in. "Thanks," she said loudly. "I—I never had friends that did shit like this before. Thanks."

Audrey smiled. "It's cool," she said, her throat already scratchy. "You're one of us now! For better or worse."

The guy behind Olivia grinned. "Oh, Liv, does that mean I can't come visit you again?"

"Please ignore Dylan," Olivia said, elbowing the guy. "He's an ass!"

Audrey laughed. Dylan was Olivia's friend from the city proper who Olivia said she had known since before she could even remember. He seemed cool, and Audrey was especially pleased that he was visiting this weekend, when Hera was playing this show, because she liked to show Julian off.

That boy who looked so at home onstage with his bass guitar, who played hard and moved hard until the sweat dripped from him, who other people looked at with awe and envy and even lust. Who wouldn't want to show him off? Maybe it was immature, but she liked people knowing he was hers, that they were each other's. Audrey, the girl with the ever-present camera and bright lipstick, and Julian, the bassist with the voice like cut glass. She liked knowing that whoever was pushing themselves on him, boys and girls wanting him after the show was done, she was the one he always looked for. Plus, being With the Band meant perks like occasional free drinks even though they were underage, and getting backstage, which was only ever a grimy room with cracked vinyl couches but still fun.

María appeared at Olivia's elbow. "Hey! Have you seen Rose?"

Audrey just about restrained herself from rolling her eyes. "No," she said. "I'm going to find Jen."

She grabbed her drink and walked over to one of the beat-up couches where Jen was sitting with Cooper and others. Up onstage the little starter band yelled over feedback, and Audrey lifted her camera to capture them as she sat down. "In my next life," Jen said, her voice loud, "I would like to be the founder of a kick-ass girl band.

Y'know, full Courtney Love style. But without the drugs and general mess."

"Courtney Love isn't all that," Audrey said. "Hole was great, yes. But there are so many other badass girls. Grace Jones. Gwen Stefani. Tina Turner!"

"How do you think Gwen Stefani gets her hair so perfect? Swear to God, she has never had visible roots for one second of her blond life." Jen took a real gulp of her beer, draining the plastic cup. "Maybe I should go blond again."

Audrey plucked the cup from her hand. "I will never, ever let you do that to yourself. Not after last time."

"Okay," Jen laughed, kicking her heels in the air. Jen was the only one of them dressed more like she was going to a club than to watch her friends at a divey bar, and sometimes the hipster-cool people crowding the room smirked behind their hands at her sequins and sparkles. And sometimes Audrey saw Jen noticing that, saw the way her fingers went to her necklaces, gripping them like a comfort, her confidence coming back full force. Audrey often wondered what it was like to have faith—Julian was Jewish, but he fell more on the agnostic side of things. Jen believed in big, mysterious things up above, plans for her life that were all laid out, waiting for her to find her way. Audrey couldn't get behind that, though; no offense to Jen, she just didn't groove to that beat. But sometimes when she looked at Jen, she especially wondered what it would be like to have that peace, that comfort.

The crowd in front of them appeared to part then, and Rose stalked through the gap, her face thunderous.

"Hi, princess," Audrey said, unsuccessfully holding back the bite in her voice.

Rose threw herself down on the other side of Jen. "This band fucking sucks," she shot back. "It's giving me a migraine. Who the hell gave them a show here?"

"Chill out," Jen said. "They're babies. Give them a chance."

Up on the stage the three pimple-faced boys pulsed behind their too-big instruments, multicolored hair whipping around. They weren't actually awful; Audrey kept catching herself moving her shoulders to the bass line.

"So what's the deal with this Dylan kid?" Jen asked. "He's kind of cute."

"He seems nice," Audrey said. She looked back to the bar for Olivia and Dylan. *He's my oldest friend*, Olivia had told Audrey. *Knows all my dirty secrets.* From the way they'd acted so far during the night, that bond was easy to see. Like right now, how they were standing by the bar with their foreheads almost touching and their faces shining. Looking at them twisted a dagger in Audrey's spine—that was how she and Rose should look right now. They should be sitting next to each other and laughing at stupid jokes that were funny only to the two of them. They should be getting up and dancing, spinning each other around the way they always did. Instead, they were . . . whatever they were right now. Fighting? At an impasse? Not right, that was for sure.

Audrey watched Dylan throw his arm around Olivia's shoulders and the way she tipped her head back, laughing at something he said.

Jen was right; he was cute, with this easy smile and teeth shining white against his dark skin. "He said I reminded him of his cousin, except not a bitch. Which is a good thing?"

Rose sat still on the couch, her pink-painted lips slightly parted. If Audrey had to name the emotion on Rose's face, she would have to call it . . . jealousy. Maybe Audrey hadn't been imagining the electricity between Rose and Olivia, even if that was what Rose would like her to believe. Ordinarily Audrey would have just asked Rose about it, needled the truth out of her—but right now? No.

"He's . . . all right," Rose said eventually, reluctantly. "I guess."

The way she was sitting right then, and the stage lights gleaming in her eyes—Audrey had her camera up to her face before she could even think about it, and the flash bloomed white. Almost perfect.

Rose whirled around. *"Audrey—"*

"What?" Audrey sat back. "You looked *intense*."

Rose sprang up, the swiftness of her movement sending the remains of the beer in her hand spraying over Jen, who let out an indignant cry.

"Not every single second of everybody's life is a fucking photo opportunity for you," Rose hissed. "Jesus! Can't I go five seconds without you getting in my face?"

Audrey instinctively pulled her camera into her chest. Standing up, Rose towered over her, and her expression had tipped from intensity to all-out rage. Audrey blinked, feigning innocence. "It was one pic—"

"I don't give a shit if it was—" Rose cut off abruptly. "You know what? Forget it."

"Rose, come on," Jen said, but Rose turned on her heel and stalked back into the crowd. "Rose!"

Audrey grabbed Jen's arm. "Let her go."

Jen threw up her hands. "God, what is going *on* with you two?"

"What?" Audrey turned. "I don't know what you mean."

"Bullshit." Jen's eyes glittered behind their layer of dark-blue shadow. "You know exactly what I mean—all the bitching and the sniping and you two cold-shouldering each other. This!" She gestured in the direction in which Rose had vanished. "It's weirding me out, and I don't like it."

"It's nothing," Audrey said. She was so used to spouting that lie by now. "Don't worry about it."

"I'm not worried," Jen said. "I'm *confused*."

"Well, don't be that, either."

A clashing riot of noise erupted up front, signaling the end of the starter band's set, and Audrey turned to watch them wave like they were gods before they left the stage. There would be a break before Hera came on, she knew, and she wanted to get closer.

Jen's fingers still gripped her arm, and Audrey shook her loose, only to clasp Jen's hand within her own. "I don't want to deal with it right now. Let's find Ree," she said. "And then let's dance like wild things."

Audrey could see the reluctance in Jen's face, could sense how she didn't want to let Audrey get away with it that easily. But the desire to dance must have been stronger than that feeling, because after a moment her face broke into a wide grin and she did a little hop.

"All right," Jen laughed. "Let's go."

By the time the lights flashed blinding white, Audrey was by the stage, Jen and María right by her side. She didn't know where Rose had gone, but it appeared that wherever it was, she'd taken Olivia with her—which was kind of annoying, because Audrey wanted Olivia to see the band and how much they kicked ass, to see Julian's musician side really come out to play. She wanted to show off: yeah, he might have gotten her pregnant, but look how much he shredded!

But Olivia had for sure gone; the Dylan kid hung back at the bar with Cooper, no sign of his friend, and actually looking perfectly unruffled by it. Which was more than Audrey could say about herself, because her brain was running on overdrive—was there something going on between Rose and Olivia, for real? Or was this Rose's way of getting back at her, latching onto somebody else so Audrey could only focus on the lack of her best friend? That wasn't the kind of trick Rose usually pulled, but right now Audrey felt like she didn't know what Rose would or wouldn't do. That was how far apart they were falling.

She shook all thought of Rose out of her head and turned her attention back to the stage. There were better, more fun things to focus on right now.

Dasha came out first, the lights flashing off her violet hijab as she took her place behind the drums. Julian came next, barely glancing at the audience before starting up a vicious bass line, which Dasha quickly added her snare to. Jasmin and Izzy appeared almost at the same time, their black and blond heads touching together before Izzy stepped up to the mic. "Hi," she said in her throaty voice. "We're Hera."

Then they were off into their first song, one that Audrey had never heard before.

María whooped over the noise, bumping her hip against Audrey's, and Audrey laughed, really laughed, like she hadn't in the longest time.

They were incredible to watch—not perfect, nowhere near, but with a pulsing energy that marked them out as different from the rest. At least, that was how Audrey felt whenever she watched them play: when she saw Jasmin tossing her cheerleader ponytail as she screamed over Izzy's voice; when she saw Julian lift his T-shirt to wipe the sweat from his eyes or hunch over his guitar, concentration burning; when Dasha bashed the hell out of her kit, like she wasn't afraid to smash the whole thing to pieces.

It wasn't just her, though; she could tell from the way the silence between songs was actual silence, how the entire tiny place began to crackle with restless electricity. Izzy had this look in her eyes, pure wanting, and as Audrey lifted her camera to capture it—of course— she had this flash of the future: Izzy holding that power over full arenas, staring out from the cover of *Rolling Stone*, killing it.

Would Julian be there with her? He always said he wasn't interested in the fame or being a "rock star," that it was about the music more than anything else. Production was where he wanted to go—but if Izzy, Jasmin, and Dasha ended up on that path, would he want to go along for the ride?

Maybe.

Jen threw her hands up in the air, jumping somehow in heels she could barely walk in, and Audrey couldn't help whipping her hair around as the band launched into the next song, a frenetic howl of guitars.

And what if he did go along? That would be incredible. Everybody Audrey knew wanted to *be somebody*; maybe her boyfriend was one of the people who would actually make it. She would never do anything to hold him back from that.

Sweat pinpricked at the base of her spine, inched down her neck as the band raced through their set, and she sang the words she knew with such voracity that her throat ached. The crowd behind her surged forward, and Audrey went with them, her heart surging, too.

Once upon a time she'd attended a show like this and watched Julian moving up there, the sweat glistening on his face, and when he'd climbed down from the stage, Audrey had walked straight over and asked him out.

Caught up in the moment, singing and yelling and dizzy with it all, Audrey forgot all about everything plaguing her. Being with her friends like this, hooked on the pulse-pounding high of the music and the dancing . . . for once there was no way she could think of anything else but the moment, the right here and right now that was so good.

TWENTY-TWO

How different today was from Saturday night. No lights, no music, and the high had worn way off.

Audrey sat in the waiting room of Dr. Miller's office, Julian on one side and her mom on the other. Her stomach grumbled, but the only food Audrey had in her bag was a granola bar, and that might as well have been nothing at all.

Her mom flicked through a magazine too fast to actually be reading it, and Julian kept shifting in his chair, feet and hands and head moving to a beat only he could hear. Like Audrey wasn't jumpy and jittery enough already. "Hey," she said tersely. "Could you stop?"

Julian folded his arms, hands tucked away tightly. "Sorry."

Her mom tossed the magazine back onto the low table in the middle of the waiting room. "All right, little miss attitude."

"You're making me nervous," Audrey said. "Both of you. I don't need to be any more nervous."

Nervous, and irritated, and ashamed. That morning, on her way downstairs, she'd heard her name in Adam's voice and stopped right before she came into the kitchen, some instinct kicking in. She'd heard Adam again: "It's Audrey's decision. You have to treat her like a grown-up, you know?"

Audrey had pressed herself back against the wall, her heart pounding a little. She should leave. She should definitely not listen in on them talking about her.

"If I had treated her less like a grown-up, then maybe she wouldn't have gotten pregnant," she'd heard her mom say. "Dr. Miller is going to judge me so hard. If she didn't think I was a shitty mom before, then she will now."

"Babe, the doctor is not going to think you're a shitty mom. She's a doctor. She's supposed to be impartial or whatever."

The clatter of a plate in the sink. "That's judges."

"Eh, same difference. Besides, you don't have to pay any attention to what anybody else thinks about you or Audrey. I think you're a fucking awesome mom."

"It sounds extrasweet with the cursing."

"It's true, though." A chair being pushed back and footsteps that made Audrey retreat farther. "You *are* an awesome mom. It's not a reflection on you that your kid got pregnant. This happens."

Silence, and Audrey had pictured her mom leaning over the sink, shaking her head. "I'm so worried about her. I don't know what she's thinking now—if she wants to keep this baby or not—and either way

I want her to be taking care of herself right now. Vitamins and eating right and all that stuff . . . I don't even know, Adam; I've never been pregnant. God, I was supposed to give her a better life and protect her and keep her from getting into situations like this! She's only seventeen. She should be thinking about school and her friends and her boyfriend, not a baby." Laura's laugh echoed round the corner then, bitter sounding. "What am I saying—she should be thinking about her boyfriend? Maybe if I hadn't gotten her birth control pills and said it was okay—"

"But it *was* okay. They're teenagers, they love each other, you like Julian, and you trusted them. You do trust them."

"I know. And they would've been having sex whether I said it was okay or not, I know that, too."

"Definitely. My high school girlfriend's mom banned us from being alone together in their house, and we still managed to do it in her parents' bed."

"Adam!"

"What? I'm just saying. Teenagers, they're wily."

"Yeah." A heavy sigh. "But if Audrey has this baby, she won't get to be a teenager anymore."

"Laura."

"She'll be changing diapers and singing nursery rhymes while her friends go out and have the fun she should be having, too, and what about college? Everything she wanted?"

"We don't know that she's going to keep it," Adam had said. "She might not, and she'll still be able to go to art school and do everything. But if she does—"

"Keep it?"

"That'll be okay, too. We'll work it out. Hey." The sound of a kiss then. "She's still our Audrey. She's a smart kid. She can take care of herself."

Another long silence. "She can't take care of a baby."

"Laura." That warning tone in Adam's voice again.

"What, you think she can?" Pause. "I hope she makes the right choice."

I hope she makes the right choice. Those words had echoed in Audrey's head all day. That meant there was a wrong choice for her to make. That meant that her mom thought she'd done something wrong, which—why had she even bothered pretending she wasn't mad? Up until now she'd felt safe in the knowledge that her mom was behind her. Except now, maybe she wasn't, and Audrey didn't know what to think.

The clock on the wall *tick-tick-tick*ed, four minutes to five. Their appointment was on the hour exactly; Julian's mom was running late, but it was okay. Less time to have to talk to her while trying not to sound weird.

Three minutes to. *Shit shit shit.*

"There's nothing to worry about," her mom said, crossing her legs in their jet-black jeans. At least some things never changed. "You know Dr. Miller's not scary, and I'm sure she's seen all this before."

Audrey nodded. "I guess."

"Julian?" Her mom leaned forward. "You doing okay?"

Julian's feet started tapping again as he pursed his lips and whistled.

"Nervous, too," he said shortly. "But other than that . . . yeah."

He slid his hand into Audrey's, and she rubbed her thumb in circles on his wrist. Two minutes to.

The doors to the waiting room opened and a harried brunette rushed in, a pinched look on her face. "Oh, my gosh, I'm so sorry—the meeting I was in ran so long."

Julian stood. "Hey, Mom." He was taller than her now, so when Audrey watched her grab him in a determined hug, her chin barely met his shoulder.

She released him and sank down into a chair opposite. "I thought I might be too late," she said, turning to Laura. "Are they running on time?"

Laura nodded. "Thanks for coming, Simone."

"Wouldn't have missed it for anything." Simone reached over to place her hand on Audrey's knee and smiled reassuringly, although it didn't quite reach her eyes. "Hey, Aud. How are you feeling?"

Do people not get sick of asking that question? Audrey pushed her irritation down and gave a shrug. "Okay, I guess." She wished they could go back in time to before all this, when Simone had no reason to distrust her and her smile was completely genuine. But there was no use thinking that, because they couldn't go back.

Simone gave Audrey's knee a squeeze before turning to Laura. "How's Adam?"

Audrey slipped her hand into Julian's and watched their moms together. Simone had these fine wrinkles around her eyes, and as Laura pulled a hand through her hair, a cluster of graying strands revealed themselves. Only recently had Audrey begun noticing her mom's age, in the laugh lines around her mouth and those gray hairs. She was still beautiful, maybe more beautiful because her face was beginning to tell a lifetime's worth of stories, but it was strange to realize she was no longer the young mom Audrey always thought of.

And, she thought, another realization hitting her, *if we keep the baby, she'll be a grandma. Weird.*

Tick. One minute to go, and a girl who looked about twenty came out of the office looking sallow. Audrey swallowed. Once this was over she could move on to the rest of her to-do list. Read birth mother's letter. Take photographs. Edit photographs. Fix things with Rose. Decide entire future. Write Spanish paper. The usual.

The office door opened again, and Dr. Miller stuck her head out, smiling wide. "Audrey Spencer?"

Audrey took a deep breath, and under her thumb Julian's pulse beat steadily, calming her. "Hi."

She got to her feet. *Ready, and . . . go.*

TWENTY-THREE

Audrey came back from her regularly scheduled throw up and slipped into her seat across from Olivia, who didn't bat an eye. She picked up her pen and stared blankly at her notebook. *Tuesdays suck. Being pregnant sucks. Everything in the entire world sucks.* "I'm so sick of being sick."

Olivia smiled slightly. "Have you tried the ginger ale–and–crackers thing?" she asked, her voice quiet even though no one around was paying them the slightest bit of attention. "My aunt swears by it."

Audrey shuddered. "That makes me feel even sicker." Like she needed any help with that. Her breath smelled acidic and sour all the time, and her knees were sore from always kneeling. "I'm so done with all this."

"Does that mean—" Olivia paused her sketching and raised her eyebrows. "Are you . . . ?"

It took Audrey a moment to realize what Olivia was asking, and then she slumped even farther over the table, letting her pen drop from her fingers. "Abortion? No. Or . . . I haven't figured anything out yet." Understatement of the century. But she did say, "I saw my doctor yesterday. Me and Julian went with both our moms."

"Whoa," Olivia said, and her eyebrows shot up so far that they disappeared under her bangs. "Intense. I didn't realize you'd told your parents. Are they okay with it? What did the doctor say?"

Audrey tapped her foot against the leg of her chair. Were her mom and Adam okay with it? Good question. She wanted to say yes, but . . . after what she'd overheard? And all they kept saying was that they'd support her and that they loved her and that they weren't mad, of course not.

And what had Dr. Miller said: A lot of medical words and some other stuff that Audrey had meant to remember but had gotten lost in the way the doctor had clasped Audrey's hand between hers on the way out, the way she'd said, "You're not on your own in this, okay?"

For the last week she'd been running those words over and over. *You're not on your own in this.* She wondered if anyone had ever said those words to the girl Mandy. If they had, would she have done things differently?

"Audrey?"

She snapped her gaze over to Olivia. "Sorry. God, my head is so all over the place. Sorry," she said again.

"It's all right," Olivia said. "When my—"

The shrill ringing of the bell interrupted her, and Ms. Fitz began speaking over it. "Everybody, remember! Individual meetings start at the end of the week! So if I were you, I'd take this week to make sure you have something concrete to show me then—whether it's a piece of work or a plan for what you're going to do, I don't care. Make sure you come with *something*!"

Audrey threw her crap into her bag and hitched the strap over her shoulder. Another thing to stress about. *Shit.*

Olivia was waiting expectantly, fiddling with the pom-pom on the end of her knitted scarf. "Coming to lunch?"

"Sure. I have to go to the bathroom first," Audrey said. "I'll tell you about the doctor later. And please—"

"Don't tell Rose," Olivia intoned. "I know, I won't. You don't have to worry about it."

"Thanks." She kicked a chair out of her way as they headed into the hall. "Not that she would even listen if you said anything. If it's not about her, she doesn't want to know."

"Oh."

Yeah, oh, Audrey thought. She wanted to say, *What's going on with you two, exactly?* But to ask felt like she'd be admitting how out of the loop she was, and also, wouldn't Olivia have mentioned something if anything were happening? They were friends—Olivia knew her secret. Wouldn't she trust Audrey the same way?

Forget it. She was making a big deal out of nothing, as per usual. Audrey shook her head and left Olivia at the top of the stairs. "I'll see you in a minute."

Audrey splashed her face with cold water in the bathroom and then made her way to the cafeteria, trying to shake off the unpleasant feeling that had settled over her in art class. Her stomach growled as she joined the end of the line and picked up a tray, banging it against her flat palm like a drum. The options were sadly limited today: limp pizza, pasta, and the dreaded fish tacos.

She bypassed the hot food and grabbed two cookies and an apple instead. Not exactly what Dr. Miller meant when she'd said Audrey needed more variety in her diet.

The line crept forward. Audrey scanned the lunchroom, looking for Julian's dark head. There—over by the windows with Cooper and the rest of his boys. He didn't see her, though—too busy laughing at something, his head thrown back and mouth wide open, showing glinting teeth. It was easier for him to fake it, somehow. He had this ability to shut off things when he needed to, compartmentalize. He could always do it—when Nate got sick, so sick he had to be in the hospital for a month, and they'd had midterms, he still managed to get straight As. Pregnancy pamphlets on one side of his brain, band practice on the other. She could lie, but when she was playing at being normal, it always felt hard.

Audrey lifted her tray high as she squeezed through a narrow gap. She was tired of lying. She needed to make a decision. She needed to talk to Rose.

It was an instinctual thought, her brain forgetting how pissed at each other they currently were. But as soon as it entered her mind, it hit her. Her heart stuttered, skipped, and then fell back into regular rhythm.

Holy shit.

Of course she needed to talk to Rose. Not just to stop lying, to have it all out in the open, but more than that. To know what to do. *Of course* she hadn't been able to make sense of any of this without her. Keeping it secret, keeping her anger so close and letting it tell her that Rose didn't deserve to know—that wasn't helping. She needed Rose to be a part of this, and how could she if she didn't know?

Audrey found them in the room, her best friend's head bent low next to Olivia's, and oh, how she ached.

Audrey needed to sit down with the girl who knew her better than anyone else and lay it all out there, not only the part about how torn she was, how she could almost see two futures unfolding in front of her completely depending on which way she chose, but also all the tiny anxieties cluttering up her brain. The part of her—the whole of her, really—that kept coming back to the same thing: Would they still love her? Julian, her mom, Adam, Rose. Herself. Whatever it was that she decided to do, would they think differently of her—would they love her less?

Audrey forced herself back into motion, swallowing the lump in her throat. All of a sudden she felt on edge, all her emotions rising dangerously close to her surface. She would get through this lunch, this moment, and at the end of it she'd tell Rose, and together they'd figure out what to do. Together they'd be okay.

She finally reached their table and put down her tray in the space next to María. "Hi," she managed.

María scooted over as Audrey sat down. "I hate cafeteria food," she said, looking sadly at her own pizza. "That cheese looks like someone already ate it and threw it back up again."

This brought laughs from Jen and Olivia sitting across from them. Even Rose, staring down at her lunch, cracked the slightest smile, a sign that ignited a cautious optimism in Audrey. *Maybe she's in a good mood today*, she thought, like that day at the coffee shop when she'd gotten so close. *I hope so. She'll talk to me, and once I tell her, she'll understand, and she'll help me, and we'll be fine. I know it.*

Audrey let out a tentative laugh. "Gross, Ree." And feeling brave then, bolstered by the laughter, she turned. "Hey, Rose—"

At the mention of her name Rose dropped her fork and stood up. "I just remembered," she said flatly. "I totally forgot to do my assignment for last period. I better go do it now."

Audrey snapped one of her cookies in two. "What?"

"See you later," Rose said, but not to Audrey, to Olivia, who she bent down to and kissed on the cheek.

Wait, *what*? Audrey felt her eyes go wide, like she was trying to take in that moment as much as possible.

Did that really happen?

So her suspicions had been *right*. Or it appeared that way, at least. How long had it been going on? Were they a Thing now? Audrey looked at Jen and María, registering their complete lack of surprise. So, no one thought this was important for her to know? Some friends.

"Rose!" Audrey called out, standing up. "Hey!"

But Rose kept walking until she was out of the cafeteria. Audrey sat with a thump, all that roiling emotion giving way to only anger now. "What the fuck?"

María shrugged. "Someone's got her bitch panties on today."

God, she was *sick* of this. Rose would rather avoid her than do the unthinkable and actually *ask* Audrey what was going on. *Had it ever even crossed her mind?* Audrey wondered. *To talk to me? That maybe this time I'm the one who needs keeping sane?* Audrey met Olivia's eyes across the table. *Well, apparently I'm not the only one keeping secrets.*

So fine. Let Rose be a bitch if she wanted to. And let Olivia look at her with an apology in her eyes. Olivia was sweet and Audrey liked her a lot, but that didn't mean she was going to let Rose get away with this.

She took a swig of María's water without asking, slamming the bottle back down on the table. Then she looked directly at Olivia and narrowed her eyes. "Rose always has her bitch panties on," she snapped. "Nothing new there."

TWENTY-FOUR

/'m so tired of this shit." Audrey banged her hands on the steering
wheel with every word: *so*—smack—*tired*—smack—*of*—smack—
this—smack—*shit*. "I don't know what her deal is! I know things
have been weird between us lately, but it's only because I've been
trying to figure out this whole *pregnancy* thing. Like, sorry this
fucking, possibly life-changing event is going on and it means I've
been a shitty friend lately. My bad!"

Julian put his hand on her knee. "In her defense—"

"In her defense? Excuse me?" Audrey wrenched the wheel to the
right and then slammed on the brakes, joining the end of the line of
cars waiting to get out of the parking lot. A few cars ahead a certain
shiny silver convertible idled, and Audrey knew, she *knew*, that Rose
was in there with María or Jen or Olivia, one of them, complaining
about her the same as she was doing to Julian right now. "She has no
defense! She's being *awful*."

"Okay," Julian said. "Jesus. I was only going to remind you that she doesn't *know* what's going on. Remember?" He hit the heat button, and dusty air came blasting out at them. "Rose probably thinks you're mad at her."

"I *am* mad at her."

"Why?"

Audrey opened and then closed her mouth, searching for the words. Why was she mad? Let's see: Because she needed Rose right now and she wasn't there for her, was never there for her. Because everything felt weird without her and things were already weird enough. Because Audrey had never felt so utterly *abandoned*. And maybe that was a dramatic way to look at it, but she was feeling dramatic today. So abandoned—yes, that was how she felt.

She pulled up the hand brake and turned to look at Julian, his face half in shadow from the sun hanging low in the clear-blue sky. "Fine. I know I've been a shitty friend lately. I know Rose has a right to be mad, but—it's not like I haven't tried. I keep trying to talk to her, but every time, she flakes out on me or makes some excuse or flat-out ignores me. So what am I supposed to do? I . . ." She grasped for words again, resorting to widening her eyes at Julian. Pathetic, but effective, always. "You know what I mean. You *know* she hasn't been herself lately."

Julian rubbed his hand over his jaw, over the slight stubble he got when he skipped shaving too many mornings in a row. "I guess she has been acting kind of different lately," he allowed. "She's been ignoring my texts, too, and then that whole thing with her and Cooper—"

From somewhere behind them came the obnoxious blare of a horn; the traffic had started moving without Audrey noticing, and a three-car gap had opened up in front. She whirled into motion, rerunning Julian's words in her head because, clearly, she'd misheard. "That whole thing with her and who?"

"Cooper," Julian repeated. "You know. On Halloween?"

"What thing?" Audrey flipped the bird at some asshole in a Camaro who cut her off. "Start making sense, please."

She felt Julian looking at her, saw out of the corner of her eye the way he frowned slightly. "Okay," he said slowly, like she needed it spelled out in order to understand. "The thing with Rose and Cooper where they slept together."

Audrey laughed. *No. No effing way.* "You're so full of it, J. Rose would never—with Cooper? Come on."

Except the way Julian was looking at her now didn't seem like he was messing around. "Please don't tell me you're only finding out about this now," he said. "You're messing with me, right?"

Audrey shook her head. "No way. Where did you hear this? Missy Trevino? You know she cannot be trusted."

"I heard it from Cooper." Julian raised his hands. "I swear to God, it's true. It was at his party, and Rose initiated, and he told me about the birthmark she has on her—"

"Okay!" Audrey threw her hand up, using the other to flick her turn signal on. She did not need to hear any more. "I believe you."

"Rose seriously didn't tell you?"

Audrey looked straight ahead. Rose's car turned left out of the parking lot, which happened to be the opposite direction from her home. "No. She didn't."

This was worse than not knowing about what was going on between Olivia and Rose. This was a real dirty little secret.

"I cannot believe her! That little—" She pulled out of the parking lot and swung the car in a wide arc, almost clipping the side mirror on some asshole's oversize matte-black truck. "This, this is *exactly* what I'm talking about. She has sex with Cooper and doesn't tell me? What else is she hiding?"

Julian twitched. "Watch out for the—"

"And you! What, you didn't think to bring this up at any point?"

"Wait, how am I the one in trouble here?" Julian said. "It's not my fault that she didn't tell you. And I didn't mention it because, oh, yeah, my girlfriend is pregnant and we're being the most indecisive assholes ever and it's kind of stressing me the fuck out. Ring a bell?"

"Don't put this on me," Audrey snapped. "You were perfectly capable of telling Cooper our secrets. What, is he more important than me? You can tell people all my business but he gets special treatment? Thanks."

"I thought you already knew! Wow, this is bullshit."

"Yeah, you're right, it is bullshit." Audrey took the next turn, toward downtown so she could drop Julian off at the restaurant for his dinner shift. "Why are you being such an asshole right now?"

"*Me?*" Julian spluttered. "I didn't even do anything!"

"That's my point! God!" She slammed on the brakes at a red light and gave an aggrieved sigh. "We tell each other everything," she said, and she wasn't sure if the *we* was her and Julian or her and Rose. Either way, she felt the heat of resentment puddling in her veins. "Always."

"Always?" Julian said, and Audrey could hear the judgment in his tone. She knew exactly what he meant. But not telling Rose that she was pregnant was not even anywhere near the same league as this.

So she nodded fiercely and kept her eyes on the road when she answered, "Always."

TWENTY-FIVE

The sour taste of bile rolled around Audrey's mouth as she shoved her books into her locker. *Disgusting*. The same thing she'd said when the contents of her stomach had splattered the inside of the toilet bowl earlier that morning.

She'd wanted to spend the day lying in bed, staring at the ceiling and musing on the joke of the cosmos that her life now was. But her mom had barged into her room and refused to listen to Audrey's indignant protests—"You are not sick," Laura had said. "And you need to go to school. So get your ass in gear, *now*."

Audrey felt an elbow in her back and stumbled forward, catching her hand on the sharp metal grate of her locker door. "Hey!" She whipped around, scanning the hall for the culprit. Was it the football team jerk giving embarrassing handshakes to his bros, or the girl in the skirt so short Audrey could see the crotch of her tights? "Watch it!"

she yelled, and the girl gave Audrey a nervous look before skittering down the hall.

Audrey turned back to her locker as she heard her name being called. Without meaning to, she looked toward the sound, and there was Rose, smiling and waving like nothing was wrong.

Is she fucking serious?

Audrey narrowed her eyes and looked into the depths of her locker, at the books and snapped-in-half paintbrushes and torn notebook pages layered like sediment. "Go away," she whispered into the pile of crap. "Go away, go away, go away." Maybe if she said it enough, it would come true.

Wrong.

"Hey." Rose broke through the cluster of kids standing next to the lockers, and there was that smile again. "What's up?"

Audrey turned her head *ever* so slowly until her eyes came to a rest on Rose, and then she pulled out this exaggerated gasp and threw her hands in front of her mouth. "Oh my God!" she said loudly. "Is it really you?"

"What?

"Wow, I can't believe it! You're . . . *talking* . . . to *me*?" Audrey shook her head, blinking rapidly. "I *must* be dreaming!"

Rose looked confused for a moment, but then her face cleared and she started to laugh. "Okay, okay, I deserved that. I've been crappy lately, I know."

This could *not* be happening. Rose *could not* be for real right now.

"And I'm sorry," Rose was saying. "And I wanted to ask you if you wanted to do something after school. The two of us. We can do coffee, or grab food at—"

"No." Audrey spat out the word like the bile still lingering acidic on her tongue. How *dare* she stroll over and ask to hang out, like nothing at all was wrong? Like she hadn't been pulling away right when Audrey really needed her, like she hadn't kept her little secret and not mentioned a single thing about sleeping with Cooper? Which, sorry, was a big fucking deal, because Rose had pledged that she would never have sex with him for fear of—that old classic—ruining their friendship. Well, she and Cooper seemed pretty fine and dandy. It was a shame the same couldn't be said about her and Audrey.

Rose took a step back, her forehead furrowing. "No?"

Audrey felt her face set in stone, grim and determined. "You heard me."

"But I—" Rose cut herself off, and Audrey heard it—the second Rose realized that Audrey wasn't playing around.

Good.

Audrey slammed her locker shut, the metal clanging loudly. "Were you ever going to tell me that you had sex with Cooper?"

Rose took three halting steps backward, her mouth dropping open. "I don't— Who told you that?"

Audrey smothered the triumphant smile she could feel coming— not that she was pleased to find out it was true, more that she had finally managed to throw something with enough spike at Rose that it hurt. Audrey already knew it was true; Cooper might be a skeeze, but he didn't lie about things like that. He didn't have any need to.

"Is that what you're mad about?"

"You think that's why I'm mad?" Audrey twisted to face Rose, holding her math textbook in front of her body like a shield. "Because you slept with Cooper?"

The second bell rang shrilly and the hall began to empty out, but Audrey held her ground. No way was she going to let Rose off the hook that easily, not now that they'd started this fight that Audrey knew had been waiting, waiting for the right moment to erupt.

Rose flinched and said, "It kind of seems like you are."

"Well, you're right," Audrey said, and the strain of keeping her voice even actually made her shake, turned her knuckles white. "I'm mad because you hooked up with Cooper, and it wasn't important enough for you to tell me. I'm *mad* because this whole fight is so like you, to make everything about yourself, to shut down and shut everyone out because you know *you* were out of line." The urge to reach out and . . . *do* something—push her, yank on her hair like they were kindergarten brawlers—almost overcame her. Her body moved as if with a life of its own, but before her fingers uncurled from her textbook she realized what a ridiculous thing she was about to do and shook herself.

Audrey tossed her hair back and spoke through gritted teeth. "I have no idea why you've been so monumentally shitty lately, but I'm done, all right? I'm so over all of it."

"Don't you think you're overreacting?" Rose said, and the lightness of her voice, the way she glanced at her nails like this whole thing was boring her—how *infuriating*.

"You're my best friend! We don't keep secrets." Like this was even about that anyway—Audrey couldn't give a shit about the dirty fact of Rose and Cooper's tryst. It was nothing, really, exactly like Rose was saying: a (maybe stupid) hookup between friends that, if things were normal, would have been revealed by Rose over morning-after breakfast for the teasing and amusement of Audrey. But she hadn't told, and now it had become so much more than that. A nail in the heart of Audrey's suspicions, that Rose was so far away, and this distance she'd been feeling was *not* all in her head.

"Oh, yeah? We don't keep secrets. Right." Rose's hand stretched out and pulled on Audrey's sleeve, the kind of gentle gesture of days past.

But looking at Rose's face, Audrey could tell this was about to be anything but gentle.

"So." Rose's tongue flicked across her lips, and for a split second Audrey imagined that the snakelike move was more, that Rose carried poison in the depths of her, until Rose's mouth moved again and suddenly she was saying, "Were *you* ever going to tell me you're pregnant?"

The word slipped from between her lips. Audrey felt the way it slithered across the inches between them, wrapped itself around her leg and bored inside her bones. "I . . ."

Yes, that was a secret.

A secret she was keeping from Rose.

That, Audrey couldn't deny. Didn't have the nerve to try to—Rose deserved better than *that*; the girl wasn't that oblivious.

But that's not the same, Audrey thought, even as she felt her mouth opening in shock. *This is my life, not some high school bullshit game.*

How can she even think this is in the same realm?

"How could you?" Audrey hadn't planned on that being what came out of her mouth, but there it was, and now that she'd said it, she realized how angry she was. Because if Rose knew, then that meant that every time she'd been cold and cruel lately, every harsh thing she'd said, everything she'd done, had been done knowing the truth. And still she'd made it all about herself? How could Rose *possibly* think that she being pregnant was anything *like* Rose's bullshit? "God, how could you just throw that in my face? That's different."

"Of course it's different," Rose said, her voice suddenly charged with fury. "Because it's *you*. Oh, how could I be mad that you didn't even tell me that you're having a *baby*? How *dare* I be upset that there's about to be a whole other thing—a whole other *person*—for you to leave me behind for? Right. I'm so *goddamn* sick and tired of you treating me like I'm the one who does everything wrong. You don't even know what's going on with me right now."

Audrey jabbed a finger in Rose's direction. "You mean what's going on with you and Olivia? Oh, I know all about that, no thanks to you."

"No, you don't. Not at all." Rose shook her head so violently that her hair shifted and swung in front of her face, almost completely obscuring her from view. "I like her, Audrey," she said. "I *like* her. She's good, she's smart, she doesn't make me feel like complete shit when I mess up—see, you would know all that; I would have told you all that if you had ever been around for me to do it!"

"Me?" Audrey said, incensed. "Get real, Rose. You're the one who's been MIA." *Oh—so sorry I wasn't there for you to whine about whatever dumb shit you did to make Olivia pissed at you. I was too busy being PREGNANT.* "And what, you like her *so* much that you had sex with Cooper? Right." She laughed, knowing how low she was aiming and ignoring the shame of it. "With *Cooper*, Rose? Come *on!*"

Audrey saw Rose's hands twitch, and how she kept glancing at the people hurrying past them to homeroom, the ones who were watching them with undisguised curiosity. *Let them look*, Audrey thought, suddenly exhausted. *I don't care.*

"What happened with Cooper had nothing to do with Olivia," Rose said, her nostrils flaring. "And yeah, it was a mistake, but I'm not ashamed of it. I *own* my shit."

"Don't you even—"

"And I wasn't even talking about Olivia to start with! See?" Rose crowed. "See how little you know about anything that's happening in my life right now? Why don't you ask me something? Ask me how my sister is. Ask me when she's coming home. No, no—ask me how long it's been since I actually saw my parents for longer than five minutes, since I've had to spend all night alone, waiting for—" She stopped abruptly before breaking into jagged, bitter laughter. "Yeah. Why don't you ask me about *any* of that?"

Audrey shook her head. She didn't need to ask about that; she knew it all already. And it made her sad and pissed off that Rose's family was so beyond belief fucked up that Rose didn't know any other way to be. Of course she never wanted to talk, of course she was fighting like this—it was the only way she knew how, and Audrey more than understood that. But that didn't make it right. That didn't make it okay. How long had Audrey been there for Rose, the one person she could and did talk to, and how many times had Rose ignored that, thrown it back in her face? How many more times was she going to do it? Audrey had had enough.

I will not let her make me feel guilty about this. She doesn't get to do that.

"I'm sorry," she started again, looking around the almost-empty hall now. "I'm sorry I wasn't always there when you wanted me to be, but I don't exist solely to serve you, Rose. Finding out I'm pregnant, it was weird and I don't know what to do so it's . . . shit. I'm sorry, but I have my own things going on, all right?"

Rose took a step back and turned her palms to the sky. "You're my *best friend*, God! Being there for each other when the shit going on in our lives is too much is what we're supposed to do. You have to let me help you, too."

Audrey's temper caught light again. "You can't," she said. "You don't know how."

"Fuck you," Rose bit out.

"Hey!"

They both jumped at the yell, turning to the source of the sound. Audrey swore under her breath as the most misogynistic teacher in school—Allen, Andrews, something like that—strode toward them in a tweed blazer and a tie that almost choked his thick gym teacher neck. "Did you ladies hear the bell? Or do you think we have that for fun?"

Audrey stared at Rose, both of them staying silent. Psychic understanding.

"Well?" Andrews or whatever his name was cocked his head expectantly. "Homeroom, now. Move it!"

"We're going," Rose said, and she grabbed Audrey's arm in a vise grip. "Come on."

Audrey allowed Rose to steer her down the corridor in the opposite direction of the teacher, until they were out of his sight. Then she wrenched her arm out of Rose's grip.

Rose made a noise of disgust. "This is such bullshit."

"At last," Audrey said faux sweetly. "Something we agree on."

Rose stopped right outside her homeroom door and flicked her hand in Audrey's direction. "Leave me alone, Audrey."

"Gladly," Audrey said, and then because she couldn't bear to let Rose have the last word, added on, "Tell your *girlfriend* I said hello."

She stomped off before Rose could do or say anything else, and her shoes made these pathetic shushing sounds as she walked through the corridors. She wished for the kind of boots Olivia sometimes wore: thick soled and steel tipped, the kind that let everybody know you were coming and exactly how much shit you could kick out of them.

But then she remembered that she was pissed off at Olivia, too, and as she slouched into her classroom to her teacher's annoyed look, she pinched her thigh through her jeans.

Fuck them, she thought, sliding onto her seat. *I don't need Rose. I don't need any of them. I am doing perfectly fine all on my own.*

TWENTY-SIX

Julian cut the engine and gave Audrey that look she was coming to hate lately, his logical, rational, listen-to-me face. "She'll get over it," he said. "You'll get over it. You always do."

Audrey looked out the window at the crowded parking lot. *I should have skipped today*, she thought. "I don't want to get over it," she said to Julian. "You didn't hear the things she said to me." Things that Audrey had replayed in her head all through yesterday, at dinner when her mom was trying to talk to her about Decisions, when she should have been sleeping late last night. They'd fought before, but not like this.

Never like this.

"Yeah, and I'm sure you only said nice things to her, right?" Julian flipped his keys in the air, a knowing smile playing on his lips. "Trust me, you'll be fine."

She buried her hands in her hair and exhaled slowly. "I can't deal."

"Hey." Julian's smile slipped into the slightest frown. "You all right?"

Audrey groaned, the noise filling the tight space of Julian's car. "I wish people would stop asking me that! I'm *fine*."

When she opened her eyes, he was looking at her very seriously, rubbing his thumb over his bottom lip. "This is terrible timing," he said. "But I—when are we going to talk? About . . . everything?"

Audrey looked at him. "You're right," she said, harsh. "That is terrible fucking timing."

"Sorry," he said. "But we have to do something," he said. "*Something.* We can't just wait around forever. Honestly, it's keeping me up at night."

He looked worried, his eyes cloudy, and then Audrey noticed the circles beneath those eyes. Her stomach twisted, and she suddenly felt horrible—more horrible. But she also didn't want to talk about it. She just wanted comfort—to be close to him again.

Audrey leaned into him, brushing her fingers across the back of his neck, that spot that made him sigh. "I know," she said. "We're going to decide. But I really want a day when we don't talk about this. Remember when we used to not talk about this at all?" She pressed her lips to his ear and felt the way his breathing quickened. "Remember when I used to be the thing keeping you up at night?"

Julian let out a quiet laugh. "Like I would forget."

Audrey kissed right below his ear, and his shiver was undeniable. He was easy to distract, sometimes. "I miss you," she said softly. "I miss hanging out, like we used to. The two of us in my room, talking about nothing. Remember that?"

In the beginning, when they'd lie on her bed swapping stories about their first crushes, playing stupid games like If I Won a Million Dollars and What I'd Do in a Zombie Apocalypse. And all the while playing a different, silent game, a game of touching. Audrey would slide her hand under Julian's shirt; he'd hook a thumb into the waist of her jeans. She'd twine her leg around his and press the ball of her foot against his calf; he'd play with her bra strap, sliding it off her shoulder. It was testing each other's boundaries, seeing who would break first.

Audrey pulled back, winding her fingers into his hair. Back then she was always the first to break, rolling on top of him and kissing him like she couldn't breathe otherwise. "Come over later," she said, quiet. "Adam's out of town. My mom's schedule's crazy with rehearsals." They hadn't slept together since finding out, but she wanted to change that. She missed the heat of him in her bed, the careful way he touched her, made her feel good.

And this time he broke. "Okay," Julian said. "You sure?"

Audrey leaned back in and pressed her mouth to his, soothed by the familiarity of the kiss, the taste and feel of him. Everything lately had been so drama filled, so much heavy talking and thinking things through and careful looks from her parents when they thought she wasn't paying attention. She wanted to forget for a little while, pretend everything was like it had been not that many weeks ago, when she only worried about her photographs and how close she was to buying a new lens, or what dress to wear on Saturday. So yeah, she thought as she gripped Julian's shoulders, she was sure.

TWENTY-SEVEN

Audrey spent every lunch period the rest of that week and the next hiding out in the art room. When she'd asked Ms. Fitzgerald if she could spend the time up there, the teacher had looked pleased.

"Of course," she'd said. "You can come in here whenever you want, whether I'm here or not. Okay?"

"Okay."

Last week she'd had her one-on-one, and although it hadn't been the shitshow Audrey had feared, it hadn't been stellar, either. They'd sat at a desk in the back of the room, the rest of the class working around them, and Ms. Fitz had looked at Audrey over steepled hands. "I'm going to cut to the chase," she'd said. "You seem off. And your standards are slipping. I know how much work you put in usually, but I'm just not seeing the results you should be achieving. As of right now, I'm not *hugely* concerned—we all have slow periods—but let this be a warning. Your work this year really matters in terms of building your portfolio. You've come a long way from where you were two years ago. I really want you to be able to keep moving up, not leveling out at a disappointing place."

"I know," Audrey had said, twisting her fingers into the hem of her sweater under the table. "I'm sorry."

"Don't apologize," Ms. Fitz said. "Make it better. I remember you talked about RISD before. That's a very good school. I think it's good that you want to try—it might be a reach, but you'll never know if you don't apply. Where else have you thought about?"

Audrey pulled in a deep breath. "Illinois Institute of Art," she said. "Maryland, Massachusetts, Parsons, Syracuse . . ."

Ms. Fitz nodded, and from the measured look on her face Audrey couldn't tell whether she was thinking *This kid's out of her mind* or *This kid's going to go far*. What the teacher actually said was "A good mix. Okay. What I want to see from you is a marked improvement in your class participation. And you haven't finalized a project yet. The clock is ticking."

Don't I know it, Audrey thought. "Okay," she said, faking as much confidence as she could. "I can do that."

So now it was Thursday night and Audrey was shut in her room, trying to figure out where it was all going wrong. Laid out on her bed were the last few months' worth of prints: black-and-white scenes from downtown, the vivid lights from Hera's show, clipped pieces of her friends.

Audrey crossed her pajama-clad legs and began sifting through the images, unsure what she was actually looking for. A theme, like Ms. Fitz always said. *The only theme my photos have is that they're all taken by me,* Audrey thought. She wished it all came naturally to her, that she didn't have to spend so much energy and time reaching for what seemed so easy to everybody else. Like, her mom could reel off a monologue in the kitchen, and it'd feel like being alone in a dark theater, spotlight on her, nothing else mattering. And Julian could take half a lyric and a wisp of a melody from Izzy, and he'd turn it into an entire song by the end of fourth period. Sometimes it felt like because it didn't come naturally to her, because she'd *chosen* art and slogged at it every day, it wasn't real. She wasn't an artist, only a fake. And usually when she thought that, she could shake herself out of it, remind herself that it wasn't true.

But lately all she could think was maybe she wasn't now or ever going to be an artist. What more sign did she need, really, than this baby inside her? A warning: *Don't get cocky. You think you deserve art school? Think again.*

Audrey sighed and shuffled the glossy images aside, opening her laptop instead. She slotted in an SD card and watched the images load up. *All I need is some inspiration.*

Right.

"Audrey!" Adam's yell came muffled through her door. "Dinner's here!"

Audrey rapped her knuckles on her computer. "Okay," she called back, forcing some cheer into her voice. "I'll be down soon!"

She waited for his feet on the stairs to fade before exhaling and beginning to click through the loaded photos. These were all old—technical practice shots in the studio at school freshman year, the cast of one of her mom's shows in rehearsal, her friends being silly.

Audrey smiled at a shot of Jen standing in the middle of some empty street. If she didn't already know it was old, Jen's chin-length hair and bangs would have made it obvious. Her eyes were closed and her smile blurred, like Audrey had caught her off guard. It must have been right after Jen's parents' messy divorce, because both the cross and the crescent moon necklaces hung around her neck—Audrey remembered taking Jen shopping the day her dad had moved out, how her face had lit up seeing the moon in a cheap jewelry store and how María had lent her the ten bucks it cost to buy it. When Jen looked that happy, it was contagious.

She clicked out of those and into a more recent folder, scrolling until she noticed a picture she didn't even remember taking, of the girls sitting on the wall out in the parking lot. María had her tongue sticking out and her eyes crossed, one arm around Rose's shoulders. Rose was almost completely obscured by Jen sitting on her lap; only the right side of her face and her jean-clad legs were visible. And then there was Olivia, their latest addition, pulling a funny face to match María and her nose ring flashing in the sunlight. What had Olivia said before? *You don't take pictures to remember what people look like? Ha,* Audrey thought. *Wrong. How would I remember these moments, these girls in this time, otherwise?*

Her hand stilled, the cursor hovering over the image. They all looked so carefree and . . . happy.

Audrey wrapped her left hand around her right wrist, her fingers curling over the veins that ran so vividly blue near the surface there. God, she wanted to look like that again, not to have the worry lines and anxious smile permanently fixed to her face. She ached to be happy and stupid again, losing sleep over practice SATs and parties she wasn't invited to instead of whether or not she'd be good at mixing formula and if an abortion would hurt more or less than the time she got her appendix out.

It was weird how much she could picture her life changing. Almost as if she were already looking back on this moment, these very moments, even as they were still happening.

Picture it: a toothless smile, soft feet kicking gleefully, a cry that could be calmed only by her. Mountains of diapers, long nights of unsettled screaming, and an unrelenting sense of exhaustion, too, of course. But those things didn't bother Audrey as much as the fact that she couldn't see further than a couple of years into the future—because any baby that she had would only be a baby for so long, as was the order of life, and yet she couldn't imagine it any older than a couple of years. She couldn't imagine what her life might be like when she and Julian would be the parents of a ten-, thirteen-, eighteen-year-old.

Parents.

It hit her so suddenly. They wouldn't just have a baby; they'd be somebody's parents. She'd be a *mom.*

The realization sent goose bumps pinpricking down her arms, and her tongue stuck to the roof of her dry mouth. *God, I'm so stupid,* she thought. *Is this really the first time I'm realizing this?*

But it was.

It would change *everything*: her relationship with Julian, with her parents, with her friends. Rose. Maybe she was right, what she'd said when they were screaming at each other, that a baby would take her away. Where would Rose go when she was lonely? There'd be no more sleepovers, no more days spent laughing at nothing, no running away to do silly things together. Who would be her refuge?

Audrey winced. Not that they were talking now anyway. Perhaps the beginning of the end had already arrived.

And then—adoption. The thought of spending the next seven months with this thing inside her and always worrying, still, and maybe it would be a good thing to do, sure. But why did she have to be good? Who decided exactly what Good was?

She hiccupped, a lone breath of remorse loud in the quiet of her room, her only company the paintings on the walls.

Maybe I don't want to be pregnant at all, she thought. But what did she want? To have fun again; to put more energy into creating art than possibly creating life; to get a full night's sleep with her brain on quiet. And what was so bad about that?

Audrey moved her hand down, skimming her chin before coming to rest on her throat. She searched out her pulse: there it was, beating slowly under her fingers, even and calm. She exhaled equally slow. How her body could be so rhythmic and regular when her brain was scrambled to the point of madness was beyond her. *I don't know what we're doing anymore*, she realized. *Have a baby, not have a baby . . . it's not like things can ever go back to the way they were before, either way.*

Not the way I wish they could.

She looked at that picture on the screen again, the joy emanating from it, the carefree feeling that was so unbelievably close, really. Five, maybe six weeks ago: had she suspected then? *No*, Audrey thought. *Wait—I must have. Did I?* She looked too happy to have been worrying about anything.

She kept looking, her chest constricting, and then a thunder of steps knocked her out of that zone. Another yell, this time from her mom: "Audrey! Dinner! Come on!"

She slammed her laptop shut and tried to ignore the tightness snaking its way into her ribs and squeezing around her spine. "Okay, I'm *coming.*"

Audrey was an expert at ignoring things now. At least *that* she could be sure of.

TWENTY-EIGHT

On her way into school the next morning Audrey was ambushed. María and Jen appeared on either side of her, linking their arms with hers as they crossed the parking lot. "Hi," María said, before Audrey even had a chance to protest. "So, I'm just going to cut to the point: *what* is going on with you and Rose? Enquiring minds want to know."

"Enquiring minds miss you at lunch," Jen said. "I hate it when we're not all together."

María steered them away from the school building. "I asked Rose, but she won't say anything."

"Whatever it is, can't you two make up?" Jen said.

Audrey pulled her arms from theirs and shook her head. "If she's not saying anything, then I'm not. And no, we can't *make up*. Sorry I'm not playing nice the way you want," she bit out. "But whatever. You wouldn't even understand if I told you, so what's the point?"

Jen and María looked at her, a mix of confusion and hurt playing on both their faces, and Audrey held up her hands, backing off before she could do any more damage. "I'm sorry," she called back. "See you later."

Now she was standing at one of the sinks in the art room, the water running a murky blend of greens and blues as Audrey scrubbed the paint from her hands. The skin under her nails bled shocking violet.

She liked the mess of painting. Sometimes photography could be too sterile, clean, especially since everything was digital. There was a pleasure in the smell of the colors, how they smeared onto the canvas and onto her clothes, through her hair if she wasn't careful enough. Mostly she kept her painting sessions at home, where no one could judge her lack of technique.

But walking into art class today, her fingers had itched to do something different, and before she knew it she was sitting in front of an easel with a brush in her hand and a moody mix of paints before her.

Audrey watched the water swirling down the drain until it ran clear and then dried her hands on scratchy paper towels. She stood there until a throat-clearing noise interrupted her introspection. "Sorry," she said, turning to see Karima Yang waiting.

"It's all right," Karima said, and she moved forward to tip her mug of water into the sink. "Thanks."

Audrey walked back to her painting, only to see Olivia standing in front of it. She darted back to her seat when she saw Audrey coming, and Audrey gave a halfhearted roll of her eyes. "You can look," she said. "If you want."

"Hmm?" Olivia looked up. "Oh. Okay." She stood and slowly crossed to where Audrey's canvas was propped up. "I like it. Did you work off one of your photos?"

Audrey folded her arms and positioned herself next to Olivia. The canvas held a basic outline of the scene she was trying to create, bold strokes of blue forming Izzy's fire-filled eyes. "Yeah," she said. "I wanted to do something different for a change."

She glanced at Olivia, who was staring fixedly at the painting. "You know, I'm pissed at Rose, but that doesn't mean you can't talk to me."

Olivia cracked a small smile. "You think I'm not talking to you because of her?" She looked properly at Audrey now. "I thought you were pissed at *me*, too."

"Why would I be mad at you?" Audrey asked the question even though she could guess at the answer; probably it had been too much to hope that she could've pinned this on Cooper. He made such a good scapegoat, though.

"You know why," Olivia said, and she looked so guilty that Audrey almost laughed. "If it wasn't for me, Rose wouldn't—" She lowered her voice. "I didn't tell her. Okay? I said I would keep your secret and I did. I tried anyway, but—God, this is going to sound so stupid—Rose guessed it. I swear to *God*. And then I told her that it wasn't any of our business, that if you wanted her to know you would tell her, and she promised me she wasn't going to say anything." Olivia did a nervous sweep of the room with her eyes, as if anybody else would even be remotely interested in their conversation. "I didn't think she was going to throw it at you like that."

"It's Rose," Audrey said flatly. "You think you know her, and then she does something like this. Trust me, you'll get used to it."

"I'm really sorry," Olivia said now. "*Really* sorry. This is—"

A clatter of plastic bangles signaled Ms. Fitz's approach and Olivia shut up fast. "Audrey," the teacher said, her eyes serious behind red plastic-framed glasses today. "Can I have a word?"

Olivia dropped back, giving Audrey a grim smile, and Ms. Fitz slipped right into the space left behind. Those bracelets clinked again as she pushed her glasses on top of her head. "This is . . . different," she said, tilting her head toward Audrey's painting, and Audrey knew she wasn't saying it in a happy way. "You remember what we talked about?"

"Yeah," Audrey said. "I mean, yes. I remember."

"Good." Ms. Fitz said, one eyebrow arching. "So I'm assuming you've worked up a project now, yes?"

"I—yes," Audrey lied. "Um, I've been working on a new series. I'm trying a mixed-media thing, and—well, I have some pieces at home. But I'll bring them in." *What? Where the hell did that come from?*

Great. Now when she didn't have anything to show, the shit was going to hit the fan worse than it would have if she'd kept her mouth shut. *Nice going, Audrey.*

Ms. Fitz gave a muted smile, as if she knew Audrey was lying but wasn't going to call her on it. "Great," the teacher said. "I'm excited to see it. Keep your focus, Audrey. Don't let yourself down."

Audrey opened her mouth to reply, but sudden heat flushed her face and this ball of frustration rose up in her throat, blocking any words she might have been able to force out. Instead she nodded tightly and stretched her lips into the fakest smile.

Ms. Fitz looked satisfied. "Good." With that she swept on to the next victim, Rami Clark bent over his block of clay.

Audrey looked down at her hands, her palms still pink from the hot water, and then to her utter mortification, tears pricked her eyes. She swore quietly and looked around, dragging her sweater sleeve over her face.

That this was the thing that finally broke her was both surprising and not. Art was the one thing she needed, the thing that she'd chosen. It was hers, for better or worse. When things were strange, when she felt bad, she found peace, beauty, fascination in a photo. She threw colors on canvas until she could breathe again, twisted the tangled threads of her heart into wires that spiraled in the wind. Until this time. The fighting with Rose, the pregnancy, everything—that felt surreal, another world, another time. But her art was real, and it was hers. If she didn't have that, then what did she have? From the first time she'd picked up the camera, Audrey had imagined going after art with everything she had, her whole heart. Now it was slipping away, and it was almost too much to bear.

The music playing out of the stereo covered Audrey's steps as she crossed the classroom and ducked into the supply closet, breathing in the sharp smell of white spirits and oils. The door closed with a soft click behind her, and in the blanketing quiet, shut away, it all burst forth.

For a brief, burning minute she sobbed, allowed herself to weep real chest-racking, mucus-leaking, salty tears for everything that was pressing at the shaky seams of her brain: the baby, and the birth mother, and the mom watching her carefully. The best friend and the fighting and the sharp press of guilt each time Rose's name came up. The future she had and might not have and the future she might be taking from her boyfriend. And the girl in California seventeen years ago, the life she might have had if it hadn't been for Audrey, forcing her way into the world without a care for anybody else.

As suddenly as she'd started, she forced herself to stop. One, two, three shuddering breaths in the dim light; one, two hands curling into tight fists.

"Okay," she whispered fiercely, swiping at her sodden cheeks. "Get it together."

Noise flooded the closet as the door opened, and Audrey moved quickly, turning into the shelves as footsteps sounded behind her. She cleared her throat loudly and pushed her hair behind her ear with one hand, stretching the other toward the bottles of white spirits on the topmost shelf.

The hand on her shoulder surprised a choked breath out of her, and she shook it off almost violently, spinning around to see Olivia standing there. "Hey," she said in this soft voice that turned Audrey's tender heart inside out. "Are you okay?"

Audrey didn't know whether to nod or shake her head or shrug—so she did all three, bursting into a shaky laugh as she did so. "Oh my God," she said, feeling fresh tears soak into her eyelashes. "Ignore me. I'm so stupid!" She flexed her fingers around the bottle she'd grabbed, avoiding meeting Olivia's eyes. "How pathetic am I, crying over *that*? I'm beyond ridiculous."

Olivia leaned against a stack of paper boxes and plucked at Audrey's sleeve. "You're not ridiculous. Don't be so hard on yourself. You're going through some major stuff right now, remember?"

"How could I forget?" Audrey hiccupped and laughed again, although it sounded more like a childish tantrum sound effect. "I know it's so not important right now, but I want Ms. Fitz to think I'm doing good, y'know? I need somebody to, like . . . *believe* in me."

Olivia nodded. "I get it."

"Shit." Audrey looked at Olivia, pressing her fingers to her cheeks and bringing them away smudged with black. *I knew I shouldn't have put on makeup today.* "On a scale of one to ten, how much of a hot mess do I look like right now?"

"About a six," Olivia said mildly, and laughed when Audrey gasped. "But that I can help with. Here."

From behind her back she produced a small black pouch and a cracked compact, pressing them into Audrey's hands. "Just call me your queer fairy godmother."

Audrey laughed through her sniffling sounds and flipped the compact open, sighing at her reflection. "I don't think we're the same foundation shade," she quipped, and then said, "But thank you."

"No sweat."

Audrey ran her thumb under her eyes, wiping away the smudged mascara to reveal circles almost as dark underneath, and then picked a worn-down lipstick out of Olivia's makeup case. She parted her lips and watched herself slick on the peachy shade in the dusty mirror. The only sounds were her rusty breathing, the creaking of the pipes against the back wall. But then Olivia spoke again.

"For what it's worth," she said, quiet but firm, "I believe in you. And *you* should believe in you. Fuck everybody else. It's all you, Audrey."

Audrey rubbed her lips together and repeated Olivia's words in her head. *Fuck everybody else*, she thought. *It's all me.*

Is it all me?

I don't know anymore.

But it felt good to think it, even for a moment. She faced Olivia again, lifting her head high and seeing the look of approval rise in Olivia's eyes. "Right," she said. "It's all me."

TWENTY-NINE

A udrey, is that you?"

Audrey cursed the squeaky hinges on the bathroom door. All she wanted was to get upstairs and put on a campy old horror movie, something that required no brain activity and that she could fall asleep to. She did not want to talk to her mother.

"Yup," Audrey said, injecting false enthusiasm into her voice. "It's me."

The door to her mom and Adam's bedroom opened. "Oh," Laura said on seeing Audrey, face washed clean and hair tied up. "Are you going to bed? It's only nine." The *on a Friday night* went unspoken.

"I know. I wanted to get an early night." Audrey pulled her robe closed and scuffed her socked feet. "Feeling pretty tired."

Wrong thing to say, Audrey realized too late as her mom's mouth twisted into a frown.

Laura reached out to press her hand against Audrey's forehead. "Have you been taking the vitamins we bought? What about the herbal tea?"

"Yes." Audrey swatted her mom's hand away. "And that tea is disgusting. It tastes like ass."

"It's good for you," her mom said. "You need to be taking care of yourself, Audrey. It's not just you anymore, okay? I know you haven't made a decision yet, but you do need to remember that right now."

"Do you think I don't know that?" Audrey closed her eyes, pinching the bridge of her nose. "Do you honestly think that I ever, for a single second, *forget* that it's not just me anymore? Forget? Yeah, right." She was aware of her voice rising, along with the heat of her blood, until she thought she might boil over and burn to the ground. *"Fuck."*

"Hey," her mom said sharply. "Watch it."

"Yeah, yeah," Audrey said. "I'll watch my language. Because you know, cursing is only the beginning—pretty soon I'll be drinking, and smoking, having sex, and then . . ." She laughed, a loud noise in the softly lit hallway. "Oh, wait. Too late!"

Audrey heard movement then and opened her eyes to see Adam halfway up the stairs, looking confused. "What's going on? Audrey, is everything okay?"

Is everything okay? What kind of monumentally stupid question was that? She couldn't remember the last time everything was anything but shit and broken pieces.

But she turned to Adam, shaking her head slightly. (Too much movement and her brain would *explode*.) "Everything is absolutely fan-fucking-tastic. Oh—" She glanced at her mom. "Sorry."

Laura's hands were clasped so tight that her knuckles were white with the effort of it. "Audrey, I understand that you're upset—"

"You don't understand *anything*," Audrey said. "How could you ever?"

Her mom recoiled from Audrey's words, and Audrey wanted to slap herself, realizing a second too late, as always, what those words sounded like. Like she was throwing her adoption in her mom's face and God, no, *no*, that wasn't what she meant.

(But if it wasn't, then why had she even said it?)

Audrey shook her head, looking between her mom and Adam. *I didn't mean it like that*, she wanted to say, *I would never say that, you're my mom, I don't care how you came to be my mom, it doesn't matter.* She opened her mouth to take it back, but she already knew that it was too late. Things like that didn't come back. "Sorry," she said automatically. "God! I'm sorry for everything, *okay?*"

Adam grabbed at her hand. "Audrey—"

"No." Audrey wrenched herself free from his grip. "Don't. I don't want to hear it. I don't want to hear anything that either of you has to say."

She stomped upstairs, hearing the wind howling around the eaves, and balled up under her duvet with her hands pressed over her eyes and her teeth chattering together. She had no idea where the outburst had come from. She wished Julian wasn't working a double shift so she could go hide at his place, for once, twined together on his couch. It would be better than being by herself. She was doing a pretty good job of pushing everybody away: her mom, Adam, Rose. Maybe it was best that she wasn't with Julian, because she'd probably only find something to hate him for, too.

I'm so tired, she thought. *Tired of it all.*

When she finally fell asleep, no dreams came. There was only emptiness.

THIRTY

Even before she slipped out of the cocoon of her bed the next morning, Audrey could feel the coldness wrapping around her limbs. The low sun offered little brightness, but she was wide awake; already she felt restless and itching to be out of there.

She got dressed quickly, piling on the layers, and packed what she needed into her bag, then wavered in front of her door with her fingers on the knob. Nothing but the sound of silence came from the other side. She hadn't heard anything else during the night, either, during the hours she'd been switching between staring at the ceiling and watching the insides of her eyelids.

Part of her had expected her mom to come after her last night, the way she usually did when Audrey yelled at her. *Don't take that tone with me*, Laura would always say. *If you want to discuss something, talk to me; don't scream it. Haven't I raised you better than that?*

She had, Audrey thought. But apparently it didn't matter how good a person she'd been taught to be: the treacherous, heartbreaking, *bad* person she truly was couldn't be confined.

The stairs creaked under her steps, and she paused outside her mom and Adam's bedroom but heard more nothing. She couldn't stop herself from remembering standing in this exact spot the night before and the look on her mom's face when she'd thrown out those words. *You don't understand* anything. *How could you ever?*

Audrey pinched herself hard on the thigh, and her feet began working again, carrying her down the rest of the stairs and through the hall and finally out the front doorway.

The trees lining the street glittered with frost, but Audrey actually felt warmer out there than in the atmosphere of her house.

She pinched herself again as she headed toward her car. *Yeah*, she thought, *and whose fault is that?*

She found herself down by the river, the wind blowing off it especially biting, and she shivered even under her two T-shirts, sweater, wool-lined coat, and jade-green scarf with a matching hat that Julian's mom had knitted for her. Her head ached and her throat felt sandpaper raw and she couldn't shake the feeling from home—

Audrey inhaled sharply. No. She was not out here to think about how much her mom hated her right now. Even if it was true—and after last night, how could it not be? But she was here to forget all that.

She lifted her camera to her eye and snapped, capturing the family coming out of the diner in colorful puffer jackets next to a woman in pale-green scrubs. Early breakfast before a day of fun and a dinner at the end of the night shift, she guessed. Instinctively she pulled back, ready to check the shot in the LCD screen, but it wasn't there.

Audrey clicked her tongue, readying herself for the next shot. When she'd grabbed her things, she'd decided to leave her DSLR behind for a change. The camera she held now was older than she was, and heavy, a remnant of her mom's years in New York and the early days of LA. There was no digital screen, no memory card, no macro setting. Just actual film and a flash that emitted a high-pitched noise as it charged up. Laura had given it to her years ago when Audrey had begun messing around taking pictures, and Audrey had played with it for a few months before falling in love with a Nikon she'd saved up for, and since then the other one had been stowed away in the bottom of her closet.

To be honest, she hadn't thought about it until she'd seen the long black strap snaking through the discarded clothes coating the closet floor. Maybe it was seeing it and remembering how happy she'd been when her mom had given it to her; maybe it was just the need to do something different. Or maybe it was thinking that once upon a time she'd been good enough for her mother, the sweet kind of child who was given nice gifts and was thankful and didn't feel the need to rain vitriol like blossoms.

Her first mistake was not thinking about the whole film situation. Her second mistake was assuming that finding film wouldn't be a problem. It took her five separate stores to find some, and then the cashier laughed in her face when she learned how much it would be.

But she'd paid the extortionate cost and wound her way to the river, and now here she was.

God knows what these will even come out like, Audrey thought as she squeezed her finger down and the shutter flashed closed and open in front of her eyes. They had a darkroom at school, which she'd known how to navigate once upon a time. Probably by the time she was finished developing them they'd be even worse than they should be, thanks to her shitty skills.

The shrill ring of her phone blasted into the calm, and Audrey barely glanced at it before answering. "Hi."

"Hey," Julian's sleepy voice answered, crackling with the remnants of dreams. "I got your message. Why are you up so early?"

"Couldn't sleep. I . . ." *I got into a fight with my mom,* she was going to say, but the thought of telling Julian what she'd said made her wish for the earth to open up beneath her. Audrey shifted on the bench that looked out over the water, ignoring the damp seeping through her jeans. "I thought coming out here would be good."

"Is it?"

Audrey picked at the polish flaking off her nails instead of answering. "Can you come over tonight?"

"No, I'm working a double today."

"Oh, yeah. Right. Sorry." Audrey said. "Yeah, I remember. Okay."

"I can swing by before, though." That was followed by a yawn and the sound of Julian clearing his throat. "Or you could come here."

As soon as he said that, Audrey ached to be there with him right then, curled up in his bed listening to his raspy voice right in her ear.

"Yeah, I'll come to you," she said, her lips stinging from the want in her words. "Go back to sleep. I love you."

"Love you more."

"Not possible," Audrey said. "Never possible."

Julian laughed low. "Whatever you say. See you later."

"See you," Audrey echoed, and slipped the phone back into her pocket.

Her hand brushed against the other thing resting in there, the paper rustling against her fingers. Audrey paused for a second to watch the way the morning light reflected off the water; this was the best view in town, no doubt, but she was hardly ever up early enough to see it.

She sighed. "You are pathetic," she said, whispering to herself fervently. "Seriously, truly, pathetically pathetic."

Because all she was doing was stalling, like she seemed to spend her whole life doing.

Time to rip the Band-Aid off once more.

She brought her hand out of her pocket, clutching the thick cream envelope. When she'd grabbed the relic of a camera, she'd taken out the hidden-away shoe box and pried open the lid. What did she have to lose? Where else did she have to look for answers? She'd pushed away her best friend by being a—she hated to admit it but she had to—hypocritical, self-centered loser. Her mom was upset; Adam, too. She felt like she'd barely spoken to Olivia lately—the one person who'd been purely nice and sweet only because she wanted to, and Audrey had taken that for granted. So now Audrey had backed herself into a corner, and the only way out was to fight through to open space again.

And this letter, this . . . lifeline, maybe? She'd waited too long for this.

The paper tore satisfyingly when Audrey ran her nail along the top of the envelope. She pulled out a single sheet, folded neatly into thirds and covered in a looping script that filled Audrey with a strange comfort.

She sucked in a breath of sharp, snow-ready air and began to read.

Dear Audrey,

 I wrote another letter like this a long time ago. I'm not sure if you ever read it, or if you even know that it exists, but I wrote it for you.

 I don't really know how to begin this one.

 With my name, I suppose: Amanda Darby. I kept my name when I got married—I wanted to keep that part of me. I used to go by Mandy when I was younger, but my husband's the only one who calls me that now, and my best friend. She's known me since I had braces and stupid purple ribbons in my hair.

 God, I'm rambling already.

 Here's the thing: I don't know if I can write this letter. I know I can physically write the words on paper, but I'm not sure I'll be allowed to get it to you. Which is my own fault—I was the one who didn't want any communication, after all. I thought it would be easier that way, and I guess it has been, in some ways, but over the past few years I've spent more and more nights awake thinking about you. My husband says I get obsessive about things, and I won't say he's not right. We went to France last year on vacation, and now I'm nearly fluent. Weird, huh?

I guess I should say, not like I haven't already, that I'm married, to a man who doesn't think my obsessions are strange and always brings me breakfast on my birthday. We have two sons, five and three. My husband wanted a daughter, but I'd already had my girl, so two boys were okay with me.

What else . . . I went to college, got my degree. Not a very good college, but I worked hard to get through it and I'm proud of that. I work in design, websites and magazines mostly, which I love. We have a dog, a Siberian husky named Poppy that I got from a rescue when I graduated college, and two goldfish that the boys called Hugo and Egg (don't ask).

There are so many questions I want to ask you. The reason I placed you for adoption was so that we could both have a chance at a good life, and now I have that good life, but I feel as if I can't rest easy until I know you do, too. Your mom is a wonderful person, so I feel confident in thinking that she will have tried her best to give you a wonderful world, and that's good.

But still, when I'm lying awake at night, I want to know whether you like cats or dogs. Do you play an instrument? Can you sing? Are you good at languages? (My boys speak Spanish and English—my husband's Puerto Rican.)

I want to know, are you happy? Do you have friends? Has

that first love hit you yet? What do you dream about? Where do you want to go?

I'm selfish, I know. I have no right to want to know all these things about you, and yet I do.

Mostly I want to know if you are happy, and I know that happiness is an oddly unquantifiable thing, but if any part of your answer could be yes, then I would be so happy.

I'm going to give this letter to the adoption agency, and maybe they'll get it to you. It's a long shot, but I'm going to try.

If you want to write me (another long shot, I admit), then please do. Of course I'll understand if you don't, so don't worry about that at all.

All my love to you and Laura—I hope the two of you are as good together as you were the day you were born, Audrey.

Sincerely,

Amanda

Audrey gripped either side of the letter, steadying it against the wind.

Amanda Darby. *Amanda Darby the graphic designer*—like Adam, Audrey realized with the beginnings of a smile—*with the husband who makes her breakfast and two little kids and a dog named Poppy.*

None of the possible lives that Audrey had imagined over the years for "the girl Mandy" (she'd never be able to think of her as that again) came close to the actuality. Audrey hadn't ever doubted that her adoption had been the best for everyone involved, but to know for certain that it was true? God, it was so— She forgot about the damp wood under her butt and the cold that made her fingers tingle and the difficult camera. None of that mattered in comparison to this.

Audrey's eyes stung, from the wind and from the letter and from the aching in her heart, and the same question kept bouncing around in her head: *why have I put this off for so long?*

Well, duh: of course she knew why, but she wished she hadn't. This—this was what she'd been searching for. The good thing she'd needed to remind her that things got better even when it didn't seem like they ever could. Look at Amanda Darby and the place she'd been in seventeen years ago, and then look at the beautiful life she had now.

Look at the life Audrey herself had: family, friends, the best boy in the world. And sure, right now everything was fucked up and confusing and so, so hard, but still, she wouldn't change it for anything.

There had been a girl exactly like her all those years ago who'd made a hard decision for a good reason, and now look where they all were.

It was as if Amanda Darby had known, somehow, that Audrey needed this. This proof that the choice Amanda had made had been the right one for her and that whatever Audrey chose would be right for her, too. Adoption had been the right decision for Amanda, and Audrey had wanted, desperately sometimes, to believe it was the right decision this time around, too.

But it wasn't.

She couldn't do it. No: she didn't *want* to do it. And as much as she wanted to believe in a fantasy world where she and Julian and their baby all lived happily ever after, she couldn't do that, either. Neither of those things was the right one; she felt that deep down in her bones. The point of deciding, of having this wondrous and heavy ability to choose what she wanted to do, was to find for herself what was best for her, and Julian. Not what she wished was right, or what she dreamed of doing, but what she knew now was the only way for her to go.

Audrey had been scared to read the letter for fear of what it contained, and what those contents might push her toward. She'd thought that if Amanda Darby regretted it at all, it would make her decision harder, and change the way she thought about her whole life. She'd thought that if Amanda Darby didn't regret it at all, it would push her closer to the adoption choice, even though she knew it wasn't right for her. But, no. Reading those words written by the woman who'd gifted her with this life, what Audrey really saw was the power available to her right now. That power to choose the beginning of the rest of her life.

So that only left one thing.

The idea of an abortion—it had been playing in the back of her head ever since she'd found out she was pregnant. Think about all the options, Julian had said. And this was an option. *The* option, the best one. The only one that would let her—and Julian—go on with their lives. And oh, she wanted to live her life. And it was scary, but knowing that she had thought it through, that all the deliberating and worrying and everything else could be over soon—it filled Audrey with calm.

She was making her choice, her own right choice. If Julian didn't feel the same way, well, then they'd have a problem. But she would explain it all to him, and hope that he would see it as clearly as she did now.

Time to be real.

THIRTY-ONE

She meant to tell Julian right away, she really did. But when she got to his house, he kissed her so sweetly and he was all excited about Hera things, and she didn't want to burden the day. Instead she let him talk, about how Izzy had finalized dates for their summer tour schedule and how he was overflowing with songs, and she felt her resolve strengthen. Next summer she wanted to be dragging her friends to those shows, not changing diapers on a screaming baby. She wanted Julian to be out there captivating new audiences, not sterilizing bottles. That was the truth of it all—maybe selfish, but real. And Audrey could hear it in Julian's voice, too, the excitement (almost mania) brewing over vans and new amps and the idea of touring, how much that was the future he wanted.

Has he realized it yet? she wondered, watching him eat leftover pizza in his kitchen while she played with her new-old camera, feeling her way around the buttons and dials, trying to learn the intricacies of it the way she knew every groove and click of her DSLR. She lifted it and snapped a shot of him waving his hands wildly. *Has he figured out what he wants—what he doesn't want?* Because it was almost painfully clear to Audrey now. He was in love with her, but he was in love with music, too. And he'd do anything for Audrey, she was pretty sure of that, but she didn't want him to do anything for her. She wanted him to choose for himself.

Maybe it didn't matter. Because she'd tell him what she wanted and that would be it. And for the first time in weeks, she felt certain.

She left his house and headed home, the letter tucked back in her pocket. She had to apologize to her mom, fix the best thing she had in her life. The first thing she did when she walked into the house was go upstairs to her mom's office. She lifted her hand to the door, ready to knock, so ready to say *I'm sorry* and *Please don't be mad at me*, but she pulled back at the last second when she heard the heavy sigh coming from inside the room.

She was ready to try again at dinner, but Adam talked the whole way through so that the silence from before didn't have a chance to return and Audrey couldn't get a word in.

Sunday morning she waited until she smelled coffee brewing and followed the aroma down to the kitchen, where she stood next to Laura for a moment before finally saying it. "I'm . . . sorry," she said slowly. "About the other night. What I said . . . you know. I'm really sorry."

She waited then, waited for her mom to turn and smile, take her in her arms and wrap her up the way Audrey loved. *Of course you're sorry*, she'd say. *I forgive you. It's forgotten. Do you want pancakes for breakfast?*

But her mom did none of that. She only nodded, watching the steam rising from the percolator. "It's fine," she said, but the stiffness of her voice said that wasn't true. "Could you take the trash out?"

Audrey opened her mouth to say it again, say it *better* somehow—but what was the point? *I can't make her forgive me.*

I hurt her.

When all she's doing is trying to do her best for me. All she's ever done is try her best for me, and what do I do?

Audrey licked her dry lips and opened the cabinet, taking out what she knew was her mom's favorite mug and setting it down between them. "Okay," she said quietly.

THIRTY-TWO

On Monday evening Audrey volunteered to go get dinner, a hopeful gesture of apology, which neither her mom nor Adam seemed to care about. But still.

Audrey intended to head downtown to one of their usual take-out places to pick up the Indian food her mom loved or maybe some soul food from the tiny place by Adam's office.

But instead she ended up at Julian's workplace with her hands in tight fists and her heart beating this steady, certain rhythm.

He hadn't called her at all yesterday, or texted. He had been quiet all day at school, too: hadn't hung out on the steps before class or visited Audrey at her locker between periods, and when she'd looked for him at lunch, she'd found him in the library sitting by a window with his headphones clamped over his ears and a distant look on his face that didn't leave even when she'd kissed him.

It's a bad day, she thought now. *A couple of bad days. Everybody has them. It doesn't mean anything.*

But still, she was kicking herself for not telling him about her decision that day. When she'd asked him what was up, he'd said, "Nothing," in that way that meant everything and then cleared his throat and said, "Dr. Morris wants me to apply to some different summer music programs at colleges. Said she'd write me a letter of recommendation."

"That's awesome!" Audrey had said. "I'm so proud of you, J."

And he'd nodded but didn't say anything else, and now Audrey was wondering exactly what he'd been thinking at that moment. Had he realized?

She thought so.

So now she was at the restaurant. It was maybe half full, and the low hum of people eating and chatting filled the space with warmth. A girl in a crisp black shirt with braids in a giant bun approached Audrey with a menu in her hands and a rictus smile on her face. "Table for one?"

"What?" Audrey pulled at the sleeves of her sweater, eyes scanning around. "No. Thank you. Sorry. I'm—"

"Hey." The girl looked at Audrey again. "Don't I know you?"

"I don't think so," Audrey said. "I'm looking for Julian. Is he around?"

"That's it!" She nodded firmly. "You're Julian's girlfriend. Audrey, right? I'm Courtney. Weird that we haven't met before, right?"

Not that weird, Audrey wanted to say, *and could we skip the small talk?* But she squashed down the urge and dipped her chin. "Yeah," she said instead. "Weird. So—"

Courtney cut her off, bobbing her head again. "I'll go find him for you. You can sit, if you want. Back in a sec!"

Audrey didn't sit—her restless feet wouldn't let her. She watched the diners instead, constructing elaborate life stories for them in her head: The black stiletto-wearing woman was in witness protection, hiding from her drug lord ex-husband. And the middle-aged couple sharing the chocolate soufflé was in the throes of a torrid affair—just not with each other. What about the silver-fox hot guy sitting at the bar?

Her name being called across the restaurant pulled her back from her daydream, and then Julian was standing in front of her looking concerned. ". . . something wrong?" he was saying as Audrey tuned in again. He cupped her face in his hands, smoothing his fingers over her flushed cheeks. "You look weird. Are you sick? Is it . . ." He looked pointedly at her stomach. "Audrey?"

Audrey swallowed hard. "I'm not sick. There's no emergency. I—I need to talk to you."

"Okay," Julian said, raising his eyebrows. "Right now?"

"Can't you get Pete to let you off early?"

"Now?" Julian repeated, and gestured to the tables that needed busing and the swinging doors of the kitchen. "I'm working. You know, that thing people have to do to make money. I can't just leave."

"Well, don't you get a break? I'll wait. It's important." She took a step toward him, attempting a smile. "Please?"

Julian glanced over his shoulder nervously and then rapped his knuckles on the order pad in his other hand. "Okay," he said. "Look, I get my break in ten minutes. All right?"

In the back Audrey sat on a crate and tried to organize her thoughts into something Julian would understand. It was hard to think of the right words to put in the right order, to make sure she was saying exactly what she wanted to. How did she tell the father of her maybe-child, the boy she unabashedly claimed as her True Love, that she didn't want It anymore?

The back door opened and Julian skipped the two steps to ground level, landing heavily. He pushed up his shirtsleeves, and Audrey shivered. How was he not freezing? She felt her blood turning to ice even as she looked at him. "Hi."

"Hi."

"Sorry," she said, rubbing her palms together. "I should have waited. I think I'm losing it."

"That's all right," Julian said with a crazy smile. "I think I'm losing it, too." He sat opposite her, leaning his elbows on his knees. "I know you want to say something, but am I allowed to speak, too?"

"You're speaking now," Audrey said.

"I mean, *speak*," Julian said, like that made things any clearer. "I have to . . . I know I was acting weird at school. I don't want to freak you out; it's— I keep getting these thoughts popping up in my head. At the most random times they'll come—I'll be clearing tables in there, or doing a problem on the board in algebra, and then they hit me."

Oh, Audrey realized. *Here it is.*

She pulled her coat tighter around her. "What thoughts?"

Julian barely paused, cracking his knuckles. "Like, say we did . . . have the baby. What would we do if there was something wrong with the baby? If it got sick? We'd have to get insurance, probably," he said, and his eyes focused on Audrey. "Then I think things like, well, maybe I'll get a job that comes with benefits. But realistically I wouldn't be able to do that right away, so if there were an emergency we'd be screwed. And what if we start fighting over shit like who changed the most diapers today or because you're mad that I say I'm tired and you were up with the baby five times in the night while I was asleep . . . I don't know, Audrey. It's thinking about college and what if you get into RISD or some other awesome school, but we can't afford it because we have to pay for kid shit?" He wiped a hand over his face roughly. "It's all this stuff that I sometimes think doesn't mean anything, but really, it means everything. Or maybe it means nothing! What does *anything* matter when there's a baby of ours in all this?"

"I don't understand," Audrey said, the truth for once. She reached over, touched his knee. "What are you saying?"

"I'm not sure. It's more than not having money." Julian stood and began pacing. "It's not having a sense of security. Or any idea what being a parent means. And now people are talking to me about college, these summer programs, and the band is doing so well right now—and I feel like I'm going to be letting people down if I don't take all these opportunities I'm being given, but I want to do what's right for us. You, too. And—this is going to sound shitty, but what am I going to tell Izzy and the others? What about Dr. Morris? I'm . . . I need you to talk me down. Okay?"

Audrey wet her lips. Shit.

Say it. *Say it.*

"Actually, this is what I wanted to talk to you about." She focused on him and pulled up every last ounce of nerve she had. "I can't do it."

"You can't talk me down?" Julian stopped pacing. "Well, can you try? 'Cause I think I'll lose my mind if you don't."

Audrey blinked and shook her head, catching her wind-whipped hair and holding it out of her face. "No," she said. "I can't do it. I can't—" She sighed, knowing that she was maybe about to ruin everything. "I can't have this baby."

"What?"

A long, stretched-out moment of silence followed her declaration. Julian stood as still as a statue.

"I know," Audrey said. "I'm sorry. I'm so, so sorry."

"I thought—" Julian's face twisted in confusion. He made a noise that was either a laugh or a groan, Audrey couldn't tell, and then he looked right at her. "I guess I assumed you wanted to keep it."

"I couldn't make up my mind," Audrey said. "One way or another. But I've been thinking—" She looked down, twisting her fingers together. "The other day, before I came over to your house, I read the letter. That my birth mom sent me? Remember? Her name is Amanda." She paused, picturing the neat script and everything those words had contained. "She has two kids now, boys, and a husband, and a dog. Poppy. Cute, right?" She stopped, reaching out to wrap her hands around his. "I love you, Julian."

"Audrey," Julian started, but she shook her head.

"Wait, please." She inhaled and tried again. "I love you, you know that. You love me. *I* know *that*. In my perfect future we stay together, and we stay happy." She watched Julian carefully, the way his dark eyes—mirrors of hers, always—skipped from looking at his feet, to the sky, to her, to the ground again. "And when we're grown-ups, maybe we'll go places. See the world together, and I'll take pictures of you in front of all the monuments like the tourists we'll be." She laughed then, pushing her thumbs into Julian's palms. "Do you see it?"

Julian's answer came softly. "Yeah."

"We'll live somewhere where the leaves go red in the fall and have kids who ride their bikes until dusk. We'll both have jobs we like— well, that we can stand, at least—and we'll do anything to keep our kids happy and safe and—" She snatched her hands out of Julian's so she could scrub at her stinging eyes. *"Fuck."*

She heard footsteps and felt the weight of Julian sitting next to her, pulling her into him so that her head fell onto his shoulder. "I can see that, too," Julian said, and his voice sent vibrations through Audrey's body. "All of it."

Of course he did. Because he was Julian, and he had all this good-ness in him and that was why Audrey had fallen in love with him in the first place and, God, she didn't deserve him. "'I want' doesn't get," Audrey said, quiet. "My mom always used to say that to me when I was little and freaking out over a Barbie or roller skates. I don't think I ever understood it until right now.

"I want so much: to be with you, to be young and stupid, to feel like myself again. . . ." She wanted to be Jen and María, dancing wild at parties and so excited for their futures, or Olivia, falling in love, taking on something new. "I want you to go and be a musician and eat ramen and live in a shitty apartment and do all the amazing things you ever wanted. I don't know if I'll even get into art school, but I want to try. I want to make my mom proud. And my birth mom. I wish this hadn't happened. So we could carry on like things were and I could stop worrying whether it's more selfish for me to keep a baby that I maybe want but know I can't give the best to, or to not keep it so I can have the life I thought I—we—would."

They sat in silence for a long minute, leaning into each other like they had so many times before. They didn't even have to move themselves; their bodies fell into place like puzzle pieces.

But then Julian lifted his shoulder, prompting Audrey to sit up properly, and turned to face her straight on. "I don't care about the music," he said, searching her face with those deep, dark eyes. "I only care about you."

"Don't say that. It's not true at all." Audrey laughed thickly. "And don't you dare try to tell me it is."

"I just want to do what's right."

"For who? Right how?"

Julian's hands clutched at the air. "God, I just don't want to be an asshole who only thinks about himself. And I don't want to make a decision we'll regret in a couple of years."

"What will we regret more? Chasing what we actually want to

do, going to California or wherever, or bringing another human being into the world without being one hundred percent sure of what we're doing?"

Julian sucked in a deep breath, loud enough for Audrey to hear. "Don't tell me what you think I want to hear. All that stuff I said, it doesn't mean I can't do this for you."

"For me?" Audrey said. "J, if we were going to do it, shouldn't it be *with* me, not *for* me? Shouldn't it be for yourself, too?" Audrey wiped her nose with the back of her hand. "It's not *just* that I don't want to. It's that—"

"You can't," Julian finished for her. He took a deep breath. "*We* can't."

"Reading the letter from Amanda—" She halted abruptly. "Wow. It's weird to say her name like that. But yeah, reading it and thinking of what she experienced when it was her turn in this situation . . ." Audrey shook her head. "She was different from me. I know she wanted me, I know it, but more than that she wanted what was best for me. So she did it. And I want to do that, too. I want to choose what's best for *me*, and having a baby right now isn't it."

Julian bit his lip, looking almost ashamed. "I wanted to believe this would work out," he said. "Y'know, I thought, 'Maybe if we both want this and we have a plan, we could do it.' I felt like . . . that's what I was supposed to do. Step up and do the right thing. Be a man and all that. And yeah, I want kids, too. Someday. It was weird, thinking about having one now, but I thought . . . fuck, I don't know what I thought." Julian's hollow laugh sent pinpricks along Audrey's spine. She hadn't missed how quickly he'd slipped into the past tense. See how well she knew him? She'd known what he wanted before he'd even had a clue. "But let's be real, what was I talking about? That we could have a baby and carry on with our lives like normal, like it's so fucking easy? Like, sure, I can be a father now, no sweat! I'm so stupid."

"If you're stupid, then so am I," Audrey said, pulling her coat sleeves over her numb hands. "We were talking about names. *Names.* Because that's the important part, right?"

Julian laughed, harder, and more real this time. "Right! Forget knowing how to change a diaper or what to do when the kid won't eat. As long as we give it a cool name, who cares?"

"Or forget the diaper stuff," Audrey said, cracking a smile herself. "How about the fact that giving birth *hurts* and that sometimes afterward they have to *sew your vagina back together.* What about that, huh?"

Julian looked absolutely horrified at that, and now Audrey was the one laughing. "See?" she said between giggles. "We know nothing!"

"They sew you up?" he repeated, eyes wide. "That sounds like torture, not helpful medical intervention. Literally sew you up? Jesus, my balls hurt just talking about it!"

"They do," Audrey said. "Aren't you glad you learned something?"

"Something I could have gone my entire lifetime without knowing," Julian said, and then he let out a short sigh. "So."

"So."

"We're not doing it," he said. "We're not . . . having a baby."

Audrey counted the seconds between his nonquestion and her

definite answer. *One. Two* . . . "No," she said simply. "I can't. And as much as I'd like to believe I *want* to, I don't. I mean, yes, I want to be a mom, but . . . one day. When I'm ready. When I have a baby, I want to do my best, and I don't think—no, I *know* that we can't give that right now."

"You're always right. It's annoying," Julian said, and then knocked his shoulder against hers. "Hey. C'mere."

He slid one hand around the back of Audrey's neck and used the other to push her hair out of her face. "We're going to be okay, you and me. Yes?"

"Yeah." Audrey nodded, sending a couple of lonely tears tracking down her cheeks. "Oh, for God's sake," she said, surprised. "I can't stop crying lately! What's wrong with me?"

"Hormones," Julian deadpanned, but he couldn't keep the anxious look off his face for long. "I can talk to Pete, get off for the rest of my shift—"

"No, don't do that." Audrey tipped her chin up to kiss Julian, only once, only quickly, but the feel of his lips on hers was like home. She pulled away and smiled. "I'll be okay. Besides, Adam and my mom are waiting; I'm supposed to be getting dinner. Which I should go do, otherwise I'll turn up at home with no food *and* the bonus news that I'm going to get an abortion. Surprise!"

Julian grabbed her hands. "Don't tell them tonight. I want to be there. Not like last time."

Audrey hesitated. She didn't want to go through the keeping-a-secret thing again, but at the same time, telling her parents that she was pregnant on her own had been hard. "Okay." She studied his face. "Are you okay with this?"

"Yes. No. No, because I wish we didn't have to make this decision, and yes, because I think you're right; this is the best thing for us to do. It was fun, though, for a while. Wasn't it?" He pressed a kiss to her open palm. "Playing make-believe."

"One day it'll be for real," Audrey said. "That's what *I* want to believe."

"Right." He squeezed her hands tight. "You and me, right?"

Audrey squeezed back. His hands were rough with guitar-playing calluses, but his fingers were the long, piano-player kind. She'd always loved how she could tell so much about him from his touch alone. They were in this together—all of it: the guilt, the selfishness, the sadness, the righteousness, the relief. They weren't perfect, but at least they could be that way together.

"You and me."

THIRTY-THREE

Dinner was quiet—that cold feeling from her mom, the awkwardness of Adam's attempted conversation starters. Audrey busied herself picking off the red onions on her pizza and turning over everything she and Julian had talked about. She'd thought that finally telling him her decision would make her feel better, and it did—at least she didn't have that nagging anxiety worming around the pit of her stomach anymore. And knowing he felt the same was better than she could have imagined. But there was fear, too, that this fantasy life they'd so briefly entertained wouldn't be there in the future.

By the time they'd finished eating it was late, and when Adam took the dishes to the kitchen, her mom stood up and stretched. "I'm exhausted," she said, more to the room than to Audrey. "I'm going to head to bed. See you in the morning."

Audrey watched her walk away, her mom's perfect posture and the hair spilling down the back of her easy gray tee and the measure of each step. If Audrey were a braver person, she would have called out, stood up and said . . . God, something. Anything would be better than the silence stretching out in this way that felt eternal.

But by the time she finished thinking about it, her mom had vanished upstairs.

She cleared the dinner debris from the table and declined Adam's offer of coffee when he came back inside. "I have homework," she said flatly, not even bothering to pretend she wasn't lying, and went up to her room.

Her phone flashed, battery on red, and she snapped the charger in before typing a text to Jen: Tell me something good, it read. I'm in a shitty mood.

Two, then ten, then twenty minutes passed without a response, and Audrey tossed her phone aside with a pissed-off sigh, opening her laptop instead.

But she didn't care about Karima Yang's statuses or the stupid video everyone was sharing or even the pictures of the band at their last show. None of it seemed to matter, and for some strange reason that fact made her want to cry more than anything else. More than her mom being mad at her and the lack of Rose's acidic laugh in her life and more, even, than saying good-bye to the baby she'd never really been going to have.

"So stupid," Audrey muttered, brushing at her stinging eyes. But it was sad, because she used to care about those things so much even if they were shallow, and now she didn't at all; she only felt the strangest kind of empty.

She got up to put the computer back on her desk and selected some music, some guy singing over a mournful mandolin. Then she changed into pajamas and turned out the lights, got into bed, and fell asleep as soon as her eyes closed.

THIRTY-FOUR

Audrey jerked awake with a sharp inhale. A tingling feeling crawled its way up her legs, and her eyes snapped wide open.

Something's wrong.

Her brain took a minute to send that message to the rest of her body, and then she sat up so she could throw off the covers and look down at her pajama pants. But there was nothing there, none of the blooming red blood that, for a fraction of a second, she'd been so sure she'd see. And as she ran her hands over her stomach, her chest, her arms, she realized that she felt no different than usual. (Well, than this new usual.)

Audrey relaxed back. That wasn't why she'd woken then. She blew out slowly, a soft hiss. That was the only sound, she noticed. No noise came from anywhere else in the house, no creaking floorboards or door hinges, not even the jingling of Marmalade's bell. Why was she awake?

A bad dream, she thought, her eyes blinking against the dark. *Or—*

The room lit up, a strobing flash.

Her phone.

The screen glowed bright in the blackness of her room, a text buzzing in, and Audrey shifted toward the nightstand, grappling for it.

She sucked in a breath when she saw the name there, and the brief contents of the message: 911.

Audrey scrambled to sit up on her knees, pressing the Call button and mashing the phone to her ear. *Pick up. Come on, pick up.*

"Hi."

The sound of Rose's voice, her raspy, thick voice, did nothing to calm Audrey's nerves, singing on high alert now. "What's wrong? Are you okay?" Audrey asked in an urgent whisper. "Rose? Say something."

"I'm okay," that voice said again, and then it hiccupped. "Well. Actually, no. I'm not okay."

"Where are you?" Audrey got to her feet, rising onto her toes so her parents wouldn't hear her footsteps through their ceiling. "Do you need me to come get you?" She was already at her closet, pulling out a sweatshirt and scarf.

It should have been weird, how easily their fight and everything else in between faded into the background in a split second. But Audrey couldn't think about that right now—the things they'd said, the hurt they'd caused; they could wait. Rose was her best friend, the girl who knew the worst parts of her and still let Audrey in. Who still loved her. There was a magic in the moments they'd had, good and awful, that couldn't ever truly be undone.

"I've ruined everything," Rose said. She sounded small through the phone, a little girl. "Like I always do."

"That's not true," Audrey said. "Rose, where are you?"

A shaky laugh. "I'm outside."

"Outside where?"

"Your house."

Audrey dropped the clothes in her hand and went to the window, peering down onto the street. Moonlight gleamed on the silver of Rose's car, waiting. "Okay," she said after a moment. "I'm coming down."

"Okay," Rose said. "Thanks."

"You don't have to thank me," Audrey said automatically. "This is what best friends are for, right?"

She waited a second for Rose's reply but heard only a smothered intake of breath. "Of course it is," Audrey said, answering for both of them. "I'll be down in a sec. It's going to be all right, Rose. Promise."

The house was still, quiet, and Audrey crept downstairs as carefully as possible in her bare feet. She got to the kitchen and was about to step out into the hall when her eyes, adjusting to the darkness, found a figure slouching over the table. Her heart kicked into overdrive, and she took an automatic step back. "Adam?"

He startled, raising his messy-hair head. "Hey, kiddo."

Audrey fumbled for the light switch, and they both squinted when the light flickered on. "What are you doing down here?"

Adam shrugged, looking at her with bleary eyes. "Couldn't sleep, and I didn't want to wake up your mom with my tossing and turning."

The glass in front of him glimmered with dark-amber liquid. "Whiskey?" Audrey guessed.

"Yup," Adam said with a small smile. "So, what's your excuse?"

Audrey shifted uncomfortably. Things were still strange between them, too—probably, Audrey thought, because now he'd seen what kind of girl she really was, the awful things she could do. He'd only witnessed the good version of her before, and now, she knew, he'd never be able to see her in the same way.

She found herself wanting to say sorry to him then, but it would only pull the tension tighter. So Audrey kept any apology to herself and instead said, "What?"

He took of a sip of the whiskey, grimacing as he swallowed. "It's one a.m., and you're not in bed. So either you can't sleep, too, or you're sneaking out somewhere. . . ." Adam looked her up and down. "Although if I were you, I'd rethink the pajamas before you go anywhere."

Audrey looked down at the holey tee (stolen from Julian) and flannel bottoms (too long for her) that served as her nightwear. "Right." Then she looked at Adam again, straightening up. "It's neither of those things. It's—I got a message from Rose, and I think she's maybe in some kind of trouble—"

"Trouble?" This made Adam sit up straight. "You need me to come with you?"

Audrey exhaled, a noisy gust of relief. See, that was why she loved Adam—no questions, no hesitation, he was there. "I'm not going anywhere," Audrey said. "She's outside. I think she's just upset and—I know it's late, but she can come in, right?"

Adam raked a hand through his hair, making it stand on end more than it already was. "I guess I'm supposed to say yes while still reminding you that I'm breaking the rules and that you should be very grateful to me for doing it. So I'll pretend I did that, and you go get her."

Her adrenaline ratcheted up a notch, and she reached for the light switch. "Will you do me another favor?"

Adam mimed zipping his lips shut. "You won't even know I'm here."

Audrey nodded and turned off the light, plunging them into darkness. "Thanks."

She stepped out into the hall. The floor chilled her toes as she walked to the door and ducked to search for her keys, tucked inside her jacket pocket. When she found them, she opened the door onto the empty night. "Rose?" Her whisper-shout fell into the silence.

Across the street, Rose emerged from her car and started across the icy asphalt. As she got closer, the moonlight lit up the angry redness of her eyes, the flush in her cheeks. Her mouth was set in a hard line that didn't falter as she mounted the steps outside the house. When she reached the top she stopped, standing there opposite Audrey, and they both stared at each other for the longest, fastest time. "Hey," Audrey said eventually. "Do you want to come in?" And it was then that Rose crumpled.

She let out a hiccup of a sob and wrapped her arms around her body, like she was holding herself together. "I didn't have anywhere else to go," she said, so quietly that at first Audrey wasn't sure she'd heard right. But then Rose cleared her throat. "I have nobody," she said, her voice catching, and she looked up to the sky. "Why do I always do this? I shouldn't have come here, I'm sorry—"

She turned like she was going to run, and Audrey grabbed Rose's arm, *hard*. "No," she said, sharp. "You can always come here. You don't have nobody, Rose; you have me. I know we're fighting, but are you really giving up on us that easily? Come on." The laugh that sneaked out was bitter and bright at the same time. "I expect more from you. And it's not just me. You have Jen and María, you have Julian, you have Olivia—"

"Not anymore." Rose shook her head. "Not after tonight."

"What do you mean?"

"I mean, we got into this ridiculous fight—no, I *started* a ridiculous fight because Olivia asked me to come to dinner one night, with her mom, and I'm a complete mess and I have this thing about parents and of course I got all weird and she got pissed and I'm pretty sure she's done with me." Rose's words ran out in one slippery stream. "Why wouldn't she be? If I were her, I'd run as far and as fast from me as I could. I should just stop, because I fuck everything up without even trying. Isn't that so *fun*?"

She rubbed her hands together, and Audrey noticed she was shivering. "Come inside," she said, tugging Rose in. "Look, it's late and you're upset and—"

Rose burst into fresh tears and pitched forward, Audrey catching her. "Whoa! I've got you, okay? I've got you."

They stayed like that for a minute, Audrey rubbing Rose's back and making the kind of soothing noises you'd make to a baby. She could feel Rose's tears soaking through her shirt, leaving a damp patch on her shoulder. For all that they'd fought, it broke Audrey's heart to see Rose like this, and she wondered how long Rose had been feeling this way. And who she could have told about it—because that was the thing; Rose didn't talk about how she was feeling to anyone but Audrey, really, and when Audrey hadn't been there . . . well.

But I'm here now, she thought. *She needs me, and I'm here, and we can get through this.*

Can't we?

Rose pulled back, sniffing and wiping the back of her hand across her nose. "I'm sorry. I'll go now. Forget it."

"No, I won't 'forget it,'" Audrey said. "Are your parents home?"

Rose shook her head. "My mom is in San Francisco," she said. "I don't know where my dad is. Some superimportant superbusiness-y trip somewhere. You know how it is."

The image of Rose all alone in that big house broke Audrey's heart all over again. "Stay here," she said. "For tonight. It's too late to go anywhere, and I don't want you to be alone."

Rose looked past Audrey and bit her lip. "Won't your parents be mad?"

"Of course not," Audrey said, and she tugged on Rose's arm again, meeting little resistance, and finally succeeded in getting Rose through the doorway. She locked it again, shutting out the cold and sinister night, and took Rose's hand. Inside felt safe, secure, and their breathing echoed in the quiet. The reassurance Audrey felt when Rose squeezed her fingers was beautiful. "You know they'd do anything for you. Besides, Adam's in the kitchen. You can ask him for yourself."

Right on cue, Adam appeared in the doorway, bleached of all color by the moonlight. "Ask me what?"

Rose took half a step back, putting herself behind Audrey, and so Audrey said the words for her. "Can Rose stay? It's so late, y'know, and . . ."

Adam looked at Rose. "Your parents away again?" he asked, carefully casual.

"Yeah," Rose said, her voice crackly.

"Okay, then." Adam tipped his head in the direction of the stairs. "Go on up. I'll let Laura know." He paused for a second, his eyes softening. "You okay, Rose?"

Audrey looked over her shoulder, curious herself, and watched Rose scrub at her cheeks, the barest hint of a smile playing on her face. "Yeah," she said. "Or I will be."

Adam nodded, satisfied. "Good," he said. "Now go up and go to sleep. You have school tomorrow." He frowned. "Did those words just come out of my mouth? Weird."

"You're a grown-up," Audrey said, leading Rose to the stairs. "Own it."

Upstairs in her room, Rose peeled off her clothes and got into pajamas from her drawer, grabbing the sweater Audrey had dropped on the floor earlier. Murmurs and movement came from beneath their feet; it was comforting, in a weird way, knowing Adam and her mom were down there talking about them, worrying about Rose. There weren't enough people in Rose's life who worried about her.

"You all good?" Audrey asked as Rose got into bed. "You're not cold or anything?"

"No," Rose said. "Just tired."

"Okay." Audrey turned off the light before getting into the other side of her bed, shuffling under the covers until she was comfortable and the heat of Rose's body was near.

As the minutes passed, she heard Rose's breathing evening out, the little snuffling sounds so familiar. Audrey couldn't settle, though, and it wasn't the remaining adrenaline or the extra body in her bed keeping her awake. She knew what it was, and she also knew that she needed to start fixing it now, while Rose was open to her, while they were together again. "Rose?" Audrey kept her voice at a whisper. "Are you awake?"

Rose's foot knocked against Audrey's shin under the covers. "Hmm," she said, which either meant yes or no, Audrey couldn't tell.

She went on anyway. "I'm sorry," she said softly. "For everything. I hate fighting with you. I wish I would have done things differently, but . . . it doesn't matter now. I wanted you to know how sorry I am, is all."

Audrey waited for Rose to say something, or move a little, but there was nothing except the sound of her breathing. Audrey let out a tiny laugh. "Okay. I guess I'll have to tell you in the morning." She searched for Rose's hand again, grabbing and squeezing her fingers as she closed her eyes. "Sleep tight."

Audrey concentrated on clearing her head, sinking into the depths of her mattress and marshmallow pillows as she finally began to fall asleep.

And then as she was tipping over the edge into peaceful oblivion, she heard Rose speak. "I'm sorry, too." The words were milky and far, but Audrey felt them clear in her heart. "But we're going to be okay."

They were going to be okay.

THIRTY-FIVE

When Audrey woke to her alarm, feeling as if she'd only gotten five minutes of sleep as opposed to five hours, she was surprised to find Rose already up and dressed. "Morning," Rose said from where she sat at Audrey's desk. "Sleep okay?"

Audrey yawned in response, stretching her arms above her head and ignoring the queasy feeling in her stomach. "Shit," she said. "I didn't do my math homework."

"You never do your math homework." Rose placed her folded arms on the back of the chair and rested her chin on them. "I'm sorry about all this."

"Stop apologizing." Audrey got up, pulled her towel off its hook, and opened the door. "I'm going to get ready, and we can get breakfast on the way to school. That'll make you feel better."

Audrey showered and dressed as fast as possible, and then she and

Rose headed downstairs. In the kitchen Marmalade looked up from his bowl long enough to ascertain that Audrey wasn't a threat to his food and then went back to eating. "Morning, kitty."

Rose crouched to stroke his striped head. "Hi, Marmalade."

The coffee in the pot was warm—Adam must have gone to work already, Audrey thought—and Audrey poured some into two travel mugs. On the counter next to the pot was a brown bag on top of a note with Rose's name on it. Audrey smiled and picked it up. "Rose—I think this is yours."

She watched Rose open it, and her face light up. "Wait—this is for me?"

The stairs creaked and Laura appeared, dressed for a full day at the theater: black jeans, black silk button-down, a thick-knit draped cardigan so long it almost brushed the floor, several thin silver chains twisted around her neck. "You're still here!" She swept through the room and grabbed the coffeepot, pouring the last bit into a mug Audrey had made in eighth grade. "Rose, I didn't know if you liked oranges or pears, so you got one of each."

Rose pulled a pink flower out of her lunch bag and twirled it between her fingers before putting it behind her ear. "I like them both," she said. "Thank you so much."

Laura shook her head, leaning against the counter with her hands wrapped around her mug. "I remember heartbreak. It's hard, I know. But you remember, Rose—anyone who doesn't make you happy doesn't deserve to make you cry."

Rose nodded, her eyes shining freshly. "I know," she said. "It's not her fault, though. Olivia's a good person."

"Well, in that case," Laura said, "you're allowed to cry."

"Mom," Audrey said. "I don't think you're helping."

Laura bristled, and Audrey remembered that they weren't supposed to be friends right now. "Rose, honey, is your mom going to be home tonight?" her mom asked, ignoring her.

Rose nodded as she rolled the brown bag shut. "Yeah," she said. "Her flight gets in at noon."

"Okay." Laura glanced at the clock. "I need to be gone. But Rose, if you need anything, you know where we are, okay? And Audrey—"

Audrey steeled herself. *What?* she thought. *Audrey, don't be a spoiled witch? Audrey, why are you such a fuckup?*

"—don't forget to take the recycling out," Laura finished.

Audrey sat in class, sketching scenes in her notebook instead of paying attention to any of her teachers. Lately, school felt so suffocating that Audrey wondered how she didn't fall down gasping for air. She'd made her decision, but she hadn't done anything about putting things into motion yet. It was causing her skin to feel itchy and tight, a size too small, and she kept thinking she was off-kilter—like everything she looked at seemed about an inch or two off its correct place.

When the bell rang for lunch, Audrey made her way to the cafeteria and found Rose hovering by the entrance. "I can't go in," Rose said when Audrey looked at her. "What am I supposed to say to her?"

Audrey glanced into the cafeteria and saw Olivia walking with Jen and María to their usual table. "Come on," she said, starting in the opposite direction. "Let's get out of here."

"You want to cut?" The sound of Rose's footsteps hurrying to keep up echoed in the halls. "Where are we going to go? How are we going to get out? We haven't planned enough for this."

True—the few times they'd ever cut school had taken detailed calculations, working out how to walk out without being stopped by the hawk-eyed monitors. But today Audrey felt reckless, and so she headed straight for the doors to the outside world with nothing but confidence. "Where are we going to go?" She stepped out into the bright winter day, throwing a hand up to shield her eyes against the sun, and she turned to watch Rose follow her out into freedom and smiled. "Wherever you want."

They got lunch from 7-Eleven—salt-and-vinegar chips, sprinkle-topped doughnuts, huge sodas—and drove around in Rose's car for a while, listening to the chirpy radio ads. Then Rose got an idea, and she took them across town to a modern building, glass front reflecting empty earth that Audrey was sure bloomed bright in the spring. Rose parked and led Audrey inside the dance studio, waving to the girl at the desk. "Hey, Fran," she said. "Are there any studios free?"

This Fran wound her hair into a bun and jammed a pencil through it before clicking something into the computer. "Basement A has a Pilates class finishing right about now," she said. "Wait. Shouldn't you be at school?"

"Maybe," Rose said. "Maybe not. You won't tell, right?"

Fran pursed her pink-lacquered lips. "All right," she said. "But you have to be out by Tap Three. And don't mess anything up."

Rose flashed a beaming smile at Audrey over her shoulder. "We won't," she said. "Thanks, Franny."

Audrey followed Rose through the maze of head shot–lined corridors, the occasional burst of music and yelling punctuating their movement. "Are we allowed to be here?" Audrey asked as they descended steep stairs.

"Senior dancers are allowed to use the space to practice whenever, really," Rose replied, pressing herself against the wall as a group of glowing middle-aged ladies filed past them. "It's fine. Trust me."

Trust me.

Audrey walked behind Rose into the studio. Rose took off her shoes, and Audrey quickly did the same before sitting with her back to the tall mirrors. Being in the basement, there were no windows, but it was brightly lit with soft-yellow bulbs, and the gray-white floor felt smooth under her bare feet.

Rose lay down perpendicular to Audrey's feet and lifted one leg, her toes pointed straight at the ceiling. "It's so peaceful here," she said, flexing and pointing her foot again. "I could live in this place."

Audrey reached into her bag and took out her camera and her phone: two missed calls from Julian and a text from Olivia. She put it facedown on the floor without reading the messages and cleared her throat. "Olivia texted me."

Silence from Rose, except for the sound of her jeans brushing together as she switched legs.

Audrey leaned back on her hands and shook her head. "Rose, what happened last night? Whatever it is, you're not going to be able to avoid her. She's our friend."

More silence. But then Rose sat up, fixing her gaze on Audrey. "We got into a fight—"

"Because she wants you to meet her mom, right."

"No," Rose said, screwing her face up. "Because I'm a freak who doesn't know how to have regular human relationships."

Audrey shuffled closer, her hands slipping on the special floor. "Yes, you do," she said. "You have one with me."

Rose's laugh filled the room. "What, the one where I got so mad at you for keeping one secret—one huge, completely understandable secret—that I turned it into some kind of vendetta against you?"

"Right." Audrey gave a wry smile. "That one."

"I'm so sorry," Rose said, the words sudden and so full that Audrey could hear their heaviness. "I don't know what happened. I—"

"*I'm* sorry," Audrey said. "It's my fault. I shouldn't have kept all of it from you, but . . . I got so twisted up trying to figure out what to do and what I was feeling that the right time never came. And . . ." She pulled a loose curl out and twisted it tight around her finger, the skin on either side of it flushing and paling alternately. "You never seemed to want to know," she said, the honest truth. "You didn't want to know that I was pregnant, or that I was scared—scared of everything going on, and of what you would think of me if you knew how awful I really am. I felt like I needed you to be there for me, the way I always am for you, but . . . you weren't."

Rose's face crumpled for the briefest moment, but she pulled it back together and inhaled. "I hate it," she said. "I hate that I made you feel that way. I hate that I wasn't there for you. God, I—I don't know what to say, Audrey. I wish I was better. Better to you. I'm going to try. Okay? I want to be the best friend that you deserve." She looked at Audrey intently. "But I promise, you didn't have to be scared. What did you think I was going to say? Maybe I would have been shocked, sure, but that's not important. I would have been there for you, whatever you decided to do. I *will* be there for you," she corrected herself. "No matter what. I mean, what else am I going to do?"

"I don't know," Audrey said. "I didn't want you to think I was stupid or naive. And I guess I was worried you would be, like, disappointed in me."

"I'm not your mom." Rose laughed. "Disappointed? I mean, how self-righteous would I have to be? I'm hardly the poster child for good decision making."

She reached across and flicked Audrey's knee. "You got pregnant. This shit happens. Statistically it was bound to happen to one of us! You just got lucky."

"Ha! Sure," Audrey said. "Lucky's exactly what I'd call it."

"And hey"—Rose sounded suddenly annoyed—"you are *not* awful. Why would you even think that?"

Audrey shrugged, her cheeks warm. "I don't know. I have done a lot of awful things these past few weeks. You should have heard the things I said to my mom. . . ." She shook her head. "She hates me right now."

"Your mom does not *hate* you," Rose said. "Don't be ridiculous.

And did you forget last night? You called me even though we weren't talking. If you were really awful, you would have straight up ignored me, right?"

"Maybe," Audrey said. "I guess." She had gone to Rose immediately, she supposed. And all she had wanted in that moment on the stoop, holding Rose while she cried, had been to make whatever was hurting her go away.

Maybe I'm not completely awful, Audrey thought, a little glimmer of hope. *I can be good. I* can.

"Have you figured out what you're going to do yet?"

Audrey threaded her wrist through the camera strap and pointed it at Rose. "Yeah," she said. "I'm getting an abortion."

The little Rose in the viewfinder nodded. "You know Katie Legrand? She's a senior; she dances here, too—she had an abortion a couple years ago. She said it wasn't as bad as she thought." Miniature-Rose tipped her head back. "Maybe you could talk to her, so you know what it'll be like."

"Maybe," Audrey said. "I think it'll be fine, though. I've thought about it, and thought about it, and *thought* about it, and this is what I want to do."

Rose raised her eyebrows. "Julian?"

"It's what he wants, too," Audrey said. "We both have so much we want to do. His music, my art. This way we get to do it."

Rose pulled her knees up and placed her palms on them. "Right," she said. "Good plan."

Audrey lowered the camera. "It's scary, though. Not the abortion and everything, I just . . . I've spent so much time thinking about the future lately. Now I feel more unsure about it than before. It's like I kept thinking that being pregnant meant no art school, maybe no more photography at all. But I realized that maybe I won't get into any art schools at all, baby or no. I don't know if I'm ever going to be good enough to be an actual artist."

Rose tipped her head to the side. "You know you can just *be* an artist, right? You make art. Therefore, you are an artist. You don't need anyone to give you permission."

"I know, but—"

"And maybe you won't get into RISD or any of the other places, but who gives a shit? Maybe I'll never be a principal dancer anywhere. I can still dance, though. It's not the end of the world."

Audrey let out a breathy laugh. "That's what my mom said. When I told her I was pregnant. *It's not the end of the world.*"

"Then you know it's true," Rose said.

It's not the end of the world. She'd never thought she'd be pregnant, but she was, and she was still breathing. If she didn't get acceptance letters next year—well, it would suck, but Rose was right. She didn't need permission to take pictures. Who was going to stop her? Nobody.

"Right," Audrey said, hooking a curl behind her ear. "So now we've covered me, can we get back to you?"

Footsteps thundered above them and Audrey looked up, half expecting the ceiling to begin collapsing. "Preschool ballet," Rose said, and when Audrey looked confused, she laughed. "I know. Who would think such tiny kids could make so much noise?"

"Huh," Audrey said. "Not me." And then she said, "About you and Coop. I shouldn't have used it to hurt you. I was only jealous, I think. That you didn't tell me. I didn't mean to judge you or anything."

"I know you didn't," Rose said with a small smile. "You never do. And, y'know, it was Halloween. You weren't there, my parents were gone. Nothing was happening with Olivia yet. I was lonely, and Coop listened to me, and he made me laugh." She laughed. "He's a good friend, really. Who knew?" Then she looked at Audrey. "Does everyone know? Am I, like, the bi girl who'll sleep with anybody now?"

"No," Audrey said, narrowing her eyes. "And I'll kick anyone's ass who says shit about you."

Rose stood then and walked to the ballet barre, placing one hand on it with a delicacy that Audrey rarely saw Rose exhibit. "I really like Olivia, you know." She stared away from Audrey. "Yeah, she's hot, and that was the beginning of it all. But she's so . . . nice. To me. For no reason."

Audrey rested her chin in her hand as she watched Rose position her feet just so. "Rose, people don't need a reason to be nice."

"No, but usually they have one anyway. They want something, you know? Not you, obviously, or the others. Cooper or Julian. But everybody else, everyone who thinks I'm their friend because they shot the shit with me outside chem class once—those people. For some reason I can't work out, I've become this girl people think they know." She bent and rolled up the bottoms of her jeans, her words quieted in her folded-over position. "But Olivia isn't one of those people. They want something from me. Olivia doesn't want anything *but* me. She looks at me and it's like she's only seeing what I hide from everybody else."

"That's good," Audrey said. "Or no?"

A moment's pause, and then Rose spoke. "Yeah, it's good," Rose said. "But then comes my inability to act like a human again. Because she said she wanted me to have dinner with her mom, and you know me—I don't do parents."

"What's so wrong with parents?" Audrey asked. "Okay, I know yours aren't the best example, but—you love my mom. And you've even met Olivia's mom before, at the mall that time."

"Right." Rose set her feet again and put her hand in front of her hip, and she looked so tall and strong standing like that, Audrey couldn't help but smile. "But I didn't know, then."

"Didn't know what?"

"About Olivia," Rose said, sweeping her arm high above her head. "That I could, like . . . love her, maybe. I don't know. Be more than a hookup. I'm not saying that I *do* love her, but . . . maybe I could."

Audrey marveled at these words coming from Rose, but she didn't want to make a big, scary deal of it, and she kept her voice level. "Okay." Audrey took her camera and snapped one shot of Rose like that, reaching, reaching. "That's amazing, Rose. Doesn't that feel amazing to you? Here you have this girl who you might be falling in love with. Doesn't that feel incredible?"

"Not at all," Rose said, and she turned away from the barre, deflating. "Because, think about it, Audrey. Think about me. The one person I might have loved before dumped me without a second thought. I don't know the last time I had a real conversation with my parents. I don't know how to do anything like this. So—"

She rushed over to Audrey and sank to her knees, almost alarmingly close—close enough for Audrey to see the flecks of green in her hazel eyes, to smell the perfume borrowed from Audrey's vanity. "So Olivia's all excited about this whole thing, us being a couple, and—I'm in her room, okay? Her mom's going to be home any minute. I'm in her room, on her bed, and we've been . . . fooling around, doing things. Having sex? I don't know, maybe." Her cheeks flushed pink, and she shook her head. "But we don't have much time, her mom's going to be home soon and we're getting ourselves together now and all I can think is 'Doesn't she want me to leave?' Aisha always made me feel like she had somewhere better to be whenever we were together. I guess Cooper might have been different, but I didn't give him the chance to show me. I've never done this before—I've never had anyone want me to stay. To eat dinner with their *mom*. But Olivia wanted that. She wanted to talk to me about nothing and everything, she wanted me to stay, she wanted to hold my hand—" Rose broke off suddenly, and the pain was palpable, sharp in the air. "I know I'm such a cliché, but it really did scare me. It scared the shit out of me. I'm looking at her and thinking that I'm going to do something to ruin this sooner or later, and I can't stand the thought of hurting her. I always ruin things."

Audrey stared at Rose for a long moment, searching her face. "Yeah," she finally said. "And if you always give yourself the excuse to, you'll keep doing it. Rose, you don't have to be this hard on yourself! No one's expecting you to be perfect. You say, 'Olivia, I've never done this before, and I don't want to mess up. Can you help me?'"

Rose closed her eyes "Easy," she said, that one word dripping with disdain.

Audrey threw her hands up. "So what if it's not?" She raised her voice. "If you don't talk to people, things get way harder. Haven't we just learned that?"

Rose opened her eyes. "You're the only person I have," she said again, sounding so sad. "My parents are always gone. They've always been gone, and they always will be, even when they're here. And Gia left; she's never coming back. I wouldn't if I were her. And that made you my only person, but then you started disappearing, too, and Olivia was there. I just . . . I fell full force into her. Now I've ruined that, too, and I don't have anybody."

"You'll always have me," Audrey said, insistent. "Even if we didn't talk for ten years, I'd still be your person. You'd still be mine." She remembered Rose's words from their fight: *There's about to be a whole other thing—a whole other* person—*for you to leave me behind for.* "And even if I were going to have this baby, it would not take me away from you. You know that, right? I wouldn't let it happen." She shrugged one shoulder. "Yeah, things would have changed. But things *are* going to change; they always do. *We're* going to change. But we're never going to leave each other behind. Come on—who else would have us?"

"No one knows me the way you do," Rose said quietly, maybe agreeing. "You're my better half."

"Not better," Audrey said. "You're no worse than me. We're both figuring shit out. Maybe you just need a little more help in certain areas."

Rose looked down at her hands, rubbing one thumb in circles on the palm of her other hand. "She was so mad," she said quietly. "She knew. I got up and was trying to find my shoes, and I'm saying I can't stay for dinner, I have to go, I have homework and I might be busy next weekend, and she started yelling at me. Completely calling me on it all, saying . . . God, everything. 'Don't run away.'" Rose exhaled. "'Walking away from me doesn't mean this is done. At least respect me enough to tell me the truth instead of lying.'"

She looked at Audrey again. "We were over before we even started."

Without meaning to, Audrey laughed, hard, earning a glare from Rose. "I'm glad this is hilarious to you. Jesus, Audrey."

Audrey shook herself, pinching her thigh to stop her laughter. "I'm sorry," she said, the last gasps easing out. "But Rose. You two are not over."

Rose looked equal parts hopeful and confused. "We're not?"

"Not if she said . . . what was it? Oh, right: 'Walking away from me doesn't mean this is done.'" Audrey pressed her hand over her heart. "I think you're fighting, is all. And what have we just learned about fights?"

Now Rose looked even more confused. "That . . . they're bad?"

"That to *fix* them you need to *talk*," Audrey said slowly. "Right?"

"Right," Rose said. "But—what, I'm supposed to just . . . say sorry? But she's so pissed."

"Yeah, and that's the point of apologizing." Audrey grabbed her things and jumped to her feet, holding out her hand to Rose expectantly. "I'll help you. It's going to be okay, Rose," she said. "Trust me."

In the flower shop, the silver-haired owner wanted to know what the flowers were for. "Lilies are traditionally a mourning flower," he said, watching Rose touch a vibrant green leaf. "But I like them in all arrangements."

Audrey touched the petal of a pink bloom. "What's good for saying sorry?"

"Roses."

They looked at each other and laughed. "We'll skip those," Rose said. "What about carnations? I like them."

Audrey waited at the counter as Rose and the owner put together a bunch of plump white carnations, pale-purple irises, and yellow daisy-like things. He wrapped the whole bunch in blue paper and tied a slippery pink ribbon around it. "Give them plenty of water," he said after Rose had paid, handing them over with a smile. "And whoever they're for, good luck."

They got back to school a little after the final bell, and the parking lot was half empty but scattered with people walking out. Audrey scanned for Olivia's blue hair, the neon hightops. "There she is." She grabbed Rose's arm and pointed toward the bus stop where Olivia was waiting. "Now go get her."

Rose bounced on the balls of her feet. "One more time?" she said.

Audrey gave a sigh, but not an annoyed one. "You say sorry," she told Rose again. "You give her the flowers, and you say sorry again, and then you explain. You tell her the *truth*." She gave Rose an encouraging shove. "Go!"

Audrey hung back as Rose walked toward Olivia, clutching those pretty flowers. She was too far away to hear anything, but when Rose reached Olivia, Audrey saw as clear as anything the hesitation in Olivia's movements. "Come on," Audrey said under her breath. "You can do this, Rose. Come on."

It was hard to tell if it was going well or not, but then Rose held out the flowers toward Olivia, and—after a long, tense moment—Olivia took them. Audrey clapped her hands together as Olivia reached for Rose, and then the flowers were crushed between them as they kissed, a long, sweet kiss, and Audrey's heart skipped.

"You did it," she whispered, and Rose broke away from Olivia, almost like she'd heard. Then she was looking directly at Audrey, her hands over her mouth, and Olivia turned, too, her face overtaken by this megawatt smile. She laughed—was it her imagination, or could Audrey really hear it carrying on the wind? It didn't really matter; all that mattered was that Rose had taken a big step and not fallen. But even if she had, Audrey would have been there to pick her back up. That was for sure.

THIRTY-SIX

Audrey was sitting in the kitchen drawing when the front door opened. She heard the telltale sounds of her mom's homecoming patterns: the clink of her keys in the glass bowl, the sigh of relief as her boots were unzipped, the similar soft exhale of the couch cushions in the living room.

Rose had been brave. Now it was her turn.

Audrey left her sketchbook open on the counter and walked on quiet feet through the hallway.

"Mom?" Audrey paused in the doorway and looked at her mom, sitting on the couch with one leg crossed over the other, exhaustion on her face. "Can I come in?"

Laura gave her a strange look before answering. "Sure."

Audrey wrung her hands together as she sat on the other couch. "Mom."

Now Laura gave an exasperated sigh. "What, Audrey?"

"I'm sorry," Audrey said suddenly, the words bursting out of her. "Mom, I'm sorry, I am. I'm so sorry for all those things I said, and the way I've been acting and I hate you being mad at me but you have every right to be, I know that—" She stopped to take a gulping breath of air as her mom turned to look at her, really look at her for the first time in days. "I'm sorry."

It was as if time stopped for a moment and they were left waiting, stuck in suspended animation. Like the moment at the top of a coin toss when which side it would fall on was still unknown.

Laura moved first, her mouth curving into a smile that didn't reach her eyes but seemed thawed from the ice Audrey had so recently become used to. "I know," she said softly. "You always are."

"I . . ." Audrey didn't quite get what that was supposed to mean. "Okay."

"You did hurt my feelings." Laura sat there, pulling the charm on the long chain around her neck back and forth, back and forth. "When you said I didn't understand."

Audrey's entire body flooded with shame. *I really did say that, didn't I?*

"I know I didn't give birth to you," her mom said now. "I haven't ever been pregnant, that much is true. But you are my *child*, Audrey. The only one I'll ever have. And I feel what you feel. I raised you and I took care of you—I take care of you because I love you and you are the light of my life. I know I wasn't the one who made you, but—"

"You made me," Audrey interrupted, her eyes hot. "Anyone can make a baby. Me and Julian made a baby, for God's sake." Her mom gave a wry nod at that. "You're the one who taught me how to do *every-thing,* and you never yell at me, and . . . somebody else chose you to be my mom because they thought you'd be amazing at it, and you are, you *are.*"

She closed her eyes, squeezed them tight as she began to cry, and then her mom was in front of her; Audrey could feel her there. "Audrey," Laura said softly. "It's okay, baby. We had a fight. It's not the end of the world."

"Do you think—" Audrey hiccupped the words, opening her eyes to see her mom standing there, that familiar tilt of her head. "Do you think I'm a bad person?"

"Love." Laura put her chin in her hands and smiled, and her eyes were wet, too. "You are one of the best people I know. You are kind, and generous, and you love with everything you have in you, even when it hurts you. You have changed my life in ways I could not have ever, ever imagined—sometimes I think about Before Audrey times and it's as if I'm looking at a stranger's memories."

She leaned in and grasped Audrey's hands, holding them tight. "So no, darling child. I don't think you're a bad person. I think you're a very, very good person."

"Even if—" She swallowed. "Even if I don't want to have a baby?"

"Yes. Even if you don't want to have a baby," her mom said imme-diately, earnestly. "I love you whatever you do. Whatever you decide to do." She paused for a second. "Is it—is that what you've decided?"

"I don't—" Audrey cut herself off. "No, I *do* know. Yeah, that is what I've decided. I can't go through with it."

There. It was out, again.

It wasn't like when she'd told her mom and Adam that she was pregnant—she didn't get that lifted-weight feeling, that beautiful moment of pure relief. Audrey wasn't sure whether it was because of everything that had already happened in the past day, that perhaps she didn't have the capacity to feel more momentous emotions right now, or if there was something else wrong with her. Maybe this was her brain's way of protecting her.

Actually, Audrey realized, it was nice not to have her heart tossing around in a wild ocean of feelings. To be sailing steady, for once.

"It's not right," she said, her head shaking slowly. "I don't want to . . . be a mother right now. I want to be me. You know?"

Her mom nodded once, and the chains around her neck chimed quietly. "Okay."

"Okay?" Audrey repeated. *Is that it? Is it this easy?* "Are you— you're not mad at me, right?"

Laura pulled a hand through her long hair and smiled so widely that her one slightly crooked tooth showed. "Why are you *always* asking me that? I'm not mad at you, love. Come here."

Audrey took the hand Laura reached out. "Listen to me," Laura said. "There are times I'm mad at you. When you leave your dishes in the sink because you can't be bothered to empty the dishwasher. When you borrow my shoes without asking first. When you eat the last slice of cheesecake that I've been saving for when I really need it. Okay?" She laughed. "Those are the things you do that piss me off. Things like this—life things, big things? I could never be mad at you as long as you're doing what you think is right and taking care of yourself along the way. Do you get that?"

"I thought maybe . . ." Audrey paused. Sitting this close to her mom felt like childhood: the scent of Laura's darkly sweet perfume and the tickle of her hair against Audrey's cheek. "You wanted a baby so bad, and here I am getting rid of my chance at that."

"Oh, baby." Laura's arm tightened around Audrey's shoulder. "This doesn't have anything to do with me. It's your life. And you'll have other chances, when you're older, if that's what you want. I don't want anything for you other than what you want for yourself, what you think will make you the happiest you can be. And I am so proud of you for making this decision for yourself. Do you understand me?"

Audrey almost burst open with all the things she wanted to say, but none of them seemed right to set free at this exact moment in time.

So instead she twisted and wrapped her arms around her mom, burying her face in the soft silk of her blouse, and that was enough.

THIRTY-SEVEN

C'mere, Marmalade." Audrey patted the bed next to her, and the cat jumped up, digging his paws into her thighs. "Good boy."

The phone rang in her ear, and she burrowed down under the covers, one hand scratching through Marmalade's soft fur. It was late, again—Adam had come home with the makings of pork dumplings, a dinner Audrey always played sous-chef for. Now she was dead tired, but in that pleasing, almost hypnotic way: getting everything out in the open had been emotionally draining, but now she felt good. Fresh and new.

The phone rang for so long that when Julian finally answered, Audrey had slipped almost completely horizontal. "Hey," he said, and his voice sent comfort rushing through Audrey's bones. "One sec, I'm leaving Izzy's."

The sound of his footsteps echoed down the line, and then a

crunching noise, and then a slam that had to be his car door closing. "All right," he said. "Hi, Rapscallion."

"What?"

"You and Rose, *Thelma-and-Louise*-ing it out of school today. Yeah, I figured it out. I'm a supersleuth."

"Oh, that." Audrey rolled onto her side. "I would have told you, but then you would have been an accomplice, right? It was for your own good."

Julian laughed. "Sure. So . . . you two have made up, then? You're not fighting anymore?"

The cautious relief in his voice made Audrey smile. "No, we're not fighting anymore," she said. "We made up. So you don't have to walk on eggshells or whatever."

"Thank God," he said. "You're so much harder to handle when you're not good with her."

"Hey!"

"I'm just saying, it's nice to know I won't have to mediate or anything."

"Like you would ever," Audrey said.

"And this means you've . . . told her, right?" Julian asked. "Everything?"

Audrey dug her toes into the sheets. "She knows. It's okay. We're okay." And they were. Maybe over these past couple of months it hadn't been that way, but times had been hard, for both of them. They had needed secrets to be kept and lies to be told. But in the end, they'd given each other the truth. That was what counted.

Shit. "Speaking of . . ."

"What?" Julian said. "What did you do?"

Audrey cleared her throat. "I told my mom about the abortion."

"Wait," Julian said. "Already? Without me?"

"Yeah. I know, I'm sorry. I should have waited to tell her with you. Are you mad?"

"Totally," Julian said. "I am *so* mad. I can't believe I didn't get the chance to tell my girlfriend's mom that her daughter, who I knocked up, is getting an abortion! And I was *really* looking forward to that."

"Shut up." Audrey laughed. "Okay, I get it."

Julian went quiet then. "Are you mad at me?"

"No. What for? You haven't done anything."

"You wouldn't have to be getting an abortion if it wasn't for me. You wouldn't be pregnant if it wasn't for me."

"Well, duh," Audrey said. "It's not like I can have sex with myself and put a baby in me." She frowned in the darkness when Julian didn't laugh. "It took both of us, you know. I seem to remember always wanting it the exact same as you did. And hey—we played by the rules. We were safe. It's not *our* fault the birth control didn't work."

She listened carefully, to the sound of Julian's breathing and what she would have bet any money was him drumming on the dash. "Still," he said eventually. "I feel like it is my fault. You're the one it's happening to—I get to stand on the sidelines and act like it's as hard for me as it is for you, but we both know it's not. So you can be mad at me if you want."

"I'm not mad at you. And I don't want to be," Audrey said. "But I will be if you keep telling me to, I swear to God."

"Do you think things are going to be different between us now?"

Audrey heard the nervous rasp in his voice, and oh, did she wish she were with him, that she could tiptoe her fingers across his lips and tell him not to be so ridiculous. That things weren't going to be any different and he was crazy for even thinking it.

But part of her worried the same way: What was going to happen to them in a month, when this was all behind them? Would they fall back into their same comfortable patterns, or would they be too changed to do that? Even if they did, they still had the future to face: college and moving across the country and growing up. *Honestly,* Audrey realized, *I have no idea what's going to happen with us. I only know what I want us to be.*

So that was what she told him. "Who knows if we're going to make it?" Audrey wrapped her arm around herself, conscious of the slow thump of her heart. "I like to think so. Because I'm real-deal, bottom-of-my-bones in love with you, and there's no way I'd let you go without a dirty fight first."

"You fight dirty, huh?" Julian said, and Audrey could hear his smile in his words. "That I'd like to see."

"Maybe one day I'll show you," Audrey said. "But until then, it's you and me. You got that?"

He laughed. "I got it, Aud. You and me," he echoed.

THIRTY-EIGHT

Audrey stood across the street from Bettie's, watching Jen and María messing around at the counter, blowing straw papers at each other. She hadn't anticipated being so nervous about doing this—hadn't she said all along that once Rose knew, she'd tell them? They were her friends. They'd be on her side.

Of course, Audrey thought. *Stop being ridiculous.*

She'd worried about what Rose would think, before. And now that nagging part of her brain had started up again, except this time it had focused on Jen. Jen, who hung out most Sundays at church and actually prayed for people when she said she was going to. Not that it meant anything—just because Jen believed in God didn't mean she wouldn't want Audrey to do this.

It doesn't, Audrey told herself. *This is Jen. These are your friends. Relax.*

Easier said than done.

"What are you doing?" Rose walked up hand in hand with Olivia, a puzzled look on her face. "You know you have to go in there, right? They don't bring the food out to you."

"You're hysterical," Audrey said flatly. "I'm—waiting."

"What for?" Olivia let go of Rose's hand and rounded Audrey to stand beside her. She stamped her boots on the slushy sidewalk. "It's freezing."

"Sorry," Audrey said. "Let's go."

She followed Rose across the street and inside, over to the corner table Jen and María had now moved to. "Oh, hey," María said on seeing them. "There you are! We've been waiting."

"We already ordered," Jen said. "Are you getting anything?"

Audrey cleared her suddenly dry throat. "I'll just get a soda," she said. "I'm not hungry."

"We'll get it," Rose said. "Coke?"

Audrey nodded, and sat as Rose and Olivia went up to order. "Aren't they so cute?" Jen sighed. "I'm so jealous."

Audrey didn't have to look to agree with Jen. Olivia and Rose were cute in all their touchy-feely, starry-eyed infatuation, and Audrey was heart-burstingly happy for the two of them. For Rose, mostly—she deserved someone exactly like Olivia. Kind and smart and strong-willed; a girl who wouldn't take any of Rose's shit.

"I'm happy for them," María said, echoing Audrey's thoughts. "And I'm even happier that you and Rose made up. I don't know what was going on with the two of you, but thank God it's over."

Audrey scrunched up her face, embarrassed. "Don't," she said. "I feel so stupid now. And also, I'm sorry. For being a bitch to you both."

María pulled her hair into a knot and stared at Audrey over the top of her glasses. "Apology accepted," she said. "Bitch."

"I have to ask." Jen spread her hands flat on the table and leaned far over it, her hair swinging. "*What* exactly happened? It's been driving me crazy trying to figure it out."

Audrey took a deep breath as Olivia and Rose rejoined them, setting down drinks. She'd been psyching herself up for this moment all day, and now it was here, and now she was going to do it.

Olivia passed Audrey a straw, and her eyes narrowed. "Audrey, what's wrong?"

"Wait," Rose said quietly.

Audrey pulled in another long breath and let it out slowly. "So, me and Rose were fighting," she said, and she was aware of everyone but Rose staring at her, a mixture of confusion and curiosity on their faces. "Yeah. I guess it started because . . . I was keeping this secret. I didn't really mean to, but it happened that way. And I'm still keeping it, really. You know, the rest of it doesn't really matter, because it all started from this one thing and I want to . . ." She paused. "Well. I'm pregnant."

No one spoke; the only noise was the scraping of María's chair as she shot back. And then: "Holy shit," María said. "Shut up. That's not funny, Aud."

Audrey raised her shoulders and tried to smile. "I'm not trying to be funny."

"Wait," Jen said in a hushed tone. "So you're for real pregnant? Rose! You knew?"

"A little," Rose said, and at the accusatory look María shot her, Rose pointed at Olivia. "She knew, too!"

"Quiet," Audrey said, holding out her hands. "Look, it doesn't matter who knew what when. Now you all know." She lowered her voice even more and plowed ahead before she lost momentum. "And you can also all know that we're not—I'm not keeping it. I'm going to go to the clinic and get it all taken care of. Okay?"

"Holy *shit*," María said again. "So that's why you've been so weird lately."

Jen twisted the end of her ponytail around her finger. "You're getting an abortion?" she asked, a curious lift to her eyebrows.

Audrey nodded firmly, focusing somewhere to the left of Jen. "Yes," she said, and the certainty felt good. "It's what we decided is best for us. Me and Julian."

"Good," Olivia said. "I mean, not good, but—no, actually, yeah. That is what I mean. I'm glad you've worked it out."

"He's not making you do it, is he? Because if he is . . ." María sliced a finger across her throat.

Rose waved the suggestion off. "Don't be stupid. It's Julian. He would never." She smiled across at Audrey, her eyes narrowing. "He knows I'd kill him in his sleep."

"Sure." Audrey managed to force out a small laugh. "And no, he's not making me do anything. Like I said, it's what we decided, together."

"Huh," María said. "Okay."

A silence descended, and Audrey busied herself drinking down half her soda. Silently, she marveled at precisely how different she didn't feel right now. Like admitting it wasn't any big deal to the others—just another piece of information about her that they needed to file away. It was kind of incredible.

The silence was broken by the arrival of food: burgers and mozzarella sticks and baskets of fries that triggered a growling in Audrey's stomach.

The interruption pushed them out of the slightly awkward silence, and María nudged her fries toward Audrey. "Have some if you want," she said. "How much did you spend on pregnancy tests? I bet you got the fancy kind," she said, poking Audrey's arm. "Did you know the scientific reliability of those is no more than the kind they give out in hospitals? They put fancy packaging on it, mark the price up, and make a killing. It's kind of genius."

"Great," Audrey said. "Well, I guess next time I'll keep that in mind."

Olivia reached for the ketchup. "You remember my friend Dylan? His cousin works at a clinic in the Bronx," she said. "She's nice. I don't think you have anything to be nervous about."

"Yeah," María said. "Mischa Cruz—she's in my government class—she got one last year. She said it went way faster than she thought it would. And I heard Katie Legrand did, too. They're both bomb chicks, like you."

"Mischa Cruz? Huh," Audrey said. "I never hear these things." Strange. How many girls did she know who had gone through the exact same thing as her—how many times had she sat next to someone in the library, thinking they were doing homework when really they were working out how much it would cost in gas money to get to the clinic and back?

Audrey glanced down the table. It hadn't escaped her notice that, aside from her initial reaction, Jen had yet to say anything. "Jen? You still with us?"

"Huh?" Jen seemed to shake herself back to the moment and then gave a tight smile that Audrey didn't buy for one second. "Yeah. It's . . . you're pregnant. And having an abortion." She took a deep breath and gave Audrey a bright smile. "That *is* a big secret. You could have told us."

"I know," Audrey said. Maybe she had been right to worry—maybe processing was going to take longer for Jen than for the others. Audrey hadn't really factored this in, one of them not being okay with it. Is that what this was—Jen being not okay with it? Or was she just reacting strangely? Audrey hoped for the latter, but she wasn't sure. "I'm sorry," Audrey said. "It's a weird thing to be dealing with, y'know?"

"Don't apologize," Jen said. "I get it."

"Mischa Cruz had one?" Rose said. "I thought she was, like, super-Catholic."

"People have their own definitions of their religion," Olivia said.

Jen nodded, that bright smile still shining "Everybody's different," she said. "And Mischa's cool."

Audrey pushed the worry aside. She was probably making a big deal out of nothing. "She is. It's kind of nice, actually," Audrey said.

"To know I'm not the only one. Not alone."

María's laugh rang out over the noise around them. "You're never going to be alone, Aud. And you're going to get through this and kick ass the way you always have. Know why?"

Rose spoke before Audrey could admit that, no, she didn't know. "Because she's Audrey." Rose reached across and laid her hand on top of Audrey's. "And Audrey Spencer is unstoppable. Right?"

Audrey looked up at Rose, at her friend watching her with nothing but love on her face, and she couldn't help smiling now. "Right," she said, her eyes stinging and her smile aching. "Unstoppable."

THIRTY-NINE

*D*r. Miller's green eyes stared piercingly at Audrey. They were bright in contrast to her creamy dark skin, almost glowing.

Audrey wondered if the doctor wore contacts. She had to, right? There was no way on earth that such emerald eyes could be real. Mostly, though, she thought it because Dr. Miller sort of scared her: she was supersmart, successful, impossibly put-together, and accepted no bullshit. So if Audrey could believe that one part of her was an enhancement of the truth, it made it a little less terrifying to be in her office.

Which was where she was now, sitting in one of the white chairs next to her mom, with Dr. Miller offering her usual cool smile on the other side of the desk.

"This is definitely what you've decided?" The doctor steepled her fingers together, her perfectly groomed eyebrows drawing together the tiniest amount.

Audrey nodded firmly and tapped her shoe against the leg of the chair. "Yes. I would like to have a termination."

"All right." Dr. Miller sat up straighter, and the overwrought concern slipped from her face. "Let's get the ball rolling."

"I have some concerns." Audrey's mom leaned in, a finger twisting a lock of hair around and around. "About the amount of time that's passed since—well, it's been a while since we found out Audrey was even pregnant. Is it going to be an issue?"

"Not at all," Dr. Miller said. "According to my notes, the pregnancy should be around twelve weeks along now. Of course that's a rough estimate, but even if we *were* off by, say, a month we're still well within the window when termination can happen. So there's no need to worry."

Laura exhaled. "Okay. Good."

They're talking about me like I'm not even here, Audrey noted. Normally that would have irritated her, but right now it was a relief to have somebody else taking charge, not to be the one making any decisions. *It's kind of nice.*

And then she thought: *Twelve weeks? Is that it?*

It felt like so much longer.

"Audrey, would you like me to talk you through the procedure?" Dr. Miller turned her smile up a fraction, from Committed to Supportive. "They'll take you through it at the clinic, too—" She looked back at Audrey's mom then. "Speaking of which, would you like me to get an appointment for you, or would you rather do that yourselves?"

It took Audrey a minute to realize that her mom was looking to her for the answer. Apparently it wasn't so easy to shrug off her responsibilities. "Um . . . I'll do it," Audrey said, and her mom looked pleased. "And I would like to hear about the, uh, procedure. Please."

Dr. Miller reached for a stack of papers on the side of her desk, the cluster of rings she wore on her left hand gleaming. "It's a pretty straightforward process," she started, flipping through the pages. "Quite quick, and you'll be given medication so it shouldn't be awfully painful. There will be some discomfort, and you may find it worsens during the recovery period, but it's nothing you won't be able to tolerate."

Outside the office's window snow fell. It wasn't enough to make Audrey hope for school to be canceled in the morning, but through the glow of the streetlights it looked postcard-pretty. She watched the thick flakes falling as Dr. Miller talked about speculums and stirrups, scraping and sucking. It kind of made her uterus sound like a cave that needed to be excavated.

At the end of the appointment Laura thanked Dr. Miller. "You've been so helpful."

"That's what I'm here for," the doctor said. "Audrey?"

She pulled her gaze away from the view outside. "Yes?"

"Is there anything else you'd like to know about? Any questions?"

Audrey had spent many nights on various websites, reading up on abortion until the early hours of the morning, and so she had enough information in her head to last a lifetime now. Some of it not so much information but the knowledge that certain sections of the country thought she was a coldhearted, soulless killer for the choice she was making. Which was such a fun thing to have in her mind.

What had Olivia said? *Fuck everybody else. It's all you.* Yeah, fuck those people. They could think whatever the hell they wanted, but in the end they didn't know her. They didn't get to make her feel like shit.

"Audrey?" the doctor repeated.

"No," Audrey said, louder than she'd intended. "I think I have everything I need. Thanks."

They walked through the fast-settling snow, leaving footprints that wove between the steps of other people rushing home from work and heading out for a midweek dinner. Audrey tried to fit her shoes into the gaps those others had left, failing mostly, and her mom walked ahead. After a minute Laura called back over her shoulder, "Come on, Audrey, Adam's making dinner."

"I'm coming." Audrey hurried to catch up and tucked her hands into her pocket. "Mom, can I ask you something?"

They turned into the street where they'd parked, and her mom glanced at her sideways. "Anything."

"How did you know adoption was the right thing for you?"

Laura stopped walking. "That's easy," she said with a smile. "I really wanted a baby. I was by myself. And I have thought all my life that adoption is this amazing thing, and so it was the only thing that made any sense to me."

"But weren't you scared?" Audrey shivered. "How did you *know*?"

Her mom's eyes creased at the edges, and she tipped her face back into the falling snow. "You can't know, Audrey. You can never be one hundred percent, totally, completely sure. And I'm not talking about this—" She waved her hand between the two of them, and in the vague direction of Audrey's stomach. "I mean in all of life. There's always going to be something you're scared about, and that's okay. Was I scared when I got you? Of course. Shitless!" She laughed. "Could I raise a daughter, all on my own? Could I, the whitest chick ever, raise this beautiful biracial girl? I took you home and put you in your crib, and God, those first few nights I remember standing over you and not believing that somebody thought I was the best thing for you. I would call up Grams, my friends, in the middle of the night and say, 'Why did I think I could do this? I'm an actor—you want me to cry on cue, I'll do it. Pretend to kill a person? I'll do it. But this? I don't know what I'm doing.' Which is— Nobody knows what they're doing when they have a baby, not really. I would wager that nobody really knows what they're doing in *anything*. Every parent every day is questioning their decisions, wondering if they should have . . . not let their kid eat Pop-Tarts for breakfast or stopped them from climbing trees and breaking bones, or given them more freedom. I think that kind of stuff all the time. Especially now—was I sending you the wrong message when I took you to get birth control pills? Is that what other people think? Do I *care* what other people think? How could I have failed you like this? Not just you, but her, too." Laura paused. "Your birth mother. She trusted me with you, because she thought I could do a better job than her, that you'd have a life she wanted for you. But here you are, seventeen, having to decide to get an abortion. I don't think that's what she wanted for you and so I feel guilty about that, too."

"But it has nothing to do with you," Audrey said. "It's not your fault. I'm so sorry I made you feel like that. I made this mess."

"Baby, you didn't *make* me feel anything," Laura said with a smile. "And don't worry about what I'm feeling. That's for me to work out, not you. But y'know, this is sometimes the way life goes. The whole world is full of people trying to get through, making the best of what they have, pretending like they have a plan and hoping they can pull it off. And there's no shame in that."

Laura stepped aside to let a brave cyclist rush past. "You make decisions that you think—that you hope—are the best thing for you in that moment, and that's all you can do. I made the decision to adopt. Your birth mother decided on me. You decided on art. And now you're deciding on this."

"I feel like . . ." Audrey pulled her hands out of her pockets so she could hold her hair out of her face, stop the biting wind blowing it into her mouth. "What if I have this abortion and then in ten years, fifteen years—what if I can't have kids then? Or what if I do this and I regret it or I change my mind?"

Her mom's face shifted then: she looked stern and the kind of imposing Audrey would never associate with her mom. "Listen to me," she said, grabbing for Audrey's hands. "Really think about this. Because it's your life, and you're in control. Do you think that's what's going to happen? That you're going to be . . . punished if you choose this way?"

"I don't know," Audrey said softly. "That's the problem."

"Or are you scared?" her mom asked. "Because fear can be a strange thing. It can do strange things to your mind. You have to see through that and remind yourself of your own truth. Getting you was the best thing that ever happened to me, and maybe it seems strange to say that what you're going through right now might be the best thing to happen to you, but it really might. You have your whole life ahead of you, Audrey. You have no idea what good things are going to happen." She stepped back and smiled wide, pulling Audrey toward the car. "And good things are going to happen for you, kid. I can feel it."

Audrey allowed herself a small smile as they got into the car and began the drive home. She closed her eyes as her mom drove, thinking about Laura's words ringing through her head.

Are you scared?

Yes, Audrey thought. *Yes, I am scared. But I hope that I'm doing the right thing.* She pressed her hands together. *No. I am doing the right thing. This baby isn't my baby,* the *baby. My baby is years away, when I'm older and wiser and hopefully happy. So I can make that baby happy, too. I know that. I know.*

They pulled up to a red light, and Audrey opened her eyes. She reached across the space between them and laid her hand on top of her mom's on the steering wheel, making Laura turn to look at her curiously. "Thank you."

"What for, love?"

"Nothing," Audrey smiled. *Everything.* "Thanks. That's all."

FORTY

When school finished on Friday, Audrey looked out from her hiding place by the stairs, watching Jen at her locker. Her red ponytail bounced as she heaved a bunch of textbooks inside before slamming it shut, and Audrey swallowed past the knot in her throat. She'd never felt weird with Jen before—they didn't really fight, only two-minute spats over stealing fries or being late for the movie. This feeling was so new to Audrey that she didn't know how to handle it. She hadn't known what to do the other day, watching Jen react to the news of her abortion with . . . uneasiness? Whatever it was that Jen had been feeling, it was definitely way less than positive. At first Audrey had thought she might have imagined it, turned it into a bigger thing than it was, but the past couple of days Jen had definitely seemed a little off with her. And Audrey had been trying not to let it get to her, because—what had her mom said? Right: she was decided on this. It was her life, and she was in control. It didn't matter what other people thought.

Audrey stepped out into the hall, filled with the usual leaving-school rush. It didn't matter what other people thought, no. Except that Jen wasn't other people. She was one of Audrey's best friends, and it *did* matter to her what Jen thought. She hadn't imagined that any of her friends wouldn't immediately support her. Arrogant? Maybe. Optimistic? Sure. But if things were reversed and Jen were the one all this was happening to, or if María decided to give up her MIT dream and join the circus, Audrey would throw everything she had behind them, no doubt. So it kind of hurt, now that she was realizing that something she'd taken for granted might not be true.

Jen was about to leave, hoisting her bag onto her shoulder, and it was now or never. Audrey pushed through the stream of people, watching as Jen joined them, and then reached a hand in her direction. "Jen! Wait!"

Jen turned sharply, that ponytail whipping around and almost taking out some short kid's eye. "Audrey?" She sounded more bemused than annoyed, but her eyes narrowed. "What's up?"

Audrey elbowed a linebacker-size kid out of her way and fell in with Jen. "Listen," she said. "Can we talk?"

Jen hesitated for a second—Audrey saw it in the twitch of her mouth—but then she nodded. "Okay."

"In here." Audrey grasped Jen's elbow and steered her into an empty classroom, the remnants of an algebra problem set smeared across the whiteboard. She made sure to shut the door before she chose a desk to sit on and pushed herself up, her feet resting on the chair. Then she focused on Jen, taking up the same position two desks down. "So."

"So," Jen repeated, and she tugged the sleeves of her sweater down over her hands. "What's up?"

"The other day," Audrey started, and then she clamped her mouth shut. No; she was sick of talking in circles around things after the past couple of months. She started over. "Jen, me getting this abortion—is this going to be a problem with us? With you?"

Jen's eyes widened. "No. Oh my God, Audrey, no, it's not. I mean . . ."

Audrey waited, but Jen didn't continue. "You mean what?"

"I mean, I hope not." Jen's voice was quiet, and she gave this almighty sigh before turning to face Audrey. "Look. It's your decision to make, your choice, and what I might happen to feel about it isn't your problem. Okay?"

"No! *Not* okay," Audrey said. "It's easy for you to say that, but if what you think I'm doing is wrong, then how is that not going to affect us?"

"It's not that I think it's wrong, but—I don't know, Audrey. I think it's that I can't feel like it's one hundred percent right. Abortion." Jen said the word carefully, as if she was afraid of it. "And I know that's terrible of me; it's supposed to be me cheering on women and their ability to do whatever they have to do, but . . ." She stopped, holding out her hands. "Okay, I'm not there yet. But one day I will be. I hope to be." She paused, her eyes narrowing as she looked at

Audrey. "Do you really think that I would let how I feel about it affect us, though? I could see it in your face the other day, when you were telling us. You didn't want to say it to me. That makes me feel like shit—I would never let what I believe change anything about our friendship. Would you?"

Audrey squeezed her shoulders to her ears. "I was worried that—I don't know. You would hate me. Think I'm wrong or whatever."

Jen rolled her eyes, a small smile on her face. "Audrey. You are not your abortion. Right? How I feel about that isn't about how I feel about *you*. I don't think you're wrong for choosing that. You know what you want to do, and I'm going to support you in whatever it is. You're one of my best, best friends." She laughed. "I'm not going to let this change anything about us."

"What if it does, though?" Audrey circled the snagged thread in her tights. "What if I come back afterward and I've had an abortion and you can't look at me the same?"

"Audrey, listen to me." Jen hopped off the desk and walked until she was in front of Audrey, staring her down. "Here's what I think. It's like . . . you don't believe God is real, and I do. You don't believe there's any such thing as fate, and I do. But do you ever make fun of me for that? Do you talk shit when I say that . . . God showed me a sign?"

"No."

"Right. So why am I going to be any different to you?"

"You're not."

"Okay, Audrey," Jen said, with a gentle shake of her head. "Now you're getting it. So . . ." She leaned back against the desk opposite, crossing her arms. "When are you going? Do you actually have an appointment?"

Audrey nodded. "Wednesday." At a clinic two towns away that Dr. Miller had directed them to, and all for the low, low price of a few hundred dollars. "It'll be fine."

"Is your mom going with you?"

"Yeah," Audrey said. "And Julian. A little family outing." She laughed, maybe a little too loud. "Sorry. I'm very weird right now."

"You're always weird," Jen said, and Audrey wanted to laugh again, but she kept it in.

Everything would be fine, soon enough. Right now was limbo, a different kind than before when she'd been going back and forth about the decision; now she was waiting for Wednesday to come and for it to be over. So she was trying to focus on other things instead—like how things between her and Rose were mostly back to normal, how Rose herself was mostly back to normal (sharply so). Now Audrey could text her in the middle of the night when she knew Rose was awake, could burrow her feet under Rose's legs when they sat on the couch in the way she knew Rose hated. Next week Julian's band was opening for a violin-playing, raspy-voiced girl María loved, and they were all going. Tomorrow Audrey had plans to clean up her room, maybe take a bag of clothes down to the Goodwill, and after that . . . well, she'd find something to do between school and sleep. Something to keep her as occupied as possible so that she wouldn't drive herself to distraction thinking about The Procedure (that was how she saw it in her head, capitalized and in big letters).

"You *are* going to be fine," Jen said. "It's like Rose said: you're the unstoppable Audrey Spencer. One day when you're properly recognized for your genius artistry—"

"Get real."

"—when everyone who is anyone knows your name, and you're living a beautiful life, you'll look back to now and be amazed this all happened."

Audrey exhaled slowly, feeling each beat of her heart vividly. "You really think so?" she asked. "Because I've been thinking about that. How one day this might be, like, a footnote in my life. But then I feel bad, because this is a big deal, right? It feels like if I forget this, then I'm a horrible person. And I've felt like that so much lately. I'm done with it."

"I don't think that makes you a horrible person," Jen said. "I think it makes you human. You know how there are those things that you think you'll never get over? They're such a big deal when you're going through it, and it feels like the end of the world that the person you like isn't interested or your friend told somebody a secret about you or your parents found out you got high and lost their shit. And when it's happening you can't imagine anything worse, but then it's a year later and you think, that person's not even worth my time. My friend made a mistake. My parents were only looking out for me. Know what I'm saying?"

Audrey looked at Jen, the gray afternoon light turning her blue eyes darker, full of wisdom. "Yeah," she said. "I get it." Maybe it was strange, to be thinking of a future so far ahead when she hadn't even made it through this moment yet, but for the past couple of months all she had felt was that even getting through it would be a miracle. And honestly, she was still scared and sometimes confused, and sometimes wondering how it was that her life had come to this point. But what Jen said was true. And one day she would look back on this with that fogginess that memory brought. At least, that was what she hoped.

And hope was a pretty powerful thing.

"Now." Jen smiled a real smile then, sweeping a lock of hair out of her eyes. "How about we go get doughnuts?"

Audrey laughed for real then, a sound full of relief. "Your foolproof cure for everything," she said, smiling. "Okay, let's go."

FORTY-ONE

ook relaxed," Audrey instructed. "Pretend I'm Sofia Coppola and
she's just yelled 'Action.'"

"You really have no idea how film sets work, do you?" Laura
laughed and pushed her hair out of her face. "Okay. Whenever you're
ready."

Audrey lifted her weighty camera and took two steps back on the
sidewalk, framing her mom in the viewfinder. Laura sat on the front
steps of their house in her winter coat and a huge white scarf, her hair
brilliant against it. This was the last set of photos she had to take for
the project that had finally crystallized in her mind: a series of portraits, a story of the people who had made her into the person she was
now, the person she might be in ten or twenty or thirty years.

She had let them choose where the pictures were taken. She'd
shot Adam in the house, sitting in front of his shelves of meticulously

organized design tomes. Julian in the music room at school, behind the piano, his hands a blur on the keys. For Rose, they'd gone back to the dance studio, and Audrey had shot what felt like a hundred frames of her sitting or dancing happily in front of the mirrors.

Laura had picked here, right in front of the house that they'd called home for ten years now, even though blustery snow was blowing. "Do you want me to move?" her mom asked. "Stay completely still?"

"You can move around some," Audrey said. "Or talk, that would be good. I know—tell me a story of something. Your favorite high school memory."

"Huh," Laura said. "Well, I only went to high school for that one year, when I wasn't working so much," she started. "The rest of the time was tutors on set. But that one year was strange, because I was starting to be known, and people thought it would be fun to have me hanging out with them. I went to a *lot* of parties that year."

Audrey shot as her mom talked, and exactly how stunning Laura was hit her all over again. Not because she had beautiful eyes or a nice smile or that rich, red hair. It was the happiness behind the smile, and love behind the eyes; that was where her beauty came from. She looked almost fairy tale–esque right now, that hair and her perfectly scattered freckles and red lipstick—the princess all grown up, Audrey thought. She still wondered at the differences between their looks, but she remembered that time when she was younger, when kids on the playground had teased her about it, how she'd cried to her mom later. And Laura had said that they didn't need to look alike to be mother and daughter, that there were plenty of kids who didn't look like their parents, some of them adopted and some of them not. "All that matters," she'd said, "is that we love each other."

Now it felt more like a game, noting their differences: holding the copper-brown of her arm next to her mom's always pale skin, mapping the irregularities of her freckles compared to Laura's uniform ones. Sure, they didn't look alike; they weren't so biologically linked. But what did that matter in the end?

Audrey watched her mom through the lens, trying to capture the effervescence of her smile. They stayed out as long as they could stand the cold. When Audrey's fingers felt frozen, she reluctantly put away the camera. "Okay," she said through chattering teeth. "That's enough."

Laura got to her feet, dusting snow from her legs. "I really like this idea," she said to Audrey. "If you need anything else, let me know. I hope they come out good."

"Me, too." Audrey smiled. Maybe they didn't look the same, but they had the same heart. That was all that mattered.

Later that evening, Audrey combed her fingers through her hair gently, teasing out her curls to their maximum volume. Her simply made-up face stared back in the mirror: mascara, a smudge of soft copper-gold highlighter on her cheeks, and a slick of plummy-red lipstick. Any minute María would be there to pick her up—they were going to hang out at Olivia's, watch movies, and talk over the parts they'd memorized long ago.

To go with her black dress she pulled on thick black tights, a pair of black boots, and the leather jacket handed down from her mom's grunge heyday—armor against the cold outside world. Five minutes until María would be there—that left her time to do something she'd been meaning to for quite a while.

"Mom?" Her boots clunked on the stairs as she ran down them, stopping outside the bathroom door. She tapped her knuckles three times. "You in there?"

"In here, honey." Her mom's voice came not from behind the bathroom door, but from across the hall in her and Adam's bedroom. "Are you looking for me?"

Audrey stuck her head around the bedroom door, covering her eyes. "You'd better be decent."

"I suppose that depends on your definition of decent."

"Mom, please." Audrey opened her eyes and breathed a sigh of relief at the sight of Laura sitting at her dressing table in a fluffy white robe, dabbing yellow moisturizer under her eyes. "Do you have a minute?"

"For you," her mom said, "always." She turned to face Audrey, smiling while she rubbed the cream into her flushed skin. She waited expectantly for Audrey to speak. "Honey?" Her mom's smile didn't drop, but her forehead creased as she moved on and began smoothing cream into her hands. "What is it?"

"Oh, yeah," Audrey said, and held out her left hand. In it was the now-crumpled and creased envelope that contained the letter from Amanda Darby. "I wanted to give you this."

Her mom stopped moving. "Is that . . . ?"

"Yeah." Audrey stepped forward, nodding in what she hoped was an encouraging way. "I thought you might want to read it."

She proffered the letter once more, waiting for her mom to make some move, to take it or stand up or something. But Laura sat there, staring at the envelope suspiciously until Audrey's hand began to shake from holding it out so long.

"Or not," Audrey said brightly, too brightly. "It's okay if you don't. It's not a big deal, I'll . . . I've read it, so I'll put it away somewhere. I only thought you might—"

"Yes," her mom said, snatching the letter out of her fingers. "I would like to read it. I wasn't sure you'd want me to or if you had even . . . That's not important." Laura took a deep breath and nodded. "Thanks, sweetie. Are you sure?"

Audrey lifted one shoulder and smiled. "It's kind of as much a letter to you as it is to me. And even if it wasn't, I would want you to read it."

Laura twisted the paper in her hands, looking down at it. "Well," she said finally. "That's very kind of you."

"'Very kind'?" Audrey laughed and placed her hands on her mom's shoulders, bending down so they were eye to eye. "How *very formal* of you!"

"Audrey!" Adam's yell rang up the stairs. "Your friends are here!"

Audrey smacked a kiss on her mom's forehead, leaving a smeared-lipstick print. "And that is my cue to leave. Have a nice evening, okay?"

"You too."

She hitched her bag onto her shoulder and had her hand on the doorknob when her mom called her name again. Audrey looked back. "Yeah?"

"You look beautiful," Laura said: "I love you, little hell-raiser."

Audrey tipped her head back and laughed. Hell-raiser? Yeah, right. "Love you, too, Mommy. Don't wait up."

FORTY-TWO

On Sunday night Audrey stood in her room with her hand-me-down camera balanced on the tripod that apparently only worked with fancy new cameras. Hopefully the duct tape–rubber band–ribbon tie method she'd rigged up would hold it in place, because she really needed this to work.

That thing about her mom being the last set of photos she'd needed was a lie. There was one more set she had to take.

Ever since her talk with Rose, and before, when Olivia had asked about it, Audrey had been thinking. She'd gone through all the many, many pictures on her computer, looked at the gallery tacked up on her wall, even searched around the various social media sites her friends were on, looking for any pictures that she appeared in.

Grand total: thirty-four.

Thirty-four! Out of the past five years of photographs, out of dozens of parties and dinners and school events, there were only thirty-four pictures of her.

And that had got her to thinking that it wasn't fair. *It's not fair at all. Here I am, asking people to lay themselves bare in front of me for the sake of my "art," or because I want a tangible reminder of a moment, or . . . because I can. Because it's my instinct now, when I see something that hits me a certain way, to pick up my camera and freeze it for myself. But I won't do the same?*

Audrey attached the shutter cord and moved backward, so that she was standing against the far wall. Underneath her feet she felt the tremors from Adam's music as he made dinner. Her mom was in the bathtub with a glass of wine and a cupcake that Audrey had slipped around the door a little while ago. Things were pretty much business as usual at the Spencer-Price household. Okay, except for the fact that their morning conversations now included phrases like "general anesthesia" and "routine procedure" and that in a few days she had an appointment at a clinic two towns away to end her pregnancy.

Other than that, yeah—completely normal.

Audrey shook her head to clear it. Her mind kept wandering off on these tangents, which would be all well and good if she didn't know she was only doing it to avoid the weirdness that was taking her own photograph.

How hard can it be? she thought. *People do it all the time. Selfie much?*

"Get over yourself," Audrey said out loud, focusing on the camera's lens staring at her. "I can do this. I'm going to do this. Any . . . second . . . *now*."

On *now* she squeezed the button clasped in her left hand, which set off a flash so bright her eyes stung and a click so familiar that she reflexively relaxed.

It still felt strange, though, a slightly alien experience to be the one fully in the frame as opposed to the one creating it. Audrey turned to the left, leaving her focus on the lens, and squeezed again. *Click.*

She ran back to the camera and pressed her eye to it, checking the framing. The thing with digital cameras was that you could see what you were doing wrong and fix it right away: tighten on some particular aspect, adjust the shutter speed, fix the focus. It was good because you were learning all along, constantly seeing and changing and moving, but using her old camera felt surprisingly freeing. You didn't know whether what you were doing was total crap or complete genius, and you wouldn't find out until the images came to life in the acetic acid.

Confident that she was at least getting her head and shoulders in the shot, Audrey went back to her spot and peeled off her shirt. She paused for a second, then removed her bra, too. Her body wasn't in the shot, so it wasn't like anyone was going to see, and the images would look so much better without bra straps cutting into her shoulders.

Click.

With each shot Audrey opened up a little. Tension easing from her neck, fog lifting from her head.

Click.

She turned in a slow circle, tilting her head this way and that, slipping her hands behind her neck and lifting her hair to expose the skin there. Raised her arms, pressed her fingers to her temples. Closed her eyes, turned; opened them, smiled.

Click. Click. Click.

When the *click* came without a flash, Audrey reloaded the film and started the whole process over again. This time, though, she stood closer to the camera, pushing herself despite how uncomfortable it made her.

They don't say "suffer for your art" for nothing, she thought.

Click.

FORTY-THREE

The day of the appointment dawned crystal clear and cold, one of those mornings when the sun high in the sky couldn't be trusted and deadly slick ice glittered underfoot.

They were supposed to leave at ten. At twenty after, Julian's car pulled up and he jumped out, breathless. "Sorry," he said. "Car died on Hampshire. I know, I know," he said when Audrey raised her eyebrows. "I'm sorry, okay?"

"Today? Really?" Audrey said quietly to him as her mom came outside, car keys in her hand.

"I said I'm sorry." Julian pushed his hair back. His mouth looked like he was trying to smile but failing, one corner lifted slightly. "Are you ready?"

Audrey slid a hand behind her neck and rubbed the tense muscles there. "I'm ready for it to be over."

"Morning, Julian," her mom said, her motorcycle boots shushing down the slush-covered steps. "Okay, Audrey. Let's go."

The drive passed quietly, the highway disappearing under the car and then bare-limbed trees waving a haunting welcome as the road turned narrow and winding. Eventually they passed inside the border of a town, and right there, sitting between a couple of generic-looking stores, was the clinic.

Audrey wouldn't have even known which building it was if not for the lone woman outside holding a sign that said, in crooked letters, SAVE YOUR SOUL SAVE YOUR BABY. "Is it wrong that I'm almost disappointed?" Julian said. "I was expecting a little more effort from the extremist side."

"It's a letdown," Audrey agreed, but she knew that they were both joking to ease the tension of the whole thing.

"Ignore it," Laura said, and her hand pressed into Audrey's back gently. "Come on, we're already late."

They hurried past the protester and into the clinic, where Audrey felt the atmosphere change. She couldn't put her finger on it—it was like half sterile hospital smell and half the feeling you get at the thought of a root canal, with an odd dash of spa serenity courtesy of the potpourri sitting on the waiting-room table. She walked up to the desk and gave her name to the woman sitting there. "Hi," she said. "I have an appointment."

Audrey sat on the table in a paper gown. The inside of her elbow was sore from the blood they'd taken and where the needle giving her sedation was placed, and her feet were cold even in the thick socks she had on.

The nurse—Hathaway, according to her name tag—pressed gently on Audrey's shoulder. "Lie back for me, hon."

The doctor and another guy—a doctor or a nurse, Audrey wasn't sure—bustled around her as she did as she was told and then put her feet up in the stirrups at the end of the bed. *Oh my God*, she thought, *they can see* everything. *This is so embarrassing.*

Then she remembered what she was there for and bit her lip so as not to laugh at her own ridiculousness. "All right, Audrey," the doctor said, and his voice was cheerful behind the surgical mask. "We're going to go ahead and get started. Are you comfortable?"

Audrey nodded, and the cap covering her hair rustled against the bed. "Yes."

"All right," he said again. "Let's get going."

"You can hold my hand if you want," Nurse Hathaway said. "And we can talk."

"Oh, we'll talk," the doctor said, and from his voice Audrey imagined him to be the kind of guy who'd always have a dollar for the tip jar, who laughed at his own jokes so hard the people around him couldn't help but laugh, too. "I'll let you know what's happening. And we can talk about anything you want—you like football?"

"My mom likes the Raiders," Audrey said, staring at the fluorescent lights above.

"Good choice," the doctor said. "They might make the playoffs this year. Okay, you're going to feel a little pressure."

When Audrey reached for the nurse's hand, it was already right there at her shoulder, and she squeezed this woman's fingers tight as the speculum was inserted. The doctor was true to his word—he talked through everything he was doing, the tube going into her uterus, the suction going on, the instrument that he was using to clear out any remaining cells.

Cells, Audrey repeated in her head. *Like I thought all along.*

The doctor also talked about his dog, asked Nurse Hathaway about her new puppy, asked Audrey if she had any pets.

"A cat," Audrey said, exhaling. "Marmalade."

"That's a good name," Nurse Hathaway said. "I like that."

Audrey hummed instead of replying. It didn't hurt so much—the sedation was taking care of that—but it was uncomfortable for sure. It was made better by the way the nurse kept rubbing her thumb across Audrey's knuckles. "You're doing great," the other doctor—or nurse—said, fiddling with a tray. "Almost over."

Audrey hummed again, loud enough so the buzzing of her own voice was the only sound in her head.

The doctor wheeled his chair back, and Audrey lifted her head at the sound of the wheels squeaking on the tiled floor. She could see that he was smiling by the crinkles around his eyes. "Okay," he said. "We're all done."

"It's finished?" Audrey let her head drop back, and the crash of relief almost shocked her with its intensity. That was it. There was not going to be a baby. She was not going to be a mother; Julian wasn't going to be a father. And she didn't have to worry about it anymore.

Life could go on.

She smiled.

After Audrey was wheeled into the recovery area and she'd sat in there for an hour that seemed like five minutes, she got dressed in her own clothes and was led out to the waiting room. Nurse Hathaway handed Audrey a bunch of pamphlets and a card with the contact details of the doctor who'd performed her D & C (letters Audrey would be glad not to think about for a while). "Remember, take it easy for the rest of today," she said. She had locs twisted into a side ponytail and the softest eyes Audrey had ever seen. "No heavy lifting, no exercise, no stress, okay?"

The doctor had said the same thing, as well as "No sex for at least two weeks, four being realistic—your body needs to heal. And of course, it doesn't have to happen after four weeks—whenever you feel ready, if you want to." Audrey had nodded without comment—she couldn't even think about that right now, but she'd filed the information away for future reference anyway.

Audrey winced as her stomach cramped again. Shit, that hurt. "No exercise? No problem."

Nurse Hathaway laughed, and Audrey could picture her as the kind of mom who'd gladly roll around in mud with her new puppy or climb up spindly trees to keep her kids happy. If she had kids, that was. "Well, that's all right, then. Remember to make that appointment with your doctor—that's important. And if you have any problems— you feel feverish, you're bleeding a lot, or if your period doesn't start up again within a couple months—call us."

Fever, bleeding, no period. Audrey filed that info away, too, and nodded. "Okay."

"Great! So." Nurse Hathaway slapped the paper file closed and gave Audrey a gentle smile. "You're all done. Do you have anybody with you?"

"My mom." Audrey turned to where Laura was waiting, biting her nails as she stared at a book. Julian sat rigidly upright next to her, drumming on his knees, much to the fascination of the toddler waiting with her mother across from him. "And my boyfriend."

"Good. You make sure they take care of you, all right?" Nurse Hathaway nodded, her locs bobbing, and Audrey felt a calm settling in. She was so, so glad they were both there with her. The other way would have been absolutely unbearable, and it made her ache to think that not everyone in her position had the same luck as she did.

The nurse patted the back of Audrey's hand. "Tell them you need ice cream and bad movies—doctor's orders."

Audrey managed to smile as another cramp attacked her body. "I will."

"Good girl," Nurse Hathaway said. "Take good care of yourself, too. You're going to be all right."

"I know," Audrey said, taking a step away from the nurse and toward her family. "Thanks. For everything."

She slept most of the drive home, in the back with her head on Julian's shoulder and a heat pack pressed to her abdomen. The cramping was killer, and her head felt like it was stuffed with cotton wool.

When they pulled up outside home it was beginning to get dark. Julian helped her up the front steps and into the hall until Audrey said, "I'm not going to break. You don't have to be quite so chivalrous." Which raised a smile from Julian, so that was good.

Adam hovered at the bottom of the second staircase, hopping from foot to foot. He began talking so quickly that it was hard for Audrey to keep up: Did she need him to get anything? Was she hungry? What about Thai for dinner? From her favorite place?

"Adam, babe." Laura's bracelets clinked as she pushed her hair back. "Let the girl breathe."

But Audrey placed her hands on his shoulders and rose up on tiptoe to kiss his (for once clean-shaven) cheek. "Thanks," she said, and Adam looked confused.

"For what?" he asked. "I didn't do anything."

"Oh," Audrey said, "yeah. You did." Then she looked at her mom. "Is it okay if I go upstairs? I'm kind of tired."

"Of course," her mom said, and she gave Julian this look that Audrey guessed she wasn't supposed to see. It was a treat-my-baby-with-delicate-hands look, an I'll-kill-you-if-you-screw-up-this-moment look. Which made Audrey happy: her mom was nothing if not fierce.

She took the stairs to her room slowly, almost weeping at the sight of her beautiful, familiar bed with the pillows scattered all over and fleece blankets to warm her feet on the bottom.

Then, curled up with Julian underneath the covers, she wept with something else. Sadness? Happiness? Mourning? Relief?

It was a mixture of all that, really, and she liked that Julian didn't try to soothe or quiet her, only rubbed the tense point between her shoulder blades while she breathed in his smell and cried harder.

"We made the right choice," he said later, when Audrey was all cried out and the sky outside was truly dark. "We did."

"I know," Audrey said, pressing her face into his chest.

And she'd know it when she woke up tomorrow, and in two weeks, and in a couple of years. Look at her birth mother—in the first letter she'd written to Audrey, everything had seemed tinged blue, pained in its sincerity, but in the second one the words had been filled with hope and happiness. Amanda Darby had a good life, now: a job and kids, a husband, a dog. If Amanda Darby could be happy, then so could Audrey. And more than that, she *should* be happy. Amanda had given Audrey the opportunity to do that, to have a mom who loved her so much even when Audrey didn't deserve it, who would make the world move to give Audrey everything she ever needed.

And maybe Audrey would grow up to be an artist, or maybe not. She could be a teacher or a mother or a person who tried to make the world a little brighter. She could do all those things because of what her mom did for her, what Amanda did for her, what she did for herself. Her life could go in ten thousand different directions, and all of them were right.

So tomorrow, and in two weeks, and in a couple of years, she'd be happy. That was a promise to herself that she'd do everything to keep.

FORTY-FOUR

When Audrey developed her rolls and rolls of film, she was pleased with the results. Her self-portraits made her the most nervous, but even they were okay. They were in focus, at least, and the angles had allowed her face to become the main point of each picture.

Since then she'd spent the entire week in art class shut away in the darkroom, messing around and experimenting with various ways of cropping and exposing and overlaying different images, the way she'd done a few months ago with her digital images. It was fun to have her hands *in* her pictures for once.

But the best part about the photographs, though—and also the hardest part—was the girl Audrey had captured in them.

Because it was her, and also not her. It looked like the girl she saw in the mirror every morning, with the slight gap between her front teeth and the brown skin that veered from deep autumn-leaves-brown to pale-sandy-gold depending on the time of the year and how much sun she'd gotten.

But this girl looked older than Audrey felt. The eyes had an intensity to them, even when they were looking past the camera or hidden away behind eyelids. Her back had more freckles mapping across it than Audrey's did—it must have, because surely Audrey would have noticed how every square inch of flesh, from her shoulders to the dip between her shoulder blades to the back of her neck, was speckled and dotted with flowering little marks. The cheekbones were more defined, the apples of those cheeks sweeter and plumper.

Mostly, though, it was the aura this girl projected: something strong and delicate at the same time, like glass, like ice. When Audrey looked in the mirror, she saw a young girl with bright eyes and a happy face. In these pictures she was knowing, older, wiser.

On the Tuesday before winter break the art studio hummed with energy and chatter. Everyone had put their best, or favorite, or most accomplished pieces on display, the way they did every year. The doughnut boxes on Ms. Fitz's desk were picked clean, and Ms. Fitz herself sat behind the desk, using her own camera to take pictures of everybody. *Art made of art*, Audrey thought.

Audrey had picked out her favorites of all her portraits and framed them before tacking them to a large piece of plywood, propping it up against the wall at the back of the room. They went in order: her mom, then Rose, and Adam before Julian. She'd picked one of her self-portraits to go last. And then, on either end, she had framed (copies) of the letters from Amanda Darby. The first one to the left of Laura's picture and the most recent one to the right of her own face. There it was: a timeline of her entire life so far.

Audrey did a circuit of the room and admired everyone's pieces, the weird and wacky, the classically clean, and tried not to notice the people pausing at her station. Reading the letters, looking at the pictures. She wasn't sure what she'd achieved with her photographs, if anything, but she liked them. *At least I managed to put something up,* she kept thinking. A few weeks ago she'd been unsure if she'd be able to keep this part of her life, and now here she was. Ms. Fitz hadn't said anything about them yet, which was good, because it meant that Audrey hadn't yet had to hear about her shortcomings. The longer she could put that off, the better.

Hovering around her display, she almost didn't notice when Olivia came to stand by her elbow, slowly taking in each photograph. "These are awesome," Olivia said. "I like mucho."

"Thank you." She paused, staring at the photo of herself. On the back of her right hand a thin, curving scar was visible, one that Audrey had completely stopped noticing over the years.

"I'm especially into this one." Olivia reached out, and Audrey was sure she was going to point at Rose's image, multiple versions of her laughing in the studio mirrors. But Olivia's hand veered off toward Audrey's self-portrait. "A picture of you! It's a miracle."

Audrey jabbed Olivia's hip. "Shut up," she said, and then she laughed self-consciously. "It doesn't even look like me."

"Are you kidding?" Olivia said. "Audrey, that's you."

Audrey folded her arms, sighing. "I know it's me, I took the pictures, I developed them, I *see* them. But . . . I don't look like myself. That's not what I look like in real life."

Olivia pointed at one in which Audrey stared off, fixated on some secret thing. "I know what you meant," Olivia said. "*That's you.* That is what you look like in real life." She put her hands on Audrey's shoulders and turned her so she couldn't avoid looking right at it. "You just didn't know it yet. And now you do."

"Ms. Lee makes an astute point."

Audrey jumped at the sound of Ms. Fitz's voice, and the teacher smiled so the edges of her eyes crinkled, the cat-flick eyeliner disappearing from sight. "Sorry," she said, sounding anything but. "I didn't mean to startle you."

Audrey unfolded her arms in the hope that it would make her look less wound up. "That's all right," she said. And then, without meaning to, she asked, "What do you think?"

"I think they're excellent," Ms. Fitz said without hesitation. "I think you've risen to the challenge and then some. You should be proud, Audrey."

Excellent? Wait—did Ms. Fitz actually say she did well, then? Did she imagine that?

Audrey couldn't contain it. "Really?" she said. "Seriously?"

Ms. Fitz laughed. "Yes, seriously. Audrey, don't be so hard on yourself. That's my job! And this time I'm telling you that you have really shown excellent growth. Not only have you told us a story here, but it's your story. Personal. People can connect to that. It's nice to know the artist behind the work."

"I . . ." Audrey faltered. "Thank you."

Ms. Fitz toyed with the thin silver chain around her neck, nodding along with everything Audrey said. "Don't thank me," she said. "You did this all yourself." She turned to scan Audrey's images, an intense focus on her face. "These images could tell a thousand different stories. That's the best kind of art, where the viewer can see the same image over and over and read something new every time. Can you see that?"

Audrey looked at her life laid out there, her face staring out. Maybe they did say something, and maybe she really *did* look like that. She didn't know how to reconcile those ideas with what was imprinted on her brain already. But she could try, at least.

"Yeah," she said, tasting the sweetness of sugar glaze and strawberry on her lips. "I think I do see."

FORTY-FIVE

Audrey pushed her bedroom door open with her toes, carrying the box of nail polish and pack of sour gummies and Marmalade in her arms. "I'm going to go full Basquiat on your nails."

Rose followed her in, laughing. "Yeah, I don't know what that means. I'm just going to assume it's good and let you do your thing."

"Philistine. Marmalade, go." Audrey shook her arms so the cat would jump to the floor, then set the snacks and polish on her bed. "What do you want to listen to?"

"Hmm . . ." Rose set down the sodas she was carrying and threw herself onto Audrey's bed. "Something with a beat. What's that group Julian's always going on about?"

"The Pharcyde?" Audrey leaned over her computer, scrolling through songs. "I got you."

Rose brandished a twisty straw, the pink plastic bent into a flamingo shape. "One day I'm going to learn about all the stuff you tell me I'm bad for not knowing. All these artists and whatever. Only because I'm getting real tired of that smug look you give me every time you go off about texture or Impressionism or Basquale."

"*Basquiat,*" Audrey said, sinking to the floor and crossing her legs. "Fine. But you know that means I'm going to do the same thing to you, and then *you* won't be able to roll your eyes when I forget the difference between third and fifth position, or what the fuck a shuffle ball change is."

"Don't you disrespect the fine art of tapping, Audrey Anne," Rose said. "The ghost of Ruby Keeler will haunt you in your nightmares."

"Ooh, I'm so scared," Audrey said teasingly. "What's she going to do, time step me to death?"

Rose tossed her head back laughing. "You don't even know what a time step is!"

"Not untrue." Audrey pulled the box of polish to the floor and began searching through the half-empty bottles: so many reds she'd lost count, purple glitter that stained like a bitch, a gold-flecked black her mom had given her last Christmas that was way too expensive for nail paint. "Come, sit. Watch me work my magic."

Rose did as she was told, mirroring Audrey's position on the floor. She spread her hands flat on the lid of the box, and Audrey set to work with a base coat. Rose never had the raggedy edges and chipped polish that Audrey sported, keeping her nails long and neatly pointed instead. Audrey's focus narrowed to Rose's nails, each one a tiny blank canvas waiting to be adorned. She applied an off-white color with slow, even strokes, occasionally kicking Rose's ankle when she kept moving to the music; when that was almost dry, she picked out an olive green and dipped one of her tiniest paintbrushes into the bottle "If you could live anywhere in the world," Audrey said, "where would you go?"

Rose's hands twitched, and Audrey steadied them with her own. "Do I have to work? Is this the kind of fantasy world where I have infinite funds and nothing tying me down?"

Audrey drew a sharp line across Rose's middle fingernail. "Yes," she said. "Whatever you want."

"Okay. I think . . . some island, somewhere, where it's crazy hot all the time and the water's that clear, clear green. I want a little house right on the beach, so close there's always sand everywhere, and I can wake up in the mornings and be in the water within thirty seconds." Rose paused. "Then again, I would love to live in Italy, too. Where my family is from—Cordovado. Always cooking and walking through the groves and sleeping under the sun. What about you?"

Audrey unscrewed the nail polish remover and tipped a small amount into the lid. "I want to live somewhere I can see the stars at night," she said, and she dipped her brush into the remover, swirling it around so the color dispersed in ribbons. "But then I want to be in a city as well. Somewhere with tons of galleries and theaters and actual culture, but where I can drive a couple of hours and be in the middle of nowhere."

"That would be nice," Rose said. Her hands twitched again. "So, guess what I'm doing on Christmas Eve?"

"Going to midnight mass?" Audrey said.

"Yeah, right." Rose laughed. "My parents haven't stepped foot in a church since their wedding. No—I'm going to have dinner at Olivia's house. *With* her mom. And some cousins or something, I don't know. But! I'm doing it."

Audrey snapped her head up, jerking her brush-holding hand up in the air so she wouldn't paint Rose's skin. "Shut up. Rose! Oh, I'm so proud of you. You are going to *kill* it. Watch—mothers everywhere will soon love you."

"All right, don't make me throw up." Rose stuck out her tongue. "It's going to be fine. Olivia's going to give me notes on her mom's entire life so I can study up and plan out exactly what I'm going to talk about."

Audrey raised her eyebrows. "For real?"

"No, of course not, that would be weird!" Rose laughed again. "But she did promise that she would lead the conversation if I get really awkward and, y'know, *me*. So. I think it'll be okay."

Audrey set down the brush and put her hands together. "Are you nervous?"

"If feeling like I'm going to pee myself every time I think about it means I'm nervous, then yes," Rose said.

"Nerves are good," Audrey said. "They mean you care. And hey— see what happens when you ask people for help?" Audrey held up her hands as Rose rolled her eyes. "I'm just saying! Saying that I was super-right and you should always listen to me."

"Yeah, whatever." Rose shook her head, setting her tawny hair swinging. "You know what, though? I am trying. To talk more about, like, my feelings."

"Like, awesome," Audrey teased.

"Shut up." Rose smiled. "I feel like it's easier with Olivia. It's like she knows when I'm not saying something, and she'll call me on it. And before, usually I would just avoid it. But now I think about what you said, and then I try to say whatever it is."

Audrey tipped her head to the side. "And?"

"And it feels good," Rose said. "Everything feels better now. Like . . . I can breathe."

Audrey broke into a smile, too, nodding eagerly. "Yeah," she said. "That's what I felt like, too. After the clinic. It's good, right?"

Rose grinned at her. "I fucking love you, Audrey Spencer. Do you know that?"

"Oh, darling," Audrey said, and she pressed her hand to her heart. "You're such a romantic."

Rose laughed, the sound uncontrolled and so wild it sent Audrey into peals, too.

She finished painting Rose's nails with her lungs sore from laughing, and when the music changed to Pharrell, Audrey let Rose drag her up off the floor and dance so hard that the floorboards creaked under their bouncing feet. And when Audrey caught the look on Rose's face, she felt like she would do anything for this girl. Because yeah, maybe the things people said about Rose were sometimes right: that she was mean, that she was a bitch. Audrey wouldn't deny it—but she wouldn't have it any other way, either. That part of Rose, and the quiet, unsure part of her—Audrey saw it all. Audrey saw, and Audrey knew, and Audrey loved that girl.

FORTY-SIX

Audrey listened to the phone ring on, and on, and on. "Come on," she muttered. "Pick up."

The line finally clicked. "Hey!"

"Jen," Audrey said. "This is *urgent*."

"What?" Jen sounded immediately concerned. "What's wrong?"

Audrey stared into her torn-apart closet and let out a wail. "I have nothing to wear!"

School was finally over, the last shrill bell releasing them until after New Year's, and on the last day every year they went out for a celebration dinner. It was always the girls, and then whoever else they could convince to tag along: Julian and Cooper this year; Izzy, Jasmin, and Dasha; and a couple of girls they sometimes hung out with at parties.

But Audrey couldn't leave until she actually got changed out of her sloppy jeans-and-sweatshirt combo. "Help me, Jen," she pleaded. "O wise one, I need your guidance."

Jen laughed. "Jesus, for a second there I thought there was an actual problem! Okay, hold on—I'll be over in ten."

By the time Jen got there, Audrey had started on her makeup instead. Jen picked through Audrey's clothes while Audrey painted on her favorite plum lipstick and smoothed serum into her curls. When she was done, she put on the outfit Jen had picked out: black jeans that were a little too tight but made her ass look great, and the shirt that she'd bought with Rose and forgotten all about. The ivory color made the gold flecks in her lipstick shimmer, and the jewels on the collar clicked against her hoop earrings. "Jen, you are a goddess."

Jen checked her own outfit in the mirror—short green dress, amazingly shiny silver flats—and blew a kiss at her reflection. "Aren't I, though?"

They drove to pick up Julian and then to their favorite Mexican place, the one that had the best guacamole and queso. Audrey ate—really ate, for the first time in months, until her too-tight jeans cut uncomfortably into her stomach. After sugar-drenched churros they piled out of the restaurant and into cars, heading for Cooper's house, where what felt like the entire rest of their class joined them. The kitchen was stocked with booze—none for Audrey, playing designated driver for the night—and Julian and Izzy dj'ed, the music turned up high enough to entice Rose to dance (admittedly, not hard to do). Audrey watched Julian, headphones on, doing whatever it was on Cooper's laptop that made the music skip and bounce, turning one song into another while Izzy bent over his shoulder, pointing at the screen. It was weird how close Julian had come to losing this. But he hadn't—*He still has the band, and me, and we still have everything waiting for us*, Audrey thought, and she smiled.

Eventually they ended up in the dining room, playing dumb drinking games with a deck of cards María had found. María leaned on Rose's shoulder, sloshing beer out of the bottle and slurring her words as she said, "I love you guys. No, don't laugh at me; why are you laughing at me? I love you guys so, so, *so* much. You're like my best friends ever. Sisters! I don't have a sister but I always wanted one but this way it's like I have four of them! Jen, what are you laughing at? Rose?"

Rose patted María's flushed cheek. "Nothing, sweetie. *Definitely* not you." She swirled her finger at the side of her head and mouthed to the others: gone.

"Oh, don't laugh!" Audrey said, even though uncharacteristically sloppy María *was* amusing. "I think that's sweet." She swirled the soda in her plastic cup and watched it bubble up. "I don't have a sister, either, so you can be my sister, Ree. And you, Jen, and Liv, and of course Rose."

Rose nodded, pouring another measure of rum into her red cup. "Okay, it's a deal. Even though I already have a sister, I could always use more. Especially if she's the nice kind of sister who lets me borrow her clothes."

Olivia put her chin in her hands. "I like the idea that you can choose your family," she said. "Imagine if you could do it for real. Like, go to the store and pick out a new mom when the one you have starts getting on your nerves."

"Oh my God!" Jen started giggling uncontrollably. "I would so do that. My dad keeps bugging me about college, and I'm, like, *stop* already. I'd love to pick out a dad who doesn't give a shit about all that and wants to watch football with me all the time."

"You are ridiculous," Audrey said. "Since when do you like football?" She caught the lime-green straw in her cup between her teeth as she considered Olivia's idea, applied it to her own life: the girl Mandy—Amanda Darby—standing in the freezer aisle, women suspended in motion behind the glass. She pictured Amanda squinting at the labels on each woman—*family history of heart disease; qualified yoga instructor; former Marine*—and nodding when she got to the one that said *actress and serial cat owner.* "Yep." She imagined Amanda saying to some clerk waiting with an oversize cart, "This one'll do."

"But don't you think that already happens?" Rose asked, pulling Audrey out of her fantasy.

Jen raised her eyebrows. "What, don't I hang out with my dad? No! If I did, I wouldn't want to go get a new one at the store!"

"No," Rose said, waving her hands in the air. "Don't you think we kind of already do choose our family? Because, all joking aside, I do think of you as family—you're always there for me, and when we fight"—here she looked at Audrey—"it's never a real fight. We're always there for each other, when we don't *have* to be."

True, Audrey thought. Imagine what life would be without her funny, flawed, wild girls—God, it didn't bear thinking about.

She thought about Olivia, this girl who'd come into her life and clicked with her so quickly, who'd turned out to be the person Rose might be falling in love with. She thought about María, whose book smarts sometimes outweighed her common sense but who never failed to make her laugh, about Jen and how hard she was trying to be true to herself. And she thought about Rose and the person she was trying to become, the heartache she held so close. She really was proud of Rose, how much she was pushing against her own boundaries to change. It made Audrey want to change, too, to be better. And together they could do that—Audrey was sure of it.

Rose leaned into Olivia, her eyes gleaming with the glassiness of being tipsy, if not flat-out drunk. Actually, Audrey knew she had to be drunk, because this lovey-dovey, sweet stuff was not Rose's usual repertoire. But honestly, Audrey liked it when this side of Rose slipped out from behind her tough-as-nails front. *This* was the Rose she knew.

"Some people never find friends like us," Rose was saying now. "So I think we're lucky. But that's not to say I don't want my real family, too. Even though we fight and fuck up and are generally a fucking mess . . . well, they're still my blood." She caught Audrey's eye again and pointed excitedly. "And look! You actually did choose your family! Or your family chose you, or . . ."

"Yeah, I think we get what you're trying to say." Olivia laughed. "Any other words of wisdom you'd like to leave us with?"

Rose closed her eyes, and Audrey watched the way Olivia looked at her, full of adoration. "Only that I love you all," Rose said, "and I wouldn't trade any of you ever."

"Ditto," Audrey said, and her voice was too quiet in the din, but she smiled anyway, not caring that no one was listening.

No one but Julian, apparently, stealthy as always. "I wouldn't trade you," his voice came in her ear, making her jump in the best way. "Not even for a pristine ninety-six Rickenbacker with gold fret inlays."

"I'm flattered," Audrey said, and she twisted around so she could tap him on his chin and press a kiss to his lips. "Really."

A whooping cheer erupted, and Rose banged the table so hard that everything on it jumped. "Let's do some shots!"

FORTY-SEVEN

The party wound down, and they fell out onto the street, Audrey ready to do her chauffeur duty. She dropped the others home—allowing Rose extra time to kiss Olivia good-bye; wasn't she nice?—until it was just her and Julian in the car.

She drove to his house with Julian holding her hand, lifting her fingers to his mouth every so often to press a kiss there. And every time he did it, she got chills racing up and down her spine.

"How bad do you think Rose's hangover's going to be?" Julian said as they cruised through the snow-and-slush-covered streets. "She was going hard on those tequila shots."

"Oh, she's a big girl," Audrey said, smiling. "She can handle it."

"I like her and Olivia together. They're good."

Audrey slowed at a particularly icy corner. "I know. God—you can practically see little cartoon love-hearts floating around their heads.

Were we like that when we first started dating?"

"Yes," Julian said. "I mean, we were worse. PDA everywhere."

"We did not!"

"Aud, we so did."

They talked the rest of the way to his house, about everything and nothing. They were different now—who wouldn't be? And Audrey wasn't sure how it was going to work out, their new way. But if there was one thing she hadn't been certain of before that she was now, it was this: she wouldn't have wanted anyone but Julian by her side during the past few difficult months. He wasn't perfect, no one was, but that didn't mean he wasn't everything Audrey needed.

She walked him to his door, waiting on the front porch under the light. "I love you," she said. "Julian Kitsch, I do love you."

"I love you," he said back, linking his hands in the small of her back. "Audrey Spencer, I do love you."

"You're the best," Audrey said, allowing herself to kiss him slow and hot in the cold winter air.

When they came up for breath, Julian said, "Yeah, I am the best," and then kissed Audrey again before she could elbow him the way she wanted to.

"I take it back," she said when they broke apart this time. "On account of your ego getting in your way."

"Whatever," he said. "There are no take-backs allowed."

"Where does it say that? *The Book of Relationships*, chapter two, verse ten?" Audrey pinched his cheek. "Charming."

She reached for him again, kissing him with a fierce intensity.

Audrey hadn't forgotten all the doctor's instructions about sex, and she and Julian had agreed that they wouldn't rush getting back there, either, that they'd go slow and not put any more pressure on the situation. Every time they touched, it was harder for Audrey to stop, though—when he kissed her so good, when she felt his warm skin while running her hands under his shirt. But it all made her feel that when the time finally came and they did do it again, it would be good.

He was the one to pull away first, laughing low. "What are you trying to do to me?"

"Me?" Audrey said, all innocence. "I'm just kissing my boyfriend."

"Yeah, you're doing something to your boyfriend," Julian said. "Now I have to go take a cold shower."

"Not for much longer," Audrey said, and she spun away from him, laughing at the expression on his face. "I'll see you tomorrow!"

At home she found her mom and Adam in the kitchen eating heaping bowls of ice cream in their pajamas like mischievous little kids. Audrey couldn't resist when her mom placed a bowl of the goodness in front of her, and so she stayed with them awhile, telling stories from dinner and none from Cooper's. Eventually her mom and Adam went up to bed, yawning and rubbing their eyes, and Audrey followed. In her room she took her time wiping off her makeup and weaving her hair into two long braids before changing and getting into bed.

Lately she'd been falling asleep as soon as her head hit the pillow, but not tonight. She lay there for a long time, reciting poems in her head, counting upward in Spanish, trying to fall into dreamland.

But it was no good, because she wasn't in the least bit tired.

Audrey scratched at the waist of her sweatpants. Something that Rose had said had stuck with her, the thought bouncing around her head keeping her awake.

You actually did choose your family!

Not exactly right—it was more that her family was chosen for her. But the outcome was the same: her perfectly imperfect, mixed-up life, the one she wouldn't change for anything.

Audrey closed her eyes and tried counting again, in English this time. *One. Two. Three. Fou*—

Wait. Yes. She knew exactly what to do.

Throwing back the covers, she rolled out of bed. She padded over to her desk, found a pen and then a clean notepad.

Audrey woke up her computer and put on some music, low enough so it wouldn't travel down through the floorboards.

Her hand holding the pen shook, but as soon as she touched the paper, it stopped. The words flowed easily, like they'd been there all along, waiting to be let out.

Dear Amanda, she began.

> *You wrote me a letter a long time ago. I can't tell you how many times I've read it. And now you've given me another one. I honestly don't know what to say.*
>
> *I think I'll start with: thank you.*

ACKNOWLEDGMENTS

I've dreamed of having a Real Book Written by Me out in the world for so many years, and now that it's here, I almost can't believe it. (I *really* almost can't believe that my story about a mixed-race girl who has an abortion, and is okay with it, is the one that made it through every obstacle to become Real.)

Biggest, truest, most heartfelt thanks to my wonderful agent, Jennifer Johnson-Blalock, and my amazing editor, Elizabeth Lynch, who are my Dream Team. Who support me even when I'm being overly neurotic and overthinking everything and tell me how much they believe in me, and this book, at every turn. Jennifer: I am so grateful for that out-of-the-blue email and that you understand everything I'm trying to say so clearly. Elizabeth: thank you for championing this book and always being on my side. I do not know what I would do without either of you. (And all the Ariana Grande gifs and Center Stage discussions.)

Everybody at Harper who made this Real Book real: Renée

Cafiero, Andrea Curley, Sarah Creech, who gave me such a beautiful cover, Steph Hoover, Christine Cox, and Sabrina Abballe. Everybody at Liza Dawson Associates, my wonderful agency home.

Those who read this story in its various early incarnations and helped me make it (so, so much) better: Jaime Morrow, Sara Biren, Stephanie Allen, Melanie Stanford, and Emily Lloyd-Jones.

I couldn't get by without the wit and warmth of so many badass ladies on the internet, most of whom I've never met in real life but who continually brighten my world, probably without even knowing it. If I were to name you all, this book would never end, but I trust that you all know who you are and that you all put a smile on my face.

Authors whose books I have loved, wept and raged over, and been so inspired by: Nina LaCour, Brandy Colbert, Courtney Summers, Sara Zarr, Stephanie Kuehn, Nova Ren Suma, Sarah Dessen, Laurie Halse Anderson, Corey Ann Haydu, and Emery Lord.

The teachers who always, always encouraged me to keep writing: Christine Martin, Ali Knowles, Toni Cain, and Joanna Price.

Emily Letts, whose video of her own abortion informed the scene of Audrey's. Thank you for sharing your experience and bringing light to the reality of abortion.

Diane Warburton, for all your help and always reminding me to take ownership of my accomplishments.

To all my friends and family. To my mum, for never saying no to books and always finding me reflections of myself. To my dad, for always believing I knew what I was doing even when I didn't.

To you, for reading.

REBECCA BARROW writes stories about girls and all the wonders they can be. A lipstick obsessive with the ability to quote the entirety of *Mean Girls*, she lives in England, where it rains a considerable amount more than in the fictional worlds of her characters. She collects tattoos, cats, and more books than she could ever possibly read. *You Don't Know Me but I Know You* is her first novel. You can visit her online at www.rebecca-barrow.com.

FOLLOW REBECCA BARROW ON